C0-AWC-953

FIRST US ED

6 —
m

Who Killed Enoch Powell?

Who Killed Enoch Powell?

BY ARTHUR WISE

HARPER & ROW, PUBLISHERS

1817 New York, Evanston, San Francisco, London

A JOAN KAHN–HARPER NOVEL OF SUSPENSE

WHO KILLED ENOCH POWELL? Copyright © 1970 by Arthur Wise. All rights reserved. Printed in the United States of America. No part of this book may be used or reproduced in any manner whatsoever without written permission except in the case of brief quotations embodied in critical articles and reviews. For information address Harper & Row, Publishers, Inc., 49 East 33rd Street, New York, N.Y. 10016.

FIRST U.S. EDITION

STANDARD BOOK NUMBER: 06–014691–5

LIBRARY OF CONGRESS CATALOG CARD NUMBER: 76–148431

Who Killed Enoch Powell?

It was a small, northern market town set in a valley. Surrounding it was rolling farmland, and beyond that hills. It had a name, but no one outside the immediate area had ever heard of it. A pleasant town, a town with a character of its own. On every other day of the year it was a quiet town. But not today. Today was an exception.

Noel Taylor—Subdivisional Chief Inspector—was supervising another inspection of the Jubilee Hall. It was the third inspection that day. Chairs had been set out in the body of the hall. On a platform at one end stood a baize-covered table and behind it five chairs. The place smelled of floor polish. Taylor stood in the doorway. A policeman, his shirt sleeves rolled up, was walking slowly along the rows of chairs. Taylor walked to the end of the row and called to him.

"All right?" said Taylor.

"Nothing, sir."

"Where's Dixon?" said Taylor.

"Think he's by the platform, sir."

Taylor walked to the platform. Constable Dixon was on his knees under the table. Only the soles of his boots were visible.

"Anything there, Dixon?" said Taylor.

Dixon backed out from under the table. He stood up and brushed his hands.

"Nothing, sir. Not a thing."

He was a young man, with broad shoulders and pink complexion. He was eager—energetic. He found it hard to stand still.

"We've checked the anteroom and the fuelroom. Nothing there, sir. Constable Simpson's checking the seating. I think it's clean, sir."

"What about the toilets?"

"Nothing, sir."

"Radiators?"

"No, sir, nothing there. Sir, I was wondering—"

"What?"

Dixon went behind the table and pulled out the central chair.

"He'll be standing here, sir—for the speech."

"Well?" said Taylor.

"He's right in line with the church tower." He pointed upward through the high windows of the hall. "I mean—someone up there with a rifle—"

"I'm putting Anderson up there. That's all right. You'll be with me this evening, Dixon."

"Yes, sir."

"With the speaker's party."

"Any more news, sir? I was wondering—"

"Another phone call."

"Another crank, sir?"

"Perhaps. Keep your eyes open. I'll be in the office if you want me."

Taylor stood at his desk, looking out of the window. He was tall, slim and erect with dark hair and sallow complexion. At thirty-five he was the youngest Chief Inspector in any of the Force divisions. But he had worked for it—courses at Hendon, correspondence courses to widen his general education and paid for out of his own pocket, nights spent with manuals of law. It had cost him friends and social life. Perhaps it would cost him his wife. But he might make Chief Superintendent by the time he was forty. And then— This was really the test, this present situation. He felt the responsibility keenly. Every year there were outside speakers in that hall. Important people. Only last year, Sir Horace Livingstone, and three months ago the secretary of the TUC. But never before a man of the caliber of Enoch Powell. Never before a man so much in the national limelight, a man around whom so much fierce controversy raged.

Taylor picked up the phone.

"Division—Chief Super."

He took a sheet of paper off the top of the tray on his left and put it in front of him.

"Chief Inspector Taylor, sir. We've had another phone call."

"That's the third, am I right?"

"Three, sir. Yes," said Taylor. "I've got it here." He looked down at the paper. "Exact words were: 'Powell—Enoch Powell. This is a warning. Tonight's his last night.' Made from a call box, sir. Timed fifteen-twelve. I've had another check made on the place. There's nothing there, sir."

"I'll let the CC know. I'll be over this evening myself."

Taylor put the phone down. He stood for a moment, then turned and opened another window. There was no sign of a break in the hot weather. The sky was a pale, cloudless blue. He could see the roof of the hall. He stood looking at it, thinking himself into every aspect of the situation, trying to imagine some security angle that might have been overlooked. The possibility of violent student protests by contingents from Hull, York and the West Riding. The use of an explosive or firearm in the hall, or of a rifle from outside. An incident with the car or in the anteroom. Nothing that he could imagine had been overlooked.

The phone rang.

"Chief Inspector Taylor."

"Mr. Taylor—Chief Constable. Thought I'd better have a word with you direct. These phone calls—treat them seriously, of course, but don't be surprised if nothing comes of them. And Mr. Taylor —ring me direct if you want me. I'll be at home."

"At home, sir?"

"That's right—at home."

At five o'clock, Sir Clinton Everard, who was to chair the meeting in the evening, rang Taylor for the police escort. The car picked up Everard's Daimler at five-fifteen and followed it into York. The divisional police were dealing with the reception on the station. Taylor, the driver and two constables remained in the car. When the Daimler reappeared, they closed in behind it and followed it back out of town.

Enid Markus had traveled up on the three o'clock train from King's Cross and taken a taxi from York. Now she stood in the queue outside the hall with her press card in her hand. They had put her on this kind of job at the time of Enoch Powell's Birmingham speech. April 20, 1968, that had been. It had been an accident. Monash was supposed to cover it. But Monash had been getting more and more difficult. He was frequently drunk. Not that that mattered in itself. As long as he produced good copy on time, what the hell did anything matter? But his copy began to fail. Not only did its quality fall off, but at times nothing materialized at all. And on the spur of the moment Jimmy Endells had called her into his office and decided that he couldn't risk sending Monash. She would have to go.

It wasn't her cup of tea. Not at all. You couldn't call her keen.

She didn't feel a sympathy. She did it because it was a job. And the more she did it, the more specialist she became—and the less chance of her being taken off it. The uproar after that Birmingham speech had given her an authority in Jimmy's eyes and the eyes of her colleagues. It was an authority she didn't want, but nonetheless she was landed with it. Wherever Powell spoke, she was there reporting it.

She was thirty-three. Lower middle class she might have described her background. Her father had been an electrician, in business on his own. But he dropped dead at work one grim afternoon before he reached fifty, and left his wife to bring up two girls and a boy. Enid was the eldest. She got herself through King Edward's, Birmingham, and took a lower second in English at the university there. She had her first affair there, with a lecturer. It hadn't been particularly pleasurable and it had filled her with a sense of guilt. Then she'd got on a local paper in the southwest, and finally made Fleet Street. That was her life, more or less.

She thought of herself as a liberal, and perhaps as an intellectual. She had admired Jo Grimond and she covenanted to Oxfam. She would have gone to Vietnam or Biafra if they'd let her. She wanted to feel involved, to feel she was able to do some good. So she didn't stand there in that queue, in a town she'd probably never see again, with any great feeling of enthusiasm or commitment. She stood because Jimmy Endells had told her to.

"He's a great man, a great man," a woman in front of her was saying. She wore a tight linen suit and a trim hat. She'd probably bought them specially for the occasion. Perhaps even made a special trip to Leeds.

"Another Churchill," her companion agreed.

"Isn't that what the country needs—another Churchill?"

They were moving gradually nearer the door. The nearer the entrance to the hall they got, the tighter did the pack of bodies become. Enid felt them squeezing in on her as she'd felt them in other places. The atmosphere frightened her. How did the man do it? she thought. Generate all this dedication, all this sense of purpose and direction? He was, she had to admit, "magnetic." She'd seen how he could draw people to him. "A political John the Baptist," someone had called him in the *Sunday Telegraph*. How apt! That singleness of purpose, that intellectual clarity that seemed to cut through so much political undergrowth and pierce to the very heart of a situation. A kind of complex simplicity.

Four policemen stood at the door, two on either side. They weren't even watching the crowd pushing past them. They simply stood, feet a little apart, hands behind backs, and stared ahead of them over the heads of the crowd. She reached them, was forced back a little, and then suddenly squeezed forward into the hall. Ahead of her an usher was holding back two young men. Both had long hair.

"Look at that hair!" said a woman behind her. "Never had a comb through it in its life."

"We only want to hear what he's going to say," said one of the young men.

"It's ticket holders only," said the usher, gently holding him back.

"It's a free country, isn't it?" said the other.

"Too bloody free!" said a heavy, tweedy man beside the young men.

"Look," said the first one. "We only want to hear him."

"Get 'em out of here," said the tweedy man. Something about the two young men seemed to fill him with fury.

"Ticket holders only," said the usher. He was repeating a formula, but he was irritable and annoyed.

"Bloody long-haired intellectuals," the tweedy man snarled.

Odd, thought Enid. Doesn't that just throw some light on something? Because here he is queuing to hear one of the purest intellectuals. And when he's heard him he'll clap and cheer with the rest.

But will he be quite sure what it is he's cheering? Or will it perhaps be something else he's cheering, something that hasn't been said?

The man looking at the tickets was harassed. He'd never faced such a press of people before. Normally he had to deal with orderly affairs like the Hunt Ball and the dinner that the Country Landowners' Association gave each February. He sat behind a little baize card table, took the tickets and spiked them on a piece of wire beside him. When he saw the press card it flustered him for a moment.

"You can't—" he began. And then: "Oh—press. You'll find—toward the front."

"Thank you," said Enid. She took the card from him before he could impale it on the spike, and squeezed past him into the hall.

The place was already full. People in front of her were gradually shuffling forward. When she got to the back row of seating, it looked as if there wasn't a single vacant seat anywhere. She stood looking over the heads of the seated audience to the raised platform at the far end, with its single long trestle table covered with heavy baize, its five armchairs and its carafe of water. Two small vases of roses stood on the table. Behind it, someone had erected a vast backing of royal blue on which was a blown-up picture of Enoch Powell, and beside it the words "England hath need of thee." That's the feeling, she thought, that's the sentiment. England with a great gaping hole in it crying out to be plugged. England waiting for direction, waiting for a philosophy to replace that of empire. A John the Baptist—or something else?

She got to the wall at the side of the hall. She'd given up the idea of a seat. She stood with her back against the wall, and her right shoulder against one of the projecting half columns that gave additional bracing to the wall at intervals down the room. She was out of the growing crush and movement of people still squeezing into the place. In that position she could still jot down the necessary notes.

At last there was a movement at the main entrance doors. Ushers were trying to close them. The crowd outside were protesting at being shut out, but it was obvious that there was no more room inside.

"I thought it was only ticket holders," said a woman in a new summer dress. She was trying to squeeze herself past Enid without success. The side aisle was packed with people ahead of her.

"Didn't you see them?" said the man she was with—a professional man by the look of his clothes and the poise of his body. "The touts outside, the wide boys from London—selling them?"

"Selling them?" She just managed to turn her head to look at him.

"They print another batch down there, bring 'em up here and sell them outside. Didn't you know?"

There were five members of the platform party waiting in the anteroom to the hall. There was Powell himself, tall, a little pale, a little gaunt. He talked easily to the chairman, Clinton Everard, and from time to time glanced down at the papers that he held in his hand. Clinton Everard himself beamed his round-faced beam constantly. He was a round dumpling of a man, bald and very red in the face. He had a handkerchief in his right hand with which he mopped at his face and neck as he spoke. Anthony Bevert, the secretary of the committee that had been responsible for the original invitation, stood foursquare, looking down at his chairman almost with disapproval. His appearance conjured up one of the popular but largely inaccurate images of country life—an image of tweed and horses. And indeed Bevert had the best hunting stable in the area. He was a stiff, unbending man with purple capillaries showing just below the surface of his cheeks and nose. His contribution to the conversation in which his chairman was trying to involve him was simply a stiff nod that didn't commit him in any way. Apart from these three central figures were two men who had traveled from London on the same train as Powell. Neither spoke, not even to one another. They were men from Special Branch. These five men comprised the group that was to take the platform.

Constable Dixon was standing at the door that opened from the anteroom into the corridor that led to the main hall. He could hear the general rumble of voices some distance away, but it was impossible for him to make out any particular words that were being spoken. He caught some of the excitement from the hall. It mingled strangely with the increasing apprehension that he felt himself. He had an odd feeling that something might have been overlooked. He ran over the corners of the hall again in his mind. He could visualize the platform and the table and the chairs that were set on it. As he remembered each item, he remembered too the way in which it had been checked and rechecked. He could think of nothing that they had overlooked, yet still the sense of having forgotten something pressed on his mind. He looked across at Chief Inspector Taylor. Taylor was standing by the outer door, the door that led from the street into the anteroom. He stood very upright, his arms folded across his chest. He wore that look of slight anxiety that had been increasingly apparent during the past few months. His face had lost a little of its color. Dixon knew that the feelings in Taylor were much the same as those that he himself was experiencing. Feelings of general apprehension, without any clearly defined cause. Perhaps, thought Dixon, such delicately balanced situations always produced such a feeling. But God, he would be glad when it was over and they had the man on the train again. He glanced at the clock that ticked away high up on the anteroom wall. Less than a minute to go. Then perhaps fifty minutes of waiting, with the voice of the speaker dimly reaching them from the hall through a half-open door of the anteroom. Perhaps fifteen or twenty minutes to get the man clear of the hall and into the Daimler. Another forty-five minutes to get him back to York and onto the train. And then . . . He could anticipate the relief that he was going to feel.

Taylor was listening partly to Clinton Everard and partly to the sounds from the hall. His face was drawn. He was caught between the desire to go through the door into the hall and see for himself that everything was normal, and the obligation he had to stay in the anteroom. He could feel a stiffness building in his neck and shoulders and the growing tautness of his abdominal wall. Quarter to ten, he was thinking. Should be clear by then. Home, perhaps, by ten o'clock. Could Beryl complain about that? It could hardly be called late—under the circumstances. He wasn't leaving her with the kids a minute longer than was necessary. It wasn't every day they had a man like Powell in the place.

Clinton Everard took a final mop at his face with his damp handkerchief. He could hear the waiting audience outside begin to cheer. From the distance, someone called out, "Good old Enoch!" Then the cheering broke into laughter. He put away his handkerchief, turned to the speaker and said, "Well, sir . . . ?" He opened the door and Powell walked through it into the corridor outside.

At last the doors to the main hall were closed. The crowd outside was shouting with fury. Someone was banging on the doors with his fists. The temperature inside the little hall began to rise. The evening sun streamed in through the windows. Men began to remove their jackets. One or two undid their collars and slackened ties. Tobacco smoke began to rise from the audience and hung about their heads in a motionless blue layer. Someone shouted, "Good old Enoch!" again. A few began stamping their feet. A man appeared from behind the blue backdrop on the platform. People mistook him and began to clap and cheer. He looked up, embarrassed, peering at them in the body of the hall. Then he gave a shy little smile, put some papers on the table and withdrew. At intervals round the hall policemen stood in blue shirt sleeves, unmoving and unmoved.

And then he came. He came briskly as if he wanted to plunge at once into the business ahead, his head a little pushed forward, a sheaf of papers in his hand. He gave an impression of being wound up, as if the mechanism inside him could hardly wait to be released. In front of him walked the chairman, and behind him the secretary and the two security men. People burst into a cheer. They began to get up so that they could get a clearer view of him, standing up there on the platform. There was a general shuffle of activity in the hall—people moving chairs, picking up coats from their laps—and still the cheering. Two young men were peering in from outside through one of the high windows. They must somehow have climbed the wall. A policeman waved to them to get down, but they took no notice.

The chairman smiled to the speaker. The speaker smiled back. They were smiles, perhaps, of nervous reaction to the tense and clamorous situation in which they found themselves. The chairman indicated a chair. Powell sat. The others sat. Powell put his elbows on the baize-covered table, leaned forward a little and clasped his hands. He was still smiling. He looked as if he was holding in check some enormous energy. Enid saw the eyes again. They were the fascination. Rather pale. What was it that they were saying? Such passion and intensity. Yet somehow a coldness.

The chairman stood at last. He turned from one side of the audience to the other. He smiled. He put up his hands to still the cheering, and at last the clamor began to subside. Individual calls of "Good old Enoch!" and "Get on with it!" to the chairman could be heard. Enid opened her notebook and turned to an empty page.

"Ladies!" called the chairman. "Ladies and—ladies and—"

At last he could be heard. He spoke in a slow, measured, resonant voice, in the accent of the area. He spoke of the honor that Powell had bestowed on the town by his presence. He spoke of his kindness and courtesy in coming such a distance to address them. He spoke of some of those pressing local problems that he thought were most closely linked with Powell's own views. He spoke in particular of "national frustration." The audience fidgeted. It was oppressively hot. But they heard him out. Enid thought of the rehearsals he must have gone through during the past ten days— standing in his bedroom in front of his mirror, taking the opinion of his wife—in order to produce such a statement. And now it was over. The relief shone from his face. He turned and put out an open hand to Powell. The audience cheered and clapped and shouted out. It was the star they had come to see and hear, and he was just rising.

He began firmly, seriously, quietly. As he spoke the quality of intensity grew in him. It shone particularly from his eyes. Enid had seen it so many times. But to the rest of the audience it was a quite new experience. It stilled. It seemed to suspend its breathing. It seemed held in that quiet, logical intensity. It seemed to give itself, almost in a religious sense. The speaker had that kind of power. Perspiration ran down cheeks unnoticed. The heat was almost debilitating, yet no one moved to cool himself. No one loosened a collar or took out a handkerchief to mop his brow. Enid looked at the faces—mouths a little open as if stopped dead in the middle of a sentence, eyes a little closed as if to shut out all other impressions except those directly connected with the speaker. One man sat with his body thrust right back in his chair, his neck drawn down into his chest, staring at the speaker. Another sat forward, on the very edge of his chair, elbow on his knee, chin resting in the palm of his hand, as if trying to get as close to the speaker as possible, to identify himself with him almost physically.

There were occasional interruptions, but only one disturbed the atmosphere. Two young men at the back of the hall started to unfold a banner. One of them called out, "On behalf of the student population—" That was all. No one saw the wording on the banner. It was ripped from them by a man standing next to them. A man suddenly incensed. He struck the young man once, in uncontrollable fury. The audience turned slowly as the incident gradually bore in on its consciousness. But few people saw anything. Simply the opening and closing of the doors at the back of the hall, and then the ushers standing again with folded arms looking toward the platform.

The anteroom door was ajar. It opened into the corridor leading to the main hall. Taylor and Dixon stood together just inside the deep frame of the doorway. They could make out the words the speaker was using and they could sense the rapt attention of the audience. But the words as such made no impact on either of them. They followed them merely as an indication of the progress of the speech, and therefore of the passage of time. Occasionally there was some interruption of the speaker's flow from some member of the audience. The interruption was followed by a pause in that flow, and then again by the speaker's voice deploring the refusal by some of his critics to listen to reasoned argument.

Taylor looked at his watch. He thought five minutes more would see a conclusion developing. He looked up at Dixon and pointed to his watch. Dixon gave a quick, nervous smile and nodded. He sighed. Taylor nodded back his understanding. Both men lowered their heads again. Taylor could feel his heart pounding inside his chest. If only the minutes wouldn't drag so!

Then, his head still lowered, Taylor seemed to see the door move toward him, and at the same time sensed some vast disturbance in the hall itself. Some great, tearing noise that his brain couldn't make sense of. There was a pressure against him, something that forced irresistibly against his body. It was the same pressure that carried the part-open door toward him. He couldn't breathe. It knocked the air out of his lungs and it flung his head back. Something had smashed the door in his face and was carrying him, turning and spinning, backward across the anteroom. As he turned, he saw Dixon already sprawling across the anteroom table. One of the table legs had given way under his weight. Still Taylor continued almost to float across the anteroom. He knocked over the stand on which the platform party had hung their hats, tripped, and saw the opposite wall, with its shiny, dark-green paint, coming straight at him. He struck it with his head, and felt himself sliding down it toward the floor.

Enid Markus was protected from the main blast by the half column against which she was leaning. She had her eyes on the speaker as he raised his hand to stress some particularly important point. It was as if the movement had touched some sensitive trigger mechanism for, as his hand rose, the platform seemed to split from end to end and then disappeared in a dense pall of acrid smoke and bursting flame, and the whole hall shook and trembled to its foundations with the violence of the explosion. The sound rang and reverberated round the high, plastered walls long after the explosion itself had ceased. And even after the echo of it had died in reality, the memory of it continued to ring and pound in the head. Only when that too had died into silence did the audience begin to come to grips with what had happened. At first there were no more than moans from the injured, lying among the rubble of the first three rows. Then those who were uninjured began to get up. They were in a state of shock. They stood. They looked about them. They looked toward the platform. Then, as if on some unheard command, they turned toward the exit doors at the back of the hall. When at last they started to move, they moved quickly. They moved straight through the chairs that stood in their way, knocking them aside, trampling through them, smashing them to pieces. Where they could, they ran. They ran into one another. They clawed one another out of the way. They trod one another to the ground. Some began to scream. Not simply women. One man, dragging an injured foot behind him, screamed and screamed as he clawed and punched his way toward the exit doors. He was screaming with shock, and the tears ran down his face. He was shouting,

"They've killed him! They've murdered him! Those blacks! Those bloody blacks!" The hysteria was catching. Others took up that or similar cries. The place began to burst with shouting and with a violence that a minute before would have been inconceivable. The sheer physical impact of the explosion—the blast, the shock that followed it—was being replaced by a sense of terrible loss, terrible personal loss. There was behind it a drive to get out of the building and avenge that loss. The nearer people got to the door, to the narrow little exit, the more savage they became. Police and ushers who tried desperately to impose some order on the exodus were simply knocked aside. Perhaps it was as well that the representatives of law and order were so outnumbered. Such was the temper of the crowd—screaming, clawing, kicking, punching its way toward the open air—that even with sufficient numbers of police on hand, it could only have been quelled by the most savage violence. Only one man might still conceivably have been able to make some impression on it, and he lay dead amid the shambles of the platform.

At the outside entrance, those trying to get out met those still hoping to get in. In a sense it was a communication problem. If those outside had been fully informed about the immediate events inside the hall, they would have moved out of the way and allowed those trying desperately to get out to do so. But communication failures seem to occur only when disaster is likely to be their outcome. So when the pushing, fighting audience tried to force its way through the highly curious and concerned crowd outside, it was met by belligerence. Fighting broke out on the steps and spread into the street outside. To add to the confusion, the explosion, which had been heard far beyond the confines of the little town, was bringing an increasing number of other curious, alarmed people to the scene. Most came on foot. A few were already beginning to arrive by car.

Taylor lifted his head and shook it. Dixon was standing over him, blood trickling down his cheek from a torn ear.

"The door's jammed, sir," said Dixon. "Can't seem to budge it."

"Let's have a look," said Taylor.

He got up and put his hand to his forehead. He felt dizzy. He picked his way past the broken table and chairs that had been thrown on their sides. He pushed the door handle, but it wouldn't move. There was a crack in the brickwork above the door. It looked as if the lintel and the entire frame had slipped. It was one of those substantial, late-nineteenth-century doors that couldn't be kicked clear of its frame. Dixon put his boot to one of the panels, but the hole he made wasn't big enough for either of them to get through. They could hear the screams in the hall. They could smell the acrid fumes left by the explosion, but they couldn't see anything. The anteroom led into the little corridor with the lavatories off it, and the hall itself was some three or four yards up the corridor.

"We'll have to go around," said Taylor, turning toward the street door. "Ring the office. Get an ambulance and some more men. Get them to seal off the area."

But the crowd was packed tight against the street entrance to the anteroom. Dixon fought his way through it. The sight of a policeman in uniform made the crowd give a little. He got clear at last and ran off toward the phone box in Dale Street. With Taylor it was different. He didn't want to get clear of it, he wanted to get through it to the front of the hall. But the crowd crushed in on him. It took him minutes to get to the front entrance. There people were packed ten deep outside the main doors. They were in a state of tremendous tension and curiosity. And to confuse an already difficult situation, the shattered and hysterical audience was trying to smash its way through the narrow doors and down the two or three steps to the street. Taylor continued to shout. He continued to pull and elbow and push. He took hold of people in front of him and dragged them out of his path. But he made no significant progress.

16

The pressure of the stricken audience bursting out from inside the hall, driven forward by shock and panic, was too much for him. He allowed himself to be carried clear and into the middle of the street.

Enid stood exactly where she was. She pushed herself as firmly as possible into the slight protection of the projecting half column and refused to be swept into the throng. It was not entirely second nature that held her there. She had had sufficient experience of much milder situations to know that if she could only hang on until the first maddened panic wore off the crowd, she stood a far better chance of being unharmed. When the immediate pressure was off her, she closed her notebook and put it in her handbag. People still forced themselves past her, but most were by now throwing themselves into the crush at the doors. The looks on their faces, she thought, would be printed indelibly on her memory. Looks of shock and of the deepest personal anguish. They had witnessed something too horrifying, and at the same time personal, for them to handle and make sense of. They simply couldn't grasp it. Dresses that had been trim and fresh five minutes earlier were torn and disheveled. Faces that had been made up with such care now ran with tears. Beyond them, at the far end of the hall, the ruined, shattered platform still smoked. The blue backing had been shredded by the blast. The blown-up picture of Enoch Powell swung a little in the breeze that came in through the glassless windows. The bottom half of the face had been torn away. Only the eyes remained looking down on the scene.

A woman in a torn blue dress was sobbing in the second row. She was bent over with both hands to her head, covering her ears and temples. Enid went to her and sat down beside her. She put an arm round the woman's shoulders and drew her very slightly toward her. The woman swayed a little from one side to the other.

"Are you all right?" said Enid.

"The only man who could have saved us," sobbed the woman. "And they've killed him!"

"You'll be all right," said Enid, trying to see if she had been hurt about the head. There was no sign of bleeding. The woman was severely shocked, but there appeared to be no physical damage. From somewhere outside the hall Enid could hear the bells of ambulances.

At last Taylor got into the hall with two uniformed men.

"God Almighty!" he said when he saw the mess. "Are those ambulances coming?"

"Should be here in a minute, sir. There's the bell. Question of how long it takes to get through that crowd."

"Get the caretaker to open up Dale Street school. We'll need somewhere to take statements."

Taylor walked to the front of the hall. He stopped when he reached Enid, still with her arms round the woman's shoulders.

"You all right, miss?" he said.

"She's badly shocked," said Enid. "I'm all right."

"There's an ambulance on its way," said Taylor.

"Can I stay with her?"

"For a moment. Till they get her into the ambulance."

"Can I get to a phone?" said Enid. "I'm a journalist. I've got to phone my paper."

"I doubt it," said Taylor.

"But look—" she said.

"You can see we've got our hands full," said Taylor.

His tension and irritability showed through at once.

"But what am I to do? I've a story to phone through to London."

"Damn your story!" he snapped. "There are other priorities."

He looked round the hall. He looked at the shattered platform and the tattered poster. He looked at the wounded lying on the floor or sunk into the few wooden chairs that remained upright at the front of the hall. Then he seemed to relent.

"I'm sorry," he said. "This—" He indicated the chaos in front of them. "You understand. You can't put through a call, not until we get a better idea of what happened."

"Are we to stay here?" said Enid.

"There's a school round the corner," said Taylor. "I'm getting them to open it. You can stay there."

He looked round. The first ambulance men were running in with stretchers.

"Down here," called Taylor.

As he spoke, firemen smashed down the door from the anteroom and began to drag hoses into the building.

Bertram Warner, the Chief Constable, had succeeded in persuading his men that the visit of Enoch Powell was a matter of routine. It was a visit that called for careful organization and for thoroughness, but it was not a visit that called for any great apprehension. Nevertheless, he was too experienced a man to pay too much attention to the advice he gave to others. He did in fact leave his office at the usual time and he did go straight home. But that was merely the smoke screen that he had to lay in order that his behavior should appear consistent to his men. Once at home he pulled a chair to the side of the telephone and prepared to sit there until news reached him that Powell was safely clear of his area. He had his evening meal in the chair and he pulled the TV set from one side of the room to the other so that he could watch it without leaving the chair. And when the phone rang he had the receiver off the rest almost at the moment the bell sounded.

"I see," he said. "I see. Yes—I see. I'll have the men sent. Expect me in—say, twenty minutes."

He rang Force Headquarters and gave instructions for the necessary reinforcements, then he rang the Government Inspector in

Newcastle. On his advice he put through a call to the Police Division of the Home Office. It was ten minutes before he could get through to someone with the necessary authority.

"Cool it off, for God's sake!" said the Home Office man. "If it gets out of hand, God knows where it could lead."

"We're holding everybody who was present," said Warner. "There are quite a lot. We can't hold them for long."

"As long as you can, that's all. Where can I reach you?"

"I'm going over there now. If I ring you in half an hour?"

"Half an hour. And another thing—for God's sake hold the press boys. If it gets out before we can do anything . . . !"

Frederick Evans, the Home Secretary and Deputy PM, was chairing the Select Services Committee in room 4B. His stomach was still giving him trouble. They said it was nothing pathological. Nothing showed under X ray. Small comfort that is, he thought. The fact that it didn't show up under X ray and barium meals and all the rest of it didn't take the pain away. It didn't make it any easier to live with. They'd told him to cut down on his alcohol intake and make sure that he had regular meals. Alcohol intake! He'd had one small Scotch a week ago, and that was it. You'd think, to hear them talk, that his job was one gay round of parties —drinks at the Soviet Embassy at lunchtime, champagne with the Patagonians at night. And regular meals—the only regular feature of his life since he came to office six months earlier had been work. The barricades in Glasgow had kept him out of bed for a week. That speech of Paisley's in Belfast hadn't made his nights any easier.

He was forty-six. A Welshman by birth, and still with the accents of his native Cardiff. He was small, dark and balding. He seemed temperamentally incapable of sitting still, of relaxing. He gave the impression of being constantly on the move, shifting his position in his chair, tapping the end of his pencil on a file or agenda paper, stretching his neck forward or from side to side, as if trying to relieve some permanent tension in his shoulders. Mike Yarwood's impersonation of him in the clubs and only last week on television was cruel but astonishingly accurate. It gave the impression of some small animal, tenacious yet disturbed. He dropped a hand into his jacket pocket, took out a tablet and slipped it under his tongue. His breath always had the smell of peppermint on it.

Patterson had just returned from Glasgow. He was painting the gloomiest picture of the situation there, with his talk of "permanent barricades" and what he called "in-built discrimination." Evans was doodling across the top of the agenda paper. The doodles took the form of sharp-pointed starlike objects, strung together by a double pencil line. From a distance they looked ominously like barbed wire. When the phone rang, his right hand continued to doodle while his left reached out for the receiver and lifted it off the rest.

"I'm sorry," he said, with a glance toward Patterson. And then into the phone: "Yes?"

Patterson took his elbows off the table and leaned back against his chair. He raised his eyebrows the merest shade to Stanton sitting opposite. Stanton gave a little resigned smile.

"I don't—" Evans was saying. "You're sure—I mean, *sure?*"

He had gone pale—not white; rather a yellowish color, jaundiced. Even his ears were yellow. His right hand had pulled a little square notepad toward him. It was making notes, apparently independent of Evans.

"If they need *carte blanche,* give it to them. Police reinforcements, troops if necessary. But for God's sake it's got to be kept cool and it's got to be kept confined. And we want to know every move they make—all of them. Put out the necessary instructions. I'll be in touch."

21

He tapped the rest three times to recall the internal operator. "PM," he said.

His mind was racing over the implications of what he'd been told. Perhaps it was Patterson who'd set the tone, with his gloomy prognostications of the Glasgow situation. Certainly Evans' immediate assessment of the position was one of unrelieved darkness. He was aware of a certain mental shock, as if his mind was still in a state of mild sedation, trying to protect itself for a few more moments from the full realization of what had happened. But his body had reacted at once. A massive dose of adrenalin had been pumped into his already overloaded system. He felt as if some powerful corrosive was eating at the lining of his stomach. He didn't believe that tissue could stand up to such treatment for much longer.

He looked round the committee, the phone still to his left ear, and said, "We shall have to adjourn. It's Powell—Enoch—some bloody madman's assassinated him."

Evans knew before he got to number 10 that the PM couldn't handle it. He knew it as soon as he spoke to him on the phone. The man's a bloody gentleman, Evans thought, and the days of gentlemen politicians have gone. They went with Munich—perhaps even before. They went with the empire, when the map was red from arsehole to breakfast time. You could send a bloody gunboat up the Niger then; now we haven't even got a gunboat. The Yanks have the gunboats now. The Yanks and the Russians—perhaps even the Chinese.

The car turned into Downing Street. It's odd, thought Evans, how news spreads. Not news, exactly. Hardly news. As far as he knew nothing had so far leaked out. But atmospheres. It seemed there was already an apprehension about the street. The clock at the bottom of Whitehall was striking eleven. It was now quite dark.

Under the street lights there were no more than half a dozen people. And yet there was an atmosphere as if something had already escaped on the wind.

The door was opened for him. He passed the police with a nod. They threw up salutes to him as he went through the door. Beckett was waiting inside.

"He's upstairs, sir," said Beckett. He looked nervous, as if for once he didn't quite know what to do.

"Upstairs?" said Evans.

"They're decorating down here. He thought, perhaps, upstairs—"

"Sir Alan Potter—Sir Philip Cleashaw?"

"They've arrived, sir. They're waiting—"

"Good. Tell them I'm seeing him alone first. Tell them I'll call them. And tell them it's good of them to come at such short notice."

He climbed the stairs to the first floor. The room door was ajar, with light showing through the opening. As he knocked, he wondered what state he would find the old man in. He opened the door, went inside and closed the door behind him.

"Ah, Freddy," said the PM, looking up and putting out a hand toward a chair. He smiled, though behind the smile there were clear indications of the strain he felt. "This matter in Glasgow—I was just refreshing my mind." He closed the file before him and put it carefully to one side.

"It's not the Glasgow matter, Prime Minister," said Evans. It was always "Prime Minister," never John or even Sir John. The PM insisted on preserving a certain formality. He liked a shape to things, an order. It made him feel secure. He was tall, angular and thin—a prime minister in the classic British style, as far as there has been any unifying style in them. He was a gentleman, with an impeccable family and educational background. He spoke and dressed like a gentleman. He looked as if he had never once been engaged in the savage in-fighting of twentieth-century politics. And yet despite that, he had emerged as the undisputed leader of the party. It was not that there was a lack of abler men, it was simply that the British as a whole, and his party in particular, preferred a "gentleman" as their Prime Minister. Preferred one, that is, when such a man was available. And Sir John Kitchin was both a gentleman and available. He was now in his seventy-first year, a fact which he relied on rather heavily to impose his authority, particularly when facing younger ministers. "We more experienced members of the party," was one of his conference cliches on which the cartoonists of the less establishment papers were always seizing. Now he was smiling across the table at Evans, his full mouth a little moist, as if he knew all Evans' problems and already his wider experience had suggested answers to most of them.

"I know it's not the Glasgow matter, Freddy," he said, twining his long, thin fingers together. "But one must preserve a sense of proportion. One must work on what is available to one at any given time."

"Of course, Prime Minister," said Evans. "But this affair—"

"Tragic," agreed the PM. "Entirely tragic. But if we don't preserve some measure of calm and control, we can hardly expect the country to do so, can we?"

"I've asked Sir Alan Potter to join us," said Evans. "And General Sir Philip Cleashaw. They're waiting downstairs. If—"

The PM's manner changed. It tightened. It hardened. He clasped his hands together more firmly and the smile went from his face.

"Have you?" he said. "On whose authority?"

Evans could have kicked himself. He'd played it badly. He'd implied a challenge to the PM's authority—an area where he was particularly sensitive. Now he had that to play down, and all the time minutes were ticking away that might have produced a line of firm and immediate action.

"I simply thought," said Evans, "that under the circumstances it might be as well to have them available—in case some specialist opinion—"

"Now, Freddy, you're going at it like a hothead. The situation's serious, of course. But things like this have happened before."

When, for God's sake, when? Evans wanted to shout. But he contained himself. He simply slipped the palm of his right hand over his stomach and pressed inward with it. It gave him a slight degree of comfort.

"I've been in touch with Briggs; he'll be along at any moment," the PM was saying. His hands had begun to relax again. He was, he felt, reestablishing his authority, the authority of a much more experienced man. "He'll probably bring Appleton with him—after all, Appleton's the man they expect to put in your shoes if they ever get into power again."

Thank God, thought Evans. If he's proposing putting the Opposition in the picture he must see some of the implications of the situation.

"And—until then, Prime Minister?" said Evans.

"Perhaps you'd better give me all the facts you have at the moment."

Bertram Warner, the Chief Constable, couldn't get through. He was in plain clothes and he arrived in his own unpretentious family sedan. He had to produce his identification card before the young constable would believe him.

"Commendable, commendable," said Warner, a touch of sarcasm in his voice.

On the steps of the shattered hall he met the Chief Superintendent.

"Couldn't get in the damn place," said Warner, but his immediate irritation had passed. "Man over there thought I was after the Crown Jewels."

He looked inside the hall. The wreckage still smoked.

"Everybody out?" he said. "I mean—the injured?"

"Just left, sir. Ambulances—just this minute gone."

"Hm. How many?"

"Nine killed outright. All the platform party—four others in the front rows. Wounded—about seven badly; ten or twelve others might be allowed home."

"And—er—*him?* The speaker?"

"Dead. Instantaneous. No chance at all."

He walked to the platform area with the Chief Superintendent a step or two behind him. His hands were thrust into his jacket pockets, with the thumbs showing outside. He was tall and finely built. The kind of man who has always kept himself in good physical shape. He was nodding his head as he looked down at the mess. He took out a pipe and lit the tobacco that was still in it. The smoke escaped from the side of his mouth.

"What was it, do you think?"

"Some kind of—bomb," said the Chief Superintendent.

"Really," said Warner, without a trace of sarcasm. "Couldn't have been a gas main?"

"We've done a preliminary check. This time of night it's a bit difficult to get at accurate records, but—it doesn't look like it. Probably have gone on burning if it had been gas."

"Probably. Any records of bombs having been dropped here during the war—some old time-fuse got shaken up by local building activity?"

"Nothing, sir."

"I'm scraping the barrel, I admit. Still, anything rather than what it looks like."

"Hm."

"You'd better get back to Division," said Warner. "Taylor can handle things. I'll be here if you want me."

"This'll stir things up, I'm afraid," said the Chief Superintendent, turning toward the exit.

"It's already started," said Warner.

"I called you in," the PM was saying, "out of courtesy. I didn't call you in to govern for me. Time for that when you win an election."

Briggs was built like a bulldog and behaved like some latter-day Churchill. He was standing now, both hands on the PM's desk, glaring down at him. "My God!" he said. "You've got a national crisis on your hands and you talk of party politics. The support that man had's enough to split the country down the middle if it gets out of hand. There are millions that think he's given them an identity—told 'em they're British, told 'em to stand up straight and look the world in the face, told 'em they matter. And there are nearly as many that think he's a kind of messiah. I tell you, he speaks for people who can't speak for themselves."

"That, coming from you," said the PM. He could still maintain a degree of bland urbanity. His background had given him a certain status in the social pecking order. He did not regard Briggs as being anywhere near him in that order. It gave him a decided assurance.

"It should damn well have come from you," snapped Briggs. "God knows we've been telling you long enough to open your eyes to the man."

"I admit he's been an embarrassment to us all," said the PM.

"Not all of us," said Briggs. "Not me. He's never embarrassed me."

"He wasn't a member of your party," said the PM.

"No," said Briggs. "He wasn't."

"Well," said the PM, pushing a little notepad away from him and smiling in that easy way that infuriated opponents and colleagues alike. It was a smile that meant he had already come to his own conclusions and that nothing was likely to shift him from them.

"All right," said Briggs with a nod toward his colleague Appleton. "You've had our views. If you choose to ignore them—all right. But by God, don't think we won't raise the devil if you do."

"Thank you," said the PM. "I propose taking the matter out of the hands of the local police and making the Home Office directly responsible for it."

"The finest way to blow up its importance," snapped Briggs.

"It could hardly be more important," said the PM. "The assassination of a Member of the House—that particular member, too. You seem to have a strange scale of priorities, I must say, if you think that's unimportant. Every right-minded man and woman in the country will want to see the most vigorous action taken to arrest whoever was responsible. I propose giving them that action." He turned to Evans and said, "Freddy, I'm making you personally responsible for the most prompt execution of the affair. Take whatever action seems to you most appropriate—and, Freddy, keep me informed."

Briggs turned to Appleton and said, "Come on, Dick." He walked quickly toward the door.

"One other thing," said the PM. "I don't want you to accuse me later of not having made you fully aware of my intentions. I'm recalling Colonel Jeffrey Monckton to handle the case, under the overall direction of the Home Secretary."

Briggs stopped. He couldn't believe his ears. He turned, looking like a gunfighter from some old Western film. His head was drawn deep into his shoulders, his hands came forward as if about to grasp something and smash it to pieces, his feet were a little apart.

"What!" he snarled. "That—butcher!"

Even Evans took a step forward and said, "But—Prime Minister!" Appleton simply threw open his hands as if it was quite the most ridiculous statement he'd ever heard.

"What you personally think of Colonel Monckton," said the PM, "is irrelevant. He has a record for toughness—very well, the situation calls for extreme toughness. He has a way of cutting through red tape—very well, that's offensive to the bureaucrat, but it's what we need now. His methods—"

"Methods!" stormed Briggs. "Good God, even in wartime there was nothing to choose between his methods and those of the Gestapo! Bribery, corruption, physical violence—those are the legitimate *methods,* are they, of a peacetime democracy?"

"I'm aware of some of the official views of him," said the PM. He waved a dismissive hand toward Briggs. "It's not the public view. He's still 'Panther' to them—they still know him by the old code name. It has a certain magic. It will be the clearest possible demonstration of the government's intention to prosecute the affair with every ounce of vigor."

"Prosecute—my arse!" shouted Briggs, walking to the desk and thumping down on it with both fists. "Do you think you can take me in with that kind of pompous drivel? What kind of a damn fool do you think I am? What's at the back of your mind is the image of the party. How's the party going to stand up to the kind of publicity that'll break in the morning? And if you manage to throw Monckton into the arena before the journalists can properly get their teeth into the thing, you'll have given them the story line before they can think up one of their own. Panther recalled from retirement—top agent to direct Powell case. And what are the police going to think of it? Shoved out of their legitimate job?"

"The police are under the direction of the government," said the PM. Evans could see that he was only becoming more deeply entrenched in his position.

"I'm wondering, Prime Minister," said Appleton, "whether Monckton's likely to accept such a job."

The PM glanced at his watch. He smiled. He said, "I've been in touch with Colonel Monckton by telephone. He's already accepted."

Briggs looked at Appleton, then turned for the door.

"My God!" he snarled as he clumped down the staircase. "What age does he think we live in? The divine right of Prime Ministers —is that what he wants us to accept? Doesn't he know what we did to Charles the First?"

News of some general explosion began to reach the London news desks in the late evening. Most of it was from free lances in the northern area, since the staff men sent to cover the speech were still being held in the hall of the local school. But it was imprecise and shadowy information. "A general explosion" and "a sheet of flame" were recurrent phrases. Nonetheless it was possible to build an alarming picture by juxtaposing such phrases with the firm fact that Enoch Powell had been speaking in the town at the same time that the explosion took place, and no reports had come in of his leaving.

Phone calls to staff men in Leeds and Hull produced no results. All reported that roads into the town had been sealed off by the police. Not a single staff man had found a policeman prepared to say a word. Phone calls to the local papers in the area—the *Yorkshire Post, Yorkshire Evening Press, Northern Echo* and *Hull Daily Mail*—were no more productive. No one knew anything but the undisputed fact of an explosion. To the Fleet Street news editors, and their counterparts in Manchester on the northern editions, the situation began to appear ominous. In case the worst had happened, obituary notices began to be set up by the printers. Blocks made from recent pictures of Powell were laid out on desks of art editors, so that if necessary the most suitable might be chosen quickly. Some of the larger papers flew reporters and photographers to Yeadon airfield. In view of what had already happened to other press men, their chances of getting through the police cordon were not good. But at least they would be ready to move in as soon as the cordon was lifted.

Phone calls to the Home Office and to the Special Security Branch only added to the confusion. The Home Office hedged. One spokesman denied having any information at all, while another confirmed that some explosion had been reported, caused, in all probability, by a fractured gas main. Special Security flatly denied having heard anything at all. In any case, it was pointed out, if there had been an explosion, that was the job of the local police force and fire service in the area. But no one on the Manchester or London news desks could get through to the local force. It seemed that all lines into the area were out of order.

Inevitably, from three areas in the country, the wildest rumors began to race outward. The journalists and photographers working suddenly on new copy in Manchester and London, the printers setting up obituary notices, began to speculate. A few press men went from the office to a club. They talked. Others heard them, added their own speculations, and talked. Near the scene of the explosion, people who had heard it without knowing what it was rang up friends. Beneath the apparent calm of the late evening, a ferment of speculation took place. No firm information appeared that might have quashed it. The late news on TV carried only the ominous announcement that an explosion had taken place in the area where Powell was to give a speech, and that no further information was as yet available.

It may have been this first trickle of information that forced Evans' hand. He wanted to hold up the normal press and TV news process long enough for him to have the situation firmly in hand. He was quite sure that if he could produce a culprit to coincide with the breaking of the story—ideally he visualized the culprit's picture appearing on the TV screen simultaneously with one of Enoch Powell—the repercussions of the assassination would be minimal. And that culprit, he hoped, was already being held for questioning in that northern school hall. With luck he would be produced by the police before dawn broke—perhaps even before Colonel Monckton arrived on the scene. And so, a little before midnight, D notices began to reach harassed news editors.

Angelo's had become an unofficial Press Club during the six months that it had been open. The reason for its sudden popularity was obvious to anyone who knew the place, for it provided a back room in which it was possible to get a drink and a snack at any time during the day or night. It lay at the back of St. Bride's Lane, very close in fact to the official Press Club, and it was hardly known outside the profession. It was here that the real speculation was taking place, speculation about the likely outcome of the assassination, for no one in that confined and smoky atmosphere was in doubt about what had happened.

Alexander Williams was sitting alone at one of the little circular cast-iron tables, eating a turkey sandwich. His round, heavy glasses had slipped a little down his nose so that when he lifted his head and glanced upward and sideways toward the group of men at the bar, he looked at them over the top of the glass. He was not a popular man. Few people spoke to him. He had a reputation for being unreliable. If you told him something in confidence, you always had the feeling that he'd break that confidence the moment it suited him to do so. He wore an old tweed overcoat, despite the heat of the evening, and his lank, dark hair dropped down over the tops of his ears. There was something a little animal about the way he sat there by himself, cramming the remains of the turkey sandwich into his mouth. As he ate, he listened. He heard the stories flying round the bar. He heard the conjectures and theories. At last he took up the paper napkin on which the sandwich had been served, wiped his hands on it and, still munching, left the place. He spoke to no one and no one spoke to him.

Outside he walked into the first telephone box he came to and rang a Covent Garden number.

"Listen, Daniel," he said. "It's Alexander Williams. . . ."

Nothing surprised Daniel Westbrook. He had a political philosophy, and there was scarcely a human event or act of God that didn't fit in with it. He was small, almost incredibly thin and acidulated. The top of his head was bald, but lower down his skull the graying hair stood out like fine twisted wire. He was almost literally skin and bone. His age was fifty-two. His weight perhaps one hundred pounds. He smoked a heavy, deep-bowled, curved pipe that seemed to pull his head forward from his shoulders. As Williams spoke to him on the phone he could visualize Westbrook sitting there in the little back room of the Covent Garden shop, surrounded by dense clouds of thick tobacco smoke.

Westbrook had begun as a Marxist. At first it had seemed to him a ready-made philosophy to which he might harness his own ambitions. But he didn't believe in the parliamentary process, and when he realized that his fellow Marxists seemed actually to believe that if they waited long enough they might be voted into power by an enlightened electorate, he spat them out—them and their philosophy together—and formed the British Union of Activists. He had in any case begun to formulate a different philosophy. He lost interest in economic and social equality, in the overthrow of capitalism and in the proletariat's ownership of the means of production. He lost interest in the proletariat, if indeed he'd ever had an interest in it. What replaced his earlier beliefs was a conviction that the real political mainspring was self-esteem. "Give the proles riches," he used to say, "and rob them of self-esteem, and you've a revolt on your hands. But give them self-esteem—a sense of distinction—and you can treat them like dogs!" And there were two ways to give the British self-esteem, he asserted to his followers. You could make them exert themselves and so *achieve* distinction. Alternatively, you could tell them that they were already distinguished, and that the reason why they failed to feel that distinction was because of the mass of non-British people who had become identified with them and who were stealing their distinction from them. "Distinction," he used to say, "increases in direct proportion to the degree of undistinction that a group can project on nonmembers." He had, he felt, discovered a fundamental political law.

"It's the beginning," he said to Williams over the phone. "We must help it to develop. We must drive the wedge home. We must isolate. You know the Annapurna restaurant in Charlotte Street? Instruct de Margolis to smash it."

Evans had counted only on silencing the official channels of information. Over the subterranean channel of rumor he had no control. All he could have done to frustrate it would have been to release as full a story as possible to the official newsmen, and that was exactly what he was determined to avoid.

In consequence, rumor did its work unhindered. It spread by word of mouth through late cinema audiences. It spread through the late drinkers in the pubs and clubs. It spread by telephone.

Muhammad Singh had a news agent's and tobacconist's shop in Soho. He had been there seventeen years, having moved from his birthplace in south Battersea when he got married. His shop was in a street with Indian and Chinese restaurants. His next-door neighbor was a Polish tailor and four of the girls in the strip club opposite were from Istanbul. It was a foreign area and he was part of it. But he felt it to be foreign, because he himself was English, with an English education, English parents and an English passport. Not that any of these facts saved him when it came to the point. He still had the characteristic facial structure and color of the race of his forebears, and that damned him to destruction that late summer evening.

He closed the shop at nine-thirty and went upstairs to watch television. At half-past ten it began to bore him. He looked at his watch. It was too early to go to bed. His wife had died the year before, and since her death he had found the evenings often unendurable. He rang a friend in Fitzroy Square and agreed to join him for coffee.

Outside, it was still very warm. He took off his jacket and laid it over his arm. He walked to the top of Wardour Street and crossed Oxford Street. Diesel fumes hung in the unmoving air. Traffic was still fairly heavy and crowds stood on street corners. Above the whole London scene, stars shone brilliantly in the night sky. What a town! he was thinking. Nowhere like it. He'd spent a week once with his wife in Paris. Long ago. But Paris couldn't match this place. Perhaps because it was his town, the place where he'd been born, the place he'd helped to fashion—in a modest enough way.

Ahead, outside one of the restaurants in Charlotte Street, there was another crowd. The weather brought them out. But he could hear voices raised as he got closer. People in the crowd were shouting. Then a sudden shattering of glass and a great roar from the crowd. A roar of satisfaction, yet at the same time one of amusement, as if they were engaged in some noisy game. Instinctively he crossed to the other side of the road. Temperamentally he was a withdrawn man, a man who kept himself to himself. It was a trait that had gained in strength since the death of his wife. He reached the other pavement and walked ahead quickly. As he passed the restaurant he saw that the whole front window had been smashed. The glass had fallen inward over the floor and tables. From the first-floor windows, two Indian women were leaning out shouting.

A man stood back on the pavement below and looked up. "It's

one of you bastards that killed him!" he shouted. He flung something upward, and the glass of the upstairs window shattered above the women's heads.

Someone in front of the shattered shop window was shouting to the proprietor inside. The proprietor was pleading with him. A man on the pavement growled. He seemed a little drunk. His movements were labored. He put a hand through the broken window and pulled a cloth from one of the tables. He held it in front of him, so that one of the corners hung down. Then he took out a cigarette lighter and set it alight. The crowd about him watched with anticipation. It knew what was going to happen. It relished the idea. It did not matter that it was happening slowly and deliberately. That simply added to its satisfaction. When the cloth was well ablaze, the man tossed it through the window. The proprietor was frantic. He rushed to the cloth and began stamping on the flames. The crowd laughed. The idea was catching. Another tablecloth was set alight, and another.

"Please, please!" cried the proprietor. "It's my home—I live here, I have children."

"I have children," someone mimicked. Everyone laughed.

"They all have bloody children."

"Sex mad!"

A piece of glass, flung by someone on the pavement, struck the proprietor in the face. He fell back with a cry and put both hands over his face. The flames began to take hold of the more inflammable materials in the restaurant. Two of the wickerwork chairs began to burn.

The drunk was wagging a finger at the proprietor. "Listen, you," he said. "For every Englishman you kill—Powell, anybody—we'll get ten of you. Understand? Hey, you! Understand?" He turned to the crowd, and as he did so, caught sight of Muhammad Singh on the opposite pavement. He pointed an unsteady finger: "There's another of 'em. Don't let 'im get away!"

Muhammad Singh turned and began to run. It was a moment before other members of the crowd caught sight of him. Then some of them broke away and began to run after him. Singh thrust his feet at the pavement and drove himself forward. He sidestepped people walking toward him. He took to the road, where his progress was less impeded. A car swerved to avoid him. The side mirror caught his jacket and tore it out of his grasp. As he looked over his shoulder, he could see three or four of them gaining on him. They were less than twenty yards behind. The first of them was shouting, "Stop him! Stop the murdering bastard!"

Fitzroy Square was just ahead. He thought that if he could get somewhere where there were more people, he might lose them. If he could bury himself in the middle of some crowd. If he could break down some turning to the right and get into Tottenham Court Road, perhaps. His heart was drumming inside his chest. The blood vessels pounded in his neck. Yet still he ran. It was as if his feet and legs understood the danger if they stopped ramming down at the pavement.

The pack behind sensed what was in his mind. It moved toward his right, and suddenly he had to swerve left and along the south side of the square. They were shouting, though he couldn't make out the words. It was more like the baying of hounds than human speech. It struck a still deeper terror into him. Then the leader began to close. Five yards, four, three. Then he leaped, body launched horizontally, both arms out, hands open to grasp the first thing they touched. The hands touched Singh's left leg. Singh snatched it up and drove down with it again. The hands couldn't hold it and for a moment he was clear.

Then something tore inside him. Something that he couldn't isolate, but something that had been the mainspring of his energy. He continued to run, against all the inner cries of his body, but something had failed. As he neared the exit from the square, one of them got a hand on his left shoulder. He jerked it clear, but as he did so the man on his right chopped at him with the outside of his left arm and struck him across the side of the head. He felt no pain from the blow, but the force of it threw him off balance. He reeled over to his left and ran his head against a row of iron railings. Still he felt no pain. His body turned, his face rolled across the railings, his right shoulder struck the ground and he slid across the pavement. He was dead seconds before they began kicking him.

There were other rumors running wild that night. Perhaps "unofficial stories" describes them better, for although they did not carry the authority of having been issued formally, they were substantially true. The story that spread through the night offices of the police, for example, was one of them. It concerned a serious rift that was developing between government and police over the assassination and how the investigation into it was to be conducted.

Evans, the Home Secretary, had to accept the PM's brief. He had to accept that Colonel Jeffrey Monckton would be responsible for the investigation. But he chose to interpret the brief as widely as possible. The PM, in his characteristically high-handed way, had refused to consult the police and army chiefs, because he felt that Evans had challenged his authority on the point. Very well. That didn't mean that Evans himself couldn't consult them. On his way out of number 10, he called on them in the downstairs library and took them back to his flat.

Sir Alan Potter was in his late forties, a tall, well-groomed man with more the appearance of a university don than a policeman. He was one of the "new men" who began to appear in top executive posts as a result of the Fortnum Committee's report into the relationship between age and leadership ability. He sat back in one of Evans' deep leather armchairs, facing the windows and the river.

"He'll never get away with it," General Sir Philip Cleashaw was saying. "He can't get away with it!"

He had his hands clasped behind his back and was walking, eyes fixed on the carpet, from one side of the room to the other.

"Oh, he'll get away with it," said Evans. "The mood of the country—the mood of the House. Everything's played into his hands. What's been the pattern of public life these past few years? Student unrest—violence in every shape and form—near civil war in Ulster—this Glasgow business. The country's sick of it. Sick of permissiveness, sick of teen-age drug merchants, sick of youth worship, sick of being 'swinging.' You know what it wants? It wants a strong man—the iron fist. And you know what keeps me awake at nights—you know what gave me this?" He prodded a finger at his rumbling stomach. "The dread that it'll get one."

"No," said Cleashaw. "Never! I don't believe it. All right, things aren't as they should be—but not that. There's something in the British makeup, something in the national character!"

He stood with his back to the window. He was below middle height, dark and with a Jewish cast to his features.

Sir Alan Potter smiled. "I think you're wrong, Philip," he said. "I think it's in the process of getting one now."

"The PM?" said Cleashaw. "Never!"

"Not the PM," said Potter. "Monckton—with the PM's backing."

"Exactly!" said Evans.

"Ridiculous!" said Cleashaw.

Evans took up a tall glass from the marble mantel and spun the contents round and round. If the others hadn't known Evans, they might have thought he was drinking Pernod. The liquid in the glass had that milky, opalescent appearance. It was in fact milk of magnesia. He measured his consumption of it by the bottle, as some men measure their consumption of Scotch.

"Look," said Potter, tapping the arm of the chair with a finger. "We know Monckton—we know his record, we know the man. Personally I've always thought him a little mad. The fact is that at this moment he's taking over power that should be in the hands of the police—and he's doing it with the authority and support of the head of state."

"Very well," said Cleashaw. "He's doing that. It's a damn shame for the police that he's being allowed to, but perhaps there's some sense in it. Damn it—it is a political assassination. It wants conducting with a certain vigor."

"That's not the real issue," said Potter. "The issue's one of power. Who's to say how he'll interpret his powers? If there's public disorder as a result of this killing, who's to be responsible for keeping the peace—us or Monckton?"

"Us?" said Cleashaw. "Damn it, it hardly affects the Army."

"It might—it just might."

"It couldn't," said Cleashaw. "That's what Parliament's there for—the preservation of democracy. First and foremost."

"Not first and foremost," said Potter. "Like any other organization its first function is to preserve itself. The first function of the PM is to keep himself and his party in power. As long as he can do that nothing can shake him, and as long as Monckton keeps the confidence of the PM he's unassailable. With the present government majority I don't see the PM losing the reins easily."

Evans put down his glass.

"You paint a pretty gloomy picture," said Evans. "But it leaves out a significant factor."

"Oh?"

"The Home Office. I have overall direction of the case. As long as I'm there, Monckton's answerable to me. Perhaps we can't get rid of him at the moment—but we can keep him in damn close check."

There were more than three hundred people in the school hall. They had been held there now for more than four hours. Some were beginning to make the most strenuous complaints to the police in charge. Some, no doubt having seen men do the same thing in television plays, were demanding to speak to their solicitors. None of it made any difference. The police were going through the enormous task of taking statements and names and addresses from everyone. Even then no one was released. The Chief Constable had given instructions that no one was to leave the school until he had given the necessary order. He had had his instructions from the Home Office. He was told to his horror that the case was to be taken out of the hands of the police. That Monckton was to direct field operations. He had expected, of course, that in a matter of such national importance London would want to send up a policeman of its own choice. Some specialist in this kind of thing. It had never occurred to him that London would put in a nonpoliceman —and such a man as Monckton.

At two in the morning, Monckton made contact with him by telephone from his Hampshire cottage.

"That Warner?" said the voice. The same voice, thought Warner, though perhaps the phone distorted it a little. It sounded a little harder, more rasping and metallic. It had, too, thought Warner, a sense of triumph in it somewhere, though what there was to be triumphant about he couldn't imagine.

"Warner here," said the Chief Constable.

"Colonel Monckton. You've been told I'm taking over?"

"I've been told," said Warner.

"What's the position?"

Warner told him. Monckton didn't interrupt. He didn't say "Yes" or "No" down the phone to show that he was following. He didn't even grunt. At one point Warner thought they'd been cut off. "You there, sir?" he said. "I'm here," said Monckton.

When Warner had finished speaking, Monckton said, "It's now two-thirty-five. I'm driving up straightaway. The place is to be kept in isolation until I arrive. Is that clear?"

"That's clear," said Warner. "I take it we're to continue with the taking of statements?"

"Of course."

"And then we can release the people we're holding?"

"Release them? What are you talking about? A state of isolation, I said. No one in or out until I get there."

"I see," said Warner.

"Something troubling you, Warner?"

"Nothing troubling me, sir," said Warner.

The caretaker had grumbled. Dixon had found him sitting in a deck chair in his small patch of garden, relaxing in his shirt sleeves in the late evening sun.

"They want the school opened up," said Dixon.

"On whose authority?" said the caretaker.

"Come on," said Dixon. "You must have heard the explosion?"

"Explosion? I thought it was one of these bloody sonic boom things they're always trying out. I said to the wife—"

"The hall—it's been blown up. We've got to have somewhere to put people."

"The hall? God almighty!"

Taylor had shepherded the crowd inside. The place smelled of children and chalk—a familiar mustiness. He organized the arrangement of chairs and trestle tables, and he persuaded Harry Rowntree to bring bread from his bakery and make sandwiches. The less formality, Taylor thought, the more readily would people cooperate. And the easier the cooperation, the quicker the thing would be over. And he wanted it over quickly, because he believed that whoever was responsible for the explosion would hardly have stayed in the audience to hear it go off. He thought it unlikely that any of the people in the hall knew a thing about the cause of the explosion. It was necessary, of course, to take names and addresses, though in the end it might prove to have been a waste of time.

Taylor spoke to the crowd in the hall. Some were sitting on chairs and a few were sitting on the floor, backs resting against the wall. Most were still standing, forming little groups, trying to make some sense of what had happened.

"I'm sorry for the inconvenience," said Taylor, standing on a chair so that he could be seen. "You know what happened—as far as any of us knows. You'll realize that we've got to take names and addresses and brief statements now, so that you won't be bothered again. We don't want to keep anyone longer than necessary. If you'd be good enough to come to the tables here."

He pointed to the six trestle tables that had been set up by the main doors into the school hall. Behind them sat his men, shirt sleeves rolled up, waiting for the first people to approach them.

Taylor sat down at one of the tables, nodded to the constable at his side, and took up a pen. He was aware of a woman approaching the table and he pulled a form toward him.

"If I could have your name," he said.

"Enid Markus," she said. "I'm a journalist."

He looked up. She was holding a large bag in front of her, clasping the handles in both hands. There was a silver clip in her hair.

"Oh yes—the hall," said Taylor. "Take a seat, will you?"

"Any news?" she said.

"For your paper?"

"I'm curious—that's all. It's natural, isn't it? I didn't expect someone to let off a bomb. Isn't it natural to be curious about it?"

"We don't know it was a bomb," said Taylor.

"Really?" she said.

"It could have been a gas main."

"I smelled the cordite," she said.

"It's this North Sea gas we're using up here," said Taylor. "Now the name again. Markus was it—Miss Markus?"

"Enid Markus."

Constable Dixon leaned over him and said, "Excuse me, sir. Chief Constable would like to see you."

Taylor got up. "She's a journalist, Mr. Dixon," he said. "Tell her nothing. She'll have the job off your back if you're not careful."

"What's his name?" said Enid Markus, watching Taylor walk out of the hall and into the corridor beyond.

"You heard him, miss," said Dixon. "No collaboration with the press."

Bertram Warner was in the headmaster's study. He looked surprisingly calm, sitting there behind the headmaster's desk. He was smoking his pipe, and looking at a map of the town and the approach roads. On each one of them was a red cross to mark the place where one of his patrols stood. He put out a hand toward a chair when Taylor came in, and said simply, "Sit down, Mr. Taylor."

Taylor sat down. He was beginning to feel the effects of lost sleep.

"How's it going?" said Warner.

"We should be through in two or three hours, sir."

"Good. Keep them there after you've seen them."

"It's going to be difficult, sir."

"I know." Warner lifted his shoulders and dropped them again, then he took his pipe out of his mouth. "Taylor," he said, "you know anything about Colonel Monckton?"

"Colonel Monckton, sir?"

"Wartime man. Used to have the code name 'Panther.' "

"Only what I've read, sir. A reputation for toughness, I believe."

"You'll be working with him."

"Working with him, sir?"

"They think it's serious enough for the Home Secretary to take a hand in it. They've appointed Monckton—Colonel Monckton—to direct it."

"Then it's out of our hands, sir?"

"You'll liaise between ourselves and Colonel Monckton."

"Then it's not to be a police matter?"

"Monckton will tell you what he wants you to do."

"I see, sir. When's he likely to arrive?"

"He left north Hampshire about two-thirty. What'll it be—two hundred fifty miles? Motorway most of the trip—say five or six hours. Say eight o'clock."

"Do you know him, sir? Colonel Monckton?"

"I've met him," said Warner. "In Germany, just after the war."

"You sound—well, a bit unsure, sir."

"Little surprised perhaps," said Warner.

"My wife, sir," said Taylor. "She'll have no idea what's happened. Could I get in touch with her?"

"You can ring her," said Warner. He picked up the phone. "Chief Constable here," he said. "Get me an outside line." He handed the phone to Taylor. "I'll be in the hall when you've finished."

Taylor dialed. He heard the door close behind Warner. He heard the phone bell ring and ring at the other end of the line. The operator—one of his own men—said, "You still holding, sir?" Taylor said, "They'll be asleep. Let it ring."

At last someone said, "Yes?"

"Beryl?"

"I've been worried out of my mind," she said.

"There's a job on. I can't get away."

"Why didn't you tell me? The children were expecting you."

"I thought I'd be home by ten."

"I kept them up thinking you wouldn't be long. They wanted to see you. Adrienne's been crying. I hope the phone hasn't woken her. When are you coming?"

"I don't know."

"I can't prepare anything if I don't know."

"I don't want you to prepare anything," said Taylor.

"Are you keeping something from me?"

"I'm not keeping anything from you," said Taylor.

"Was it the explosion?"

"I'll tell you when I see you."

"And you don't know when?"

"I've said I don't know."

"All right."

"Beryl—I'm sorry."

"I'm used to it," she said.

By four-thirty in the morning, Evans began to sense a breathing space. He had conferred and phoned and sent memos. Monckton was on his way north from Hampshire. Warner had appointed one of his Chief Inspectors as Monckton's aide. No new information had been forthcoming during the past hour. He thought that with luck he might manage two hours' sleep. He took off his shoes and tie and loosened his collar. He set the alarm for six-thirty and lay down on the bed. He was used to snatching sleep when he could, and he fell into unconsciousness almost at once. Within half an hour he was wide awake. The pain in his stomach was almost unbearable. When he pressed it with the palm of his hand—a movement that had become instinctive to him—instead of easing the pain as it usually did, it increased it sharply. It made him cry out. He recognized that his body had suddenly revolted against its usage. It was not the usual pain, something that would pass in time, something that could be eased by a tablet under the tongue or a glass of milk. Something inside him had broken—collapsed under the strain. He lifted his knees toward his chest. It gave him some slight ease. He managed to roll a little to his left and pick up the phone. The first number that came to mind was for the emergency services. He dialed and called for an ambulance. His flat was locked, he said. He couldn't get up to open it. If they couldn't get in they had his permission to break the lock. But would they please hurry.

He was unconscious when they lifted him onto a stretcher. They took him to St. George's at Hyde Park Corner. By six-thirty that morning they had opened up his abdominal wall and exposed the perforated ulcer.

People in the hall seemed reconciled to their virtual imprisonment. They felt no less bitter about it, but they were less inclined as the night wore on to protest to the police. They had collected in small groups, discovering people with whom they had some small thing in common. Many were already known to one another—it was only to be expected in such a small town—but others were not. A number had traveled considerable distances to hear the speech.

The journalists made up one such group. There were fifteen of them, and journalism was perhaps the only thing they had in common. Many of those from the nationals were already well known to one another. They had met a dozen times before on similar jobs. The two free lances knew no one. Bob Arnold, who had met Enid Markus on three or four occasions, was saying to her, "You're resigned to it—OK. I'm not. I don't give a damn what they say, I'm getting out. I've got a story and I'm getting to a phone with it."

"How?" said Enid. "I mean, all right, supposing I agree with the sentiments—just how are you getting out of here?"

She looked around. People were still queuing to be interviewed at the trestle tables. Beyond them, a policeman stood at the main entrance doors. There were two other doors into the hall. Both were guarded by policemen. She turned back to Bob Arnold.

"I've been to the gents," he said. "I can get the window open there."

"Fine," she said. "Why are you telling me?"

"Cover for me if you can, will you? That's all. Some story when they want to know where I am—just long enough to let me get to a phone."

"Why?"

"Why?"

"You get away. You get an exclusive, if they hold us long enough. What do I get?"

"Look," said Arnold. "When I've rung my paper and they've got the copy, I'll ring yours. I can't be any fairer."

She thought for a moment, then she said, "All right. When are you going?"

"I'll go now, if that's OK with you."

"It's OK with me," she said.

He nodded and turned away. She watched him walk across to the policeman at one of the doors and explain what he wanted. The policeman nodded and he passed through the door.

Someone was asking about "Reggie." He turned to her and said, "Reggie—you know Reggie? Short, fat guy with specs—you know?" She nodded. "Well, you seen him?" She shook her head. "Been gone half an hour; can't see him anywhere."

"Where did he go?" she asked.

"Said he was going for a pee."

She looked across to the door and saw Bob Arnold coming back to her.

"They must have caught on," he said. "Some bastard's screwed the bloody window down."

"Did you see Reggie? Reggie Deacon? You know?" she said.

"Yes, I know. No—he's not there. Why?"

"No one's seen him for half an hour."

"But he'd never get through that window," said Arnold. "Not

with those legs and that fat arse. You sure?"

"That's what they're saying."

Certainly it had been a struggle. Reggie Deacon had spotted the window much earlier in the evening. He didn't know why it registered at the time, but he remembered it in a flash when the police made it clear that even after the preliminary statements had been taken, no one was going to be released. He got it open all right, but he got through it only with the greatest difficulty. It was an agonizing few minutes for him. He had had to leave the door unlocked so that no one would suspect there'd been an escape from the place —not, at least, until he'd got a ten-minute start. Then his legs were too short for him to be able to step through the open window. He had had to go out headfirst. He was hopelessly out of condition. The metal projection on the bottom frame of the window that was used to secure the lock stuck into his belly as he struggled to drive himself through the hole. When his center of gravity was on the outside of the window sill, and he began to topple forward out of the window, he put down his hands flat on the brickwork of the wall and tried to control his descent. It worked for an inch or two, and then he began to feel gravity seize his body and pull it downward. Increasingly he lost control. He began to fall forward, headfirst toward the asphalt surface of the playground below. For a moment he was held. The metal projection that had been sticking into his belly now caught at the base of his fly. It slowed his progress forward, without actually stopping it. For a second it seemed to hold his weight, and then, inexorably, he continued to slip downward. When he finally lost control and the metal projection began to rip his trousers apart, he was some three feet above the asphalt. He turned his head a little, his glasses fell off and he crashed down on one shoulder. The fall knocked the breath clean out of him. He thought he would never breathe again. He lay, an overweight, amorphous heap, wedged upside down at the junction of wall and playground. Then at last he began to find his feet. He had rubbed the side of his head down the last few inches of brick-work. It was bleeding, though only from superficial grazing. He sat up and groped for his glasses. When he found them he put them on and dragged himself to his feet. His trousers hung from him— two separate legs, held together only at the waistband. But he was out. He was clear of the hall, and as far as he could tell, unseen. It was now simply a question of getting to a phone.

Police reinforcements were continuing to arrive in the area. Monckton had already given his instructions for the place to be sealed off, held in a state of hermetic isolation, until he arrived. Local Army units were also standing by. Deacon had thought that his only problem was to get out of the hall. It proved to be the easiest part of his escape. He climbed the railings at one corner of the playground and dropped heavily into Dale Street. He hung in a doorway until a police patrol had passed the corner ahead, and then began to move. It dawned on him that all the local phone boxes would be out of action, or controlled at the exchange by the police, and he realized with a certain sinking of his spirits that he would have to get clear of the town—perhaps clear of the sur-rounding area—before it would be safe to use a phone.

The patrolman saw the white Rover in the distance. He had been looking for it for the past fifteen minutes. It was seven-thirty-five in the morning. He picked up the car microphone and said, "Car approaching now—white Rover. Might be him."

As he put down the microphone, the Rover drew alongside. The driver wound down the window and said, "Colonel Monckton. I'm looking for the Chief Constable."

The patrolman directed him to Subdivisional Headquarters, then picked up the microphone again.

"What's he like?" said control.

"Cropped hair—thinnish build—moustache. Seems a pleasant enough sort."

Noel Taylor was on the steps when Monckton's car drew up. He opened the door and Monckton got out. He was shorter than Taylor had expected. He stood with a slight stoop. Taylor saluted and Monckton nodded in response.

"Chief Inspector Taylor, sir. Chief Constable's expecting you."

Taylor turned and walked up the steps to hold the main door open for Monckton. The policeman on the door of the headmaster's study stood aside. Taylor knocked and pushed open the door for Monckton to walk in.

"If you'd take a seat, sir," said Taylor. "Can I get you a cup of tea?"

"Tea? Thank you. No milk."

"Of course, sir. I'll tell the Chief you're here."

Warner was in the hall. He looked tired. He was explaining with infinite patience to the group of journalists why it was necessary to hold them. Taylor caught his eye. They walked together to the hall door.

"He's here, is he?" said Warner.

"In the study, sir."

"Think you can work with him?"

"I think so, sir—seems quite easy."

"Right. Let's go and meet him."

Monckton was sitting behind the desk. How the sight of him again took Warner back! He'd hardly aged at all. The same cropped hair, the same moustache, the same slight blend in the top of the body. Monckton looked up, then stood up and put out a hand. The pale eyes still had that distant look, as if not quite focused on what they were looking at. The wrinkles on the forehead were deeper, the cheeks a little more sunken.

Warner took the hand. It was still firm and strong.

"Well, Warner," said Monckton. "Where was it the last time?"

"Düsseldorf, I believe, Colonel. The von Kuffstein investigations."

"Ah, yes. Von Kuffstein. Some little misunderstanding between us. I remember."

"It's a long time ago, Colonel."

"Yes," said Monckton, dropping his hand to his side.

There was no warmth between them.

"I see you have the area sealed," said Monckton, running a finger over the map on the desk.

"No one's been in or out since the explosion," said Warner.

"Good. Where are you holding them?"

"Just down the corridor—the school hall."

"How many?"

"About three hundred."

"And the bomb itself—what news have you there?"

"Forensic are inside. They'll give us a preliminary report as soon as they've finished."

"But it was a bomb? No doubt about that?"

"None at all. No mains services within thirty yards—no bombs dropped on the area during the war."

"No old mine workings, no natural gas pocket?"

"Nothing, Colonel."

"Hm!" said Monckton. "Then we shall have to wait for forensic. What about motive—any light that can be thrown on that?"

"Mr. Taylor was on the spot the whole time," said Warner.

"Very little in the way of demonstrators, sir. There'd been arrangements to transport students from the universities, but they didn't arrive," said Taylor.

"None of them?"

"One or two by private car. None in the official coaches."

"Why not?"

"The local police delayed them."

"On whose orders?"

"Well—mine, sir," said Taylor.

"Good," said Monckton. "How did people get into the hall?"

"It was an all-ticket meeting, sir," said Taylor. "Just the one entrance, through the main doors. The committee had a man checking the tickets. I had two men with him."

"Nothing unusual there?"

"Nothing, sir. My men recognized most of the audience."

"What about other ways in?" said Monckton.

"Just the one into the anteroom, sir. I was in there myself before the meeting and up to the time of the explosion."

"You weren't in the hall itself?"

"No, sir. Just in the anteroom."

Warner took out his pipe and put it in his mouth.

"I'd rather you didn't," said Monckton.

"Sorry," said Warner. "I forgot."

"How many men did you have in the hall?" said Monckton.

"Ten, sir. Then myself and a constable in the anteroom."

"Was anything thrown?"

"No, sir. I've been through it with all the men I had in the hall—nine of them, that is; one's still unconscious in hospital—head injuries. Nothing was thrown."

"So it was there before the meeting—the bomb, whatever it was?"

"It must have been, sir. I don't know where. We made three searches of the hall. I supervised them personally. We found nothing. Platform, lavatories, radiators, seating—nothing at all."

"What time did you make the last search?"

"Just after three, sir. After that I had men on both doors and two inside the hall."

"This man of yours who was injured—how close to the speaker was he?"

Monckton lifted his head. He was looking more beyond Taylor than at him.

"Front row, sir—very close. That's how he came to be knocked about."

"If there was anything to be seen, he would have seen it?"

"Yes, sir. But I don't think there was anything to be seen. He had a personal radio with him—all the men had. He had instructions to keep it in his hand. Control was listening the whole time. They heard nothing."

"Sounds to have been a very professional job," said Monckton. "What do you think, Warner?"

"Someone who knew what he was doing, Colonel—yes."

"I've checked the local quarries, sir, and the Army Explosives Depot at Wheaton," said Taylor. "There've been no break-ins—no explosives or detonators missing. No local men known for this kind of thing."

"Safebreakers?"

"No one, sir. I don't think it was a local man. It feels too—professional."

"Any militant organizations in the area—immigrant organizations?" said Monckton.

"It's not an immigrant area, Colonel," said Warner.

"These people are all over, Warner," said Monckton, turning to look at the Chief Constable.

"No local organizations, sir," said Taylor. "Not known to us. The West Riding police are checking there. Perhaps Leeds or Bradford—perhaps Hull."

Monckton continued to look at Warner.

"The people you're holding," said Monckton. "They've all made preliminary statements?"

"On the desk, sir. There." Taylor pointed to a pile of documents.

Monckton turned over the first two or three. "Anything significant in them, Chief Constable?"

"The Chief Inspector's been through them, Colonel," said Warner.

"You leave a good deal to your Chief Inspector."

"He has my absolute confidence," said Warner.

"They're the usual forms, sir," said Taylor. "Names, addresses, nationality—brief statements."

"Yes," said Monckton. "So I see. This man"—he tapped the form in front of him—Kerick—Jan Kerick?"

"He's the local brewery manager, sir. Been here for—"

"Since the war," said Warner.

"He was born in Warsaw, I see. You've got him down as British."

"He was naturalized after the war. He was a pilot with the RAF," said Warner.

"Any more like him, Mr. Taylor—non-British in origin?"

"Well—some, sir—yes."

"How many?"

"Well—" Taylor looked at Warner. The Chief Constable had his hands in his jacket pockets. He was standing very upright. His expression was stern, controlled. "I suppose seven or eight, sir."

"I'd like to see them," said Monckton.

"In the hall, sir?"

"In here. You can release the others—except the journalists. Now I want to have a look at this Jubilee Hall, Warner, and I want to have a word with forensic. Are they on the phone down there?"

"There's no phone in the hall, Colonel," said Warner.

"Have an internal line run down there, will you?"

It was some time before the authorities at St. George's Hospital could identify their patient. Evans had been picked up from his bed, half dressed. He had no jacket with him which might have contained a diary or an address book. Now he still lay unconscious under the postoperational effect of anesthesia. He was one of the PM's newer men, so that his face had not received that press and TV publicity that would have made him instantly recognizable to the hospital authorities. In any case, even if the face had been well known, it might still not have been recognized under the circumstances in which he now lay. The robust face of a political figure as it appears in the press—full of confidence from some political success—bears little resemblance to the same face lying strained with pain or actually unconscious. When he was finally identified through police channels, the Home Office was immediately informed.

The Home Office official who took the call was in something of a quandary. The PM would have to be told, particularly in view of the Powell case, but was this particular official the man to disturb the PM at such an hour? Could he really insist that the PM be woken up and told? He hesitated. He walked twice round his desk. Finally he picked up the phone and made the necessary call.

In many ways the PM was an excellent leader. He was particularly good at quiet, unofficial diplomacy. He could swing a conference with a well-argued speech. But on the point of his authority, he was sensitive. And his authority had been challenged. It had been challenged by Briggs, the leader of the Opposition, and to some extent it had been challenged by Evans. Like many weak men, he saw the only way to meet such a challenge as being a massive—almost excessive—reassertion of that authority. He met all such challenges with a total, inflexible stubbornness. Evans might have exercised a considerable control over Monckton's activities. But Evans now lay unconscious. The Evans-Monckton relationship was quite different from the PM-Monckton one. Monckton was the PM's personal choice. It was a choice that had been challenged. It was not unreasonable, then, for the PM to decide that, right or wrong, Monckton must be backed to the hilt. Any hesitation in that backing would imply a doubt in the PM's own mind about his own judgment, and such a doubt he could never allow himself to admit. Monckton had been given in effect *carte blanche* to conduct his inquiries as he wished. The removal of Evans now meant that the massive and unswerving support of the PM would back up whatever Monckton decided to do. There was one established fact from which the PM drew a good deal of comfort. Whatever Monckton's methods, he produced results quickly. The objections to those methods by some of the PM's colleagues, and certainly by the Opposition and the press, would take a little time to organize. Monckton, the PM was certain, would produce a culprit within the next forty-eight hours. The PM was confident that he could contain any opposition for at least that time. And once the assassin was named, the PM's action would be entirely vindicated. Whatever methods Monckton had used would be seen to have been justified.

From Taylor's office in Subdivisional Headquarters, Bertram Warner rang Her Majesty's Inspector in Newcastle.

"Perhaps you'd just confirm Colonel Monckton's standing, sir," said Warner.

"He has Home Office authority to investigate the Powell assassination."

"Is he responsible to you, sir?"

"No—not at all. I don't come into it. He's directly responsible to the Home Secretary."

"What's our position, sir? The local force? Are we to drop the investigation?"

"Certainly not. You're to continue as vigorously as possible—under his overall direction."

"We're to cooperate fully, sir?" said Warner.

"I don't understand, Mr. Warner—is something wrong?"

"Nothing's wrong, sir—now I understand the position. And if

he gives me a direct order, I'm to carry it out?"

"Certainly. Look, I know what you're thinking. You're not alone. But that's the position. I've been on to the Home Office—the fullest cooperation, they say."

"Thank you, sir."

"You can see their point of view. It's not every day we have a Member of Parliament killed. Not that kind of Member. Not in this country."

"No, sir."

Constable Dixon had been through the statement forms and arranged them in two batches. Taylor took the smaller batch into the main school hall. People got up from the floor where they had been sitting. They walked toward him. A woman was crying. One of the journalists tapped him on the arm and said, "Come on, Chief Inspector—what gives?"

Taylor stood on a chair. He called out, "If I could have your attention for a moment, please!" People moved nearer to him. It left the back of the hall empty. He called out again and put up both his arms. Eventually the talking stopped. Everyone looked at him.

"If the people from the press would stand well over on the left, please—the rest of you well over on the right."

"Discrimination!" one of the journalists called out. One of his colleagues blew a raspberry.

The main body shuffled slowly to the right. There were no protests. Sleeplessness and shock had made them obedient.

"Now if these people would go to the back of the hall." Taylor read out ten names. Individuals detached themselves from the main group and walked to the back of the hall. Taylor nodded to a constable, who made his way up the hall and stood with them. Taylor looked at the main group on his right and said, "I'm sorry we've had to keep you so long—if you'd just like to file out."

A policeman opened the main doors and the first people began to move through them.

"Thank God for that!" someone called out.

Taylor got down off the chair. Five or six press men came across to him.

"Hey, what the hell, mate?" said one of the press men.

"What about us? What do you want us for?" said another.

Enid Markus said, "What about those at the back? Why are you holding them?"

"They're foreigners, aren't they?" said the man on her left. "They've got foreign names."

"Is that why you're holding them?" said Enid Markus.

"We need fuller statements," said Taylor. "That's all."

"But they are foreigners?" said Enid Markus.

"Not all of them," said Taylor.

"But some of them?"

"Are they?" said Taylor.

"And that's why you're holding them?"

"Is it?" said Taylor.

He walked toward the doors. Two constables were standing ready to close them. Another constable stood between the press men and the people moving through the doors. A journalist called out, "You're a bloody racialist, mate." Taylor turned and said, "Call me that again and I'll have you inside!"

Monckton was back in the headmaster's study. He was sitting behind the desk when Taylor walked in.

"Knock, would you, Chief Inspector?" said Monckton.

"Sorry, sir. I didn't know you were back."

Taylor put the ten statement sheets on the desk.

"They've gone, sir," he said. "The others are waiting."

"Where did you look, when you searched the hall?"

Monckton had the plans of the Jubilee Hall in front of him.

"Well—every possible hiding place—"

"Under the platform?"

"No, sir—not under the platform."

"Oh?"

"It's bolted to the floor, the whole structure. I checked the bolts myself. They hadn't been touched. The old paint covering hadn't been broken. Nobody's had the platform up, sir."

"And the floor?"

"We went over every board. Nobody's been under there, sir. Dust still in place, no cracked tongues, nailholes still full of dust."

"Forensic says the thing was under the platform."

"Have they said how it got there, sir?"

"Were you in the Army, Chief Inspector?" said Monckton, lifting his head from the plan on the desk and looking at Taylor with his pale, expressionless eyes.

"The Army, sir?" said Taylor. "National Service, sir, that's all—Aden mostly."

"You've had no war experience?"

"Well—action, sir. Local guerrilla activity. Pretty violent at times. But not war, I suppose, in that sense."

"We lost Aden, Mr. Taylor. Does that strike you as being significant?"

"It was simply a police action, sir. We were just policing the place. I didn't know we were trying to hang on to it."

"A police action. Hardly the attitude that made the country great. And this was just a police action too, wasn't it? You have the greatest figure in British politics in that hall—one of the century's great men—but your police action doesn't prevent some renegade scum from assassinating him under your nose. I'm losing confidence in this 'police action' of yours, Chief Inspector. It lacks thoroughness. It lacks dedication. You know why I'm here, don't you?"

"Yes, sir. To conduct an inquiry into this—affair. To bring the culprit to justice as soon as possible."

"I'd credited you with more insight, Chief Inspector. I thought you'd be able to see beyond the propaganda aspect. I thought you'd appreciate the sensitive position that exists in the country, the position that lies behind his assassination. Don't you realize the knife edge on which we're balanced? On the one hand, the last shreds of a great and disciplined community; on the other—total collapse into permissiveness and anarchy. That's the real issue. Do you think that I'd have been recalled from retirement for anything less than that?"

Taylor looked at him, at his gaunt figure and his pale eyes. The terms of reference implied in Monckton's statement were immensely wider than any Taylor could have guessed at.

Cigarette ends and matches had been trodden into the floor of the school hall. The air smelled of stale smoke. At the far end, the ten people whose names had been called out by Taylor sat in one line against the wall. No one spoke. In front of them stood a young policeman, his hands behind his back. The group of journalists near the main doors was silent. Two were asleep on the floor. One stood looking out of a window at the bare playground, his hands flat against the glass. A policeman standing near them yawned.

Taylor pushed open one of the main doors and looked down the hall. The sun cast brilliant shafts of light across the floor. Half a dozen people turned and looked toward him. Taylor stood and lifted a hand to the policeman at the far end of the hall. The man turned to the people sitting along the wall behind him. He spoke to them and they began to get up. He pointed toward Taylor and they moved down the hall.

"Listen, Chief Inspector," said Enid Markus, walking over to Taylor. "How much longer?"

"Not long," said Taylor.

"But why this muzzle on the press? What's so damn mysterious that you want it kept quiet?"

"We need fuller statements, that's all. Nothing mysterious in that. Usual practice, isn't it?"

"But why from us? What kind of information have we got that nobody else has?"

"We shan't know till we get fuller statements," said Taylor.

He was holding the door open for the other group to pass through.

"You don't care much about your press image, do you, Chief Inspector?" she said.

"Not much," said Taylor.

He followed the last of the group through the door, and let it swing closed after him.

The man at the window took a cigarette out of his mouth and stubbed it out on the paintwork. He turned and said, "For Christ's sake, ducky, what you worried about? I'll lay you fifty to one we're out of here in sixty minutes flat. When Reggie Deacon gets to a phone there'll be no point in holding us any longer."

Reggie Deacon had in fact got clear. It had not been easy for him. He was quite out of condition and could hardly cope with the obstacles he found in his way. Three police barriers had blocked his exit, and at each he had had to climb a wall, drop into a back yard or an alley and find a way around. But he had done it. He had got clear of the town and beyond the blocks on the approach roads. He was tired and hot. His clothing was torn. He wanted a drink and something to eat.

He walked through the woods and open fields in order to avoid two villages. In the third it seemed safe to try the phone box. He walked some seven or eight miles. It was nine o'clock in the morning, the sky cloudless and the sun already hot.

His story was the first hard news that Fleet Street had had. It threw his London office into a state of immediate confusion. The editor, Bill Hobbs, was still at home and still in bed. The phone call from the office got him up. He sat for a moment on the edge of his bed, staring at the floor. It couldn't have happened at a worse time. If they waited till the next morning when the next issue was due, everybody would have the story. Then there was the D notice, designed to stop the publication of just such a story as Deacon had phoned in, on grounds of national security. It didn't place an absolute embargo on such publication, but if Hobbs was going to ignore it he would have to have some damn good reason for doing so.

Bill Hobbs dressed and went to the office. He read the story as the copy-taker had recorded it. He looked at the D notice. He knew the policy of his paper. If he consulted the chairman, Hobbs would have to fall in with the D notice. No other decision was open to the chairman. Yet Hobbs knew the chairman. He knew what decision he would hope his editor would take. Hobbs called an editorial conference for ten o'clock and sat down to rough out a leader. At noon a special edition appeared. The front page headline read: WHO KILLED ENOCH POWELL? The story was substantially as Deacon had phoned it in.

So the story broke. And through the D-notice breach rushed every other medium through which news is transmitted. By twelve-fifteen independent TV stations were putting out news flashes, still of necessity based on Deacon's story. And by one o'clock the BBC had decided that something must appear on "The World at One," something that would not only state the known facts but serve to cool off the situation as much as possible.

But no one had really calculated the strength of feeling associated with Powell. No simple intellectual presentation of the facts could stem that feeling. The whole country seemed to be lined behind one of two views of Powell—those who had seen him as a savior and those who had seen him as a demon. All was black and white. And black and white became the principal issue. It seemed for the moment that the PM's action had been right. The only thing that would check the most alarming consequences was the arrest of those responsible for the killing at the earliest possible moment. It seemed as if any means would justify that end.

Monckton came out of the headmaster's study. He looked at the people waiting in the corridor outside. They stood with their backs to the opposite wall, facing him. They were tired. Most looked unsure of themselves and their position. A few looked defiantly at Monckton. Monckton's expression didn't change as he looked from one face to the next. No one spoke. Taylor stood on Monckton's left, waiting. At last Monckton looked down at the documents in his hand. He said, "I'm sorry it's been necessary to keep you."

To Taylor he didn't sound sorry. He looked as if he found even this cursory association with the people in the corridor distasteful. Yet what he said had a controlled civility about it. Taylor felt that if Monckton had been able to smile he would have done so.

"There are a few more questions" said Monckton, as if he thought it necessary to offer some brief explanation. "Perhaps we could begin with Mr. Kerick—Mr. Jan Kerick?"

He looked along the line of faces in front of him. A dark-haired man, slight and well dressed, nodded and said, "I'm Kerick."

"Do go in, Mr. Kerick," said Monckton.

Monckton stepped to one side and indicated the door. Kerick turned and looked at the others on his right and left. He looked at Taylor. Then he walked past Monckton into the room.

"Sit down, Mr. Kerick," said Monckton, still standing in the open doorway. "Smoke if you wish." Monckton turned to Taylor and said, "Send out for some cigarettes and matches, will you, Chief Inspector? Tell the Chief Constable I'd like to see him at twelve-thirty. And put a constable on this door."

Monckton closed the door of the study behind him. Taylor heard him say, "You don't find it oppressive in here, do you, Mr. Kerick?"

Bertram Warner was sitting in the Chief Inspector's room. When Taylor walked in he got up. He sighed a little wearily. He gave the impression of being not only tired but also a little bored—as if he had seen this kind of thing so many times before it had ceased to interest him.

"There's been a multiple crash north of Leeming Bar," said Warner. "You don't mind my using your room?"

"Of course not, sir," said Taylor. "Is it bad?"

"Three trailer trucks in convoy. Someone ahead of them shed a slick of oil across the road. They've closed both lanes."

"Colonel Monckton would like to see you at twelve-thirty, sir."

Warner looked at his watch. "Would he?" he said.

"He's let most of them go now—except the press and the ones he wanted to see himself."

"What's he doing now?"

"Mr. Kerick's with him."

"He didn't want you to stay?"

"He asked me to tell you he'd like to see you, sir," said Taylor.

"He doesn't want you to go back?"

"He didn't say so, sir."

Warner sat on the edge of the desk and looked at Taylor for a moment. He had seen him rise very quickly in the service. Fifteen years or so from constable to Chief Inspector. Well deserved, thought Warner; a first-class policeman. But this was out of the ordinary, having to deal with a situation like this, having to cope with a man like Monckton.

"How's that son of yours?" said Warner.

"Jimmy, sir? Oh, he's fine. Fine."

"Settled down all right?"

"Oh, they both have—he and the girl."

"And your wife—Beryl? It must have made quite a difference to her life. A lot of changes in routine."

"I suppose so, sir. Seven years without children—it's a long time," said Taylor.

"Well, it was the right decision. I'm glad of that."

"Adoption? Oh, yes. It was the right decision, sir. A bit of opposition from parents at the time—particularly in Jimmy's case with his mother being half-Jamaican. You knew that, sir?"

"Yes," said Warner.

"But that's all gone now. People don't think about it for long—not people you've known all your life."

Warner got up and put his hands in his jacket pockets.

"What do you think of him now you've seen him—Colonel Monckton?" said Warner.

"Well, sir—"

"That's all right. I only ask out of interest. I knew him once."

Warner took a pipe out of his pocket. "Do you mind?" he said.

"Of course not, sir," said Taylor.

"I thought I'd better ask," said Warner, looking over the top of the pipe bowl as he lit it. "I was ticked off earlier."

Taylor smiled. "I think it's just pipes he has an objection to. He sent out for a packet of cigarettes before he talked to Kerick."

"Not for himself?" said Warner.

"For Kerick, I believe."

"Perhaps the objection's to pipe smokers," said Warner, "rather than pipes."

"Perhaps," said Taylor. "Tough—that's how he strikes me, sir. But not a policeman."

"Oh?"

"I've a man out now, sir, checking the hotels and boarding-houses. He's not even suggested that. And British Rail police here and in York are getting me details on the stations of origin of all passengers who passed through their barriers yesterday. He's said nothing about that. And this preoccupation with foreigners—"

"It could have been a foreigner," said Warner. "The policies associated with Powell—it could well have been a foreigner."

"But not one of those he's talking to at the moment, sir. No one's going to plant a bomb in an enclosed space like that, then sit down and wait for it to go off. Whoever it was was miles away at the time of the explosion. It was a planned, professional job."

"You may be right," said Warner. "But hadn't it occurred to you that whoever it was had to get previous information on the hall, the timing, the rest of it—and if that man was a foreigner then a foreigner in the hall might well have had contact with him?"

"Frankly, no, sir. No, it hadn't. Only two of those people he's holding are foreigners—the others are naturalized British subjects."

"To you that makes a difference—"

"All the difference."

"But to Monckton—does Colonel Monckton make that distinction?"

An Army Land-Rover went down the street below Taylor's window. It turned in front of the Jubilee Hall and backed up to the main entrance doors. Four soldiers began unloading lifting gear and taking it into the hall.

Taylor picked up the phone and said, "See if you can get hold of Sir Clinton Everard's secretary for me. Ring me back here."

Suppose I'd been doing it, thought Taylor. Suppose I was going to kill a man with a bomb. I'd have one chance to get away with it. A first-time job it would have to be. I'd study the man—habits, behavior, how he stood when he spoke, how he traveled. Then I'd pick the spot—a meeting as far away from my home base as possible. Devon, Norfolk, Cumberland—miles away. I'd go to the hall. I'd listen to other speakers there until I knew the disposition of every damn piece of furniture blindfold. Then the bomb itself—something transportable, something easily concealed. Something that would let me get well clear of the place before it went off. But how the devil would I have got it under the platform without leaving some kind of clue?

The phone rang. A woman's voice said, "Yes?" It was a flat, dead voice.

"Sir Clinton Everard's secretary?" said Taylor.

There was a pause.

Taylor said, "I'm trying to get hold of Sir Clinton Everard's secretary. Chief Inspector Taylor."

"I'm sorry," said the woman. "I'm still—shocked. I didn't hear until I came into the office. It's terrible."

"Of course," said Taylor. "I'm—very sorry."

"Tragic!"

"Tragic," said Taylor. "I'm trying to fill in the background—could you tell me how long ago the date of the meeting was fixed?"

"About six weeks. Just a minute—the eighth of last month. We had a committee meeting then to confirm the date."

"To confirm it?"

"It wasn't our date. Mr. Powell fixed it. We'd been trying to make an arrangement with him for months. He had a very heavy program. This was a cancellation, I think."

"So before the eighth no one knew the date of the meeting?"

"No. It hadn't been fixed."

"And after the eighth there was a press announcement?"

"In the local papers, yes. On the tenth. I don't know about the nationals."

"Thanks," said Taylor.

"Is there any more news? Is there anything anyone can do to help?"

"Not at the moment," said Taylor. "But thanks."

About five weeks then, thought Taylor. During that time some-one had been in the town twice—once to go over the hall and once to plant the explosive. At least twice. Someone, surely to God, would remember him.

There was a knock at the door and a constable came in with a plate of sandwiches and a chipped mug of tea.

"Thanks," said Taylor, clearing a space on the desk.

"Mr. Kerick's downstairs, sir," said the constable. "Sergeant Price wonders if you'd see him."

"Kerick? What about?"

"He's kicking up a fuss about Colonel Monckton, sir."

"Give me a minute to get a bite of this, then send him up."

Kerick stood in the doorway of Taylor's room. "I didn't ask to see you, Mr. Taylor," he said. "I didn't want to see you. They insisted down there."

He was out of breath. His shirt collar was undone and his tie loosened. He had a handkerchief pressed to his forehead.

Taylor took a chair from against the wall and put it in front of the desk. "You'd better have a seat, Mr. Kerick," he said.

"I don't want a seat," said Kerick. "I don't want anything."

"What's happened? Come on—tell me."

"British justice!" said Kerick, as if the articulation of the words caused him real effort. He was rapping the back of a hand against the door. "You know—we hear about it everywhere. This *fairness*. This *gentlemanly* system. This being innocent until proved guilty. You know what? You know who I blame? Me! Myself! For even believing it." He swallowed. Emotion caused him to tremble. "That man," he said. "The accusations, the suggestions, the dirty innuendos! Not only me—my wife, my daughter, my friends, every-one I've touched! He hated me. I'd never seen him before in the whole of my life—but he hated me. You know why? Because I was born in Warsaw. The greater part of my life I've lived here, in this town. But no—nothing, it means nothing. I was born in Warsaw and that damns me."

"Mr. Kerick—you must have misunderstood him."

Taylor walked toward him.

"Mr. Taylor," said Kerick. "How long have you known me? Fifteen—twenty years, is it?"

"I suppose it is."

"You think of me as a Pole—an outsider—every time you see me?"

"No."

"No. Of course you don't. I have been a naturalized Englishman longer than I was Polish. So allow me to know when someone thinks otherwise. Allow me that, will you? And allow me a memory—allow me to remember when I last saw this kind of man!"

"Do you want to make a formal complaint?"

"I have made a statement—downstairs."

"I'll look into it, Mr. Kerick."

"Yes, look into it, Mr. Taylor. And let me tell you what I refused to tell him: I don't belong to any immigrant society, I don't know of the existence of such a society, and if I did I should not join it. The war cured me of joining anything ever again. I am a brewer, that's all. I know nothing about explosives. There is nobody to whom I wish any kind of harm."

He turned in the doorway.

"What happened to your head, Mr. Kerick?" said Taylor.

"Hm?" said Kerick. "I walked into something—that's all."

The constable outside the closed door of the headmaster's study nodded to a colleague. He pointed behind him with his thumb and whispered, "Dishing it out in there!" Monckton's voice growled through the door.

70

Inside, Warner was standing patiently facing the desk like some recalcitrant schoolboy who knows he must endure the headmaster's rage, yet is sufficiently used to it for it not to bother him unduly.

Taylor heard the raised voice and the acrimonious words as he walked down the corridor. "What is it, constable?" he said, nodding toward the door.

"Chief Constable, sir. I think Colonel Monckton's upset by something."

"How long's he been in there?"

"About five minutes, sir. He was in the hall—I had to fetch him."

Taylor looked at his watch. It was a little before twelve-thirty. He knocked and walked in. Monckton stopped talking and turned to Taylor. He looked at him as if he didn't recognize him. Then he took a sheet of paper from the desk and thrust it at Taylor. Taylor looked at it. It was a typed copy of Reggie Deacon's story.

"Well?" said Monckton.

"Well—it's out, sir."

"I can see it's out, man, but how? You had my instructions to let no one out. How did this Deacon man get away?"

"I didn't know anyone had got away, sir. I had men on all the doors, the windows were secured—"

"All right! My God, am I the only one who can see where this could lead? This sentimental liberalism that surrounds us, this national disease—Powell gave us a lead against it. At this moment millions support him. Where are they going to direct their energies when they find themselves leaderless? That leader struck down by the hand of some madman? Someone, some strong man must step into that gap before the situation dissolves into anarchy. If we could have held the press for a day— Now it's too late. I'm leaving for the Home Office. Do whatever you need to do here, Taylor, then join me tomorrow."

Taylor looked at Warner.

"I've all the authority necessary," said Monckton. "There's no need for you to consult the Chief Constable."

"The journalists, Colonel Monckton?" said Warner. "I take it they can be released now?"

"Get them out," said Monckton.

"Do you wish to make a statement to them, Colonel? They'll be anxious for some explanation."

"Just get them out!"

Enid Markus said, "For God's sake, Mr. Taylor, you can't just clam up like this!"

"Look, we've been here the whole bloody night! Everybody else has gone! We want some kind of explanation!"

"Come on, Chief Inspector. Come off it. If you don't tell us anything, we'll have to make it up."

Enid Markus said, "Are you holding anyone? Can we say somebody's helping you with the investigation?"

"No, you can't," said Taylor.

"This D-notice breach—what effect's that going to have on the situation?"

"Have to wait and see," said Taylor.

"For Christ's sake!"

"Well, thanks, Chief Inspector," said Enid Markus. "Any time you want any help from me—just give me a ring."

"Christ, I'm starving! Let's get a bloody drink."

Johnny de Margolis was sitting on the table in the back room of Daniel Westbrook's antique shop in King Street. He was a square-built, powerful young man, with tight-curled black hair and an easy, quick smile. He swung his legs as he listened to Daniel Westbrook.

Westbrook had heard his account of the attack on the Annapurna restaurant in Charlotte Street. The news had excited him, though not to that frenetic pitch which he occasionally reached when he paced the back room like some madman and cried out in his high-pitched, penetrating little voice. He was, even at his most calm and relaxed, little less than a dynamo of energy, never still, always applying another match to the bowl of his pipe, always turning over this pile of papers or that. Now he was on his feet, moving to the curtained window, moving back to the door that led into the shop, pouring out his theories, considering aloud this plan and that. He filled the room with a kind of desperate energy that caught up de Margolis in it.

On the table was the special edition carrying the story of the explosion.

"You see," he was saying, rapping the paper with the back of a hand, moving away from it, then returning to rap at it again. "It's an inevitable movement. Nothing can stop it. The seeds were sown years ago, the crop is pushing its way to the surface. On this movement we shall be carried to power! Power—do you know what it means, de Margolis? Can you sense it? Can you feel it rising up in you like some force you can't control? Power to mold a nation in the best image of itself! Power to cleanse, power to purge and expunge, power to eradicate! I see a new Jerusalem—with Britain the high priestess."

"There'll be counterdemonstrations," said de Margolis.

His eyes were alight with the exciting possibilities that he saw ahead.

"Of course," said Westbrook. "And we must harness them. We must be in the van of them all, directing, steering, developing."

"It'll need a bit of organizing," said de Margolis.

"Do you think it hasn't been organized?" cried Westbrook. "Do you think all the plans haven't been laid months—years ago? Listen, de Margolis. Some of the left-wing political philosophers of the nineteenth century had a dream. They dreamed that revolution would come first in Britain. They were wrong. It came first in Russia. Why? Why were they wrong?"

He turned, thrusting his narrow face toward de Margolis and stabbing at him with a finger.

"They were wrong because they forgot the British empire! They forgot that poverty and squalor and long working hours for little pay are less important to a man than a sense of identity!"

De Margolis had heard it before. Every member of the British Union of Activists had heard it before—or something very like it. It was almost a set speech that Westbrook burst into from time to time, as if he were rehearsing it for the final, significant occasion. Yet still de Margolis marveled at the frenzy behind it.

Westbrook turned away from de Margolis, still seated on the edge of the table, and moved more freely about the room. He seemed to be freeing himself of the last traces of a self-control that had been holding him in check, and as he freed himself his voice increased in volume, as if he were no longer aware of the smallness of the room.

"The empire gave the British workingman that sense of identity," Westbrook cried. "He could still lift his weary, work-blackened face from the sight of his starving children and say, 'I'm British! I own a thousand million square miles of the earth's surface! I own a thousand million other human beings on that surface!' That gave him the necessary sense of identity. He was identified with the biggest and most prosperous system the world had ever seen. Against that identity, what did poverty matter! What did it matter that he had little share in that prosperity? There was a chance, if he smashed the system, that he might have a bit more money in his pocket. But set against that the possibility that he might lose his sense of identity in the process. And it was a real sense of identity, backed up by hard facts. He knew the system was dependent on his personal efforts. He knew that the steam engines he was making were opening up the dark continent. He knew that the mining equipment and blankets and textiles he was producing were pushing out the frontiers of empire. So the thing grew by his efforts. And as it grew, so his sense of identity increased. He had a significance that made his poverty seem insignificant. Wasn't it the same in the war? Didn't everyone work from morning till night —not for the wage envelopes, but because they were identified with something clearly defined and vastly greater than themselves? And now where's it gone? Where's the empire that gave a Briton distinction in the eyes of the world? Gone! And what is there to replace it? Nothing! We have sagged from world eminence into this gray mediocrity! And the nobility of war—what of that? Outrages against it at the Cenotaph, and the medals of heroes on sale to callow adolescents in the back streets of Soho! This is the philosophical vacuum that the erosion of empire has caused and this is the vacuum we must fill!"

He stood staring at the closed curtains, his back to de Margolis. He was panting from shortage of breath. His pipe had gone out in his hand. When he turned he was pale. His skin had a jaundiced look, yet perspiration ran down his cheeks, and de Margolis saw the look of frenzy in his eyes.

Westbrook stood for a moment, then he pulled out a chair from under the table and sat down. He put his elbows on the table and let his head sink onto his hands. De Margolis couldn't decide whether he had his eyes closed, or whether he was studying the newspaper more closely. At last, Westbrook lifted his bony head, the graying hair still in disarray around the base of the skull.

"The demonstrations will be no more than stepping-stones. The Wimbledon final will be a more fitting setting for a major exhibition of power."

At two in the afternoon, Bertram Warner returned to Force Headquarters. At two-thirty the forensic team produced an interim report. The cause of the explosion had been a substantial charge of explosive contained in a narrow metal cylinder. The device had been constructed with considerable ingenuity and skill. It had been in four parts which could be easily carried and fitted together on the spot. It had been placed under the platform through a two-inch hole drilled through the side woodwork and held against the under surface of the flooring by the magnetic attraction between the casing and the metal straps used in the construction of the platform. After insertion, the hole had been plugged with a previously prepared wooden bung and the junction between bung and surrounding woodwork had been filled with stained putty. Even a close examination of that particular section of woodwork would probably not have revealed the position of the hole. The device had contained two separate transistorized systems. One, coupled to a microphone and small transmitter, would have allowed the monitoring of any sounds within fifteen feet of it. The other was an electronic trigger activated by a radio signal. Using a portable transmitter/receiver, a man sitting five miles from the hall could have monitored the police conversations that had taken place near the platform during the day, then listened to Powell's speech and chosen the exact moment at which to trigger the device. Detonation would have been instantaneous.

Taylor phoned the Chief Superintendent at Division.

"Going to London?" said the Chief Superintendent. "What's the CC say?"

"Well, he knows, sir," said Taylor.

"And he approves?"

"I don't know that he approves. He didn't say. It's a bit awkward, sir, with Colonel Monckton's authority."

"What arrangements are you making?"

"I'm seeing Inspector Marston. I'll put the routine follow-up in his hands—with your approval, sir."

"You sure about Marston? Has he got the drive? I could put someone else in."

"Quite sure, sir," said Taylor. "It'll be mostly legwork now. Forensic makes it pretty clear it was someone from outside—the interim report and our own inquiries."

"All right, Taylor."

"There's one other thing, sir. There's been a complaint about Colonel Monckton. I've just read the statement. It'll have to be passed to Division."

"What kind of complaint?"

"About his behavior, sir—during an interview."

"Well—that's not likely to get very far, is it? All right, Taylor, send it on."

Inspector Ted Marston weighed a little over two hundred pounds. He was affable and easy going. He was older than Taylor and he had passed the point where ambition still drove him on. He was hard working, solid, reliable, but he knew how much he was prepared to let police work dominate his life.

"For God's sake, Ted," said Taylor, "drop your jacket somewhere. Too damned hot in here as it is."

"Gardening weather, sir," said Marston, taking off his jacket and sitting down.

"Better have a look at this," said Taylor, handing the forensic report across the desk.

Marston reached for his jacket, took out a pair of glasses and looked at the report.

The phone rang. "Damn!" said Taylor. He picked up the receiver. "Chief Inspector Taylor."

"Your wife, sir. Could she have a word with you?"

"Tell her—no, put her on."

He looked at Marston. "Beryl," he said.

Marston smiled at him.

"I don't know what you think I am or how you suppose I'm to run a house—" said the voice.

Marston looked back at the report.

"I've somebody with me," said Taylor.

"What about your lunch?"

"I've had some sandwiches."

"But I've cooked this meat. I've been keeping it hot."

"I told you I wouldn't be home."

"You said in the morning. It's three o'clock."

"All right, it's three o'clock."

"I might as well throw it out."

"You might as well," said Taylor.

He put the phone down.

Marston looked at him and said, "They never quite understand police work."

"Somebody ought to lay on a course," said Taylor.

Marston put the report on the desk. "Pretty clear it's an outsider," he said.

"I think so, Ted. But I still think the real answer's here. It means a lot of legwork but it's got to be dug out. And you'll have to organize the digging. I have to go to London to join Colonel Monckton and you'll be in charge—I've told Division."

"You joining his staff?"

"That seems to be the idea."

"Well, that's a bit of good news. Could mean promotion."

"I suppose so," said Taylor.

"I can let you have that information you wanted on hotel and boardinghouse guests—about fifteen minutes all right?"

"Good. We can go through it together."

Only when he reached the Home Office did Monckton hear of the

Home Secretary's collapse. At once he saw his new position. In the absence of the Home Secretary, he was directly responsible to the Prime Minister. The changed situation was full of new possibilities. If he could maintain this special relationship, his power might be almost without limit. With the government's overwhelming majority in the House, there was no issue on which it could be defeated. Equally, the Prime Minister's position was no less secure. He had the backing of the constituencies and the support of the majority of Parliamentary party members. Briggs and the Opposition could howl at him inside and outside the House, but they couldn't topple him. With the personal backing of such a man, Monckton began to glimpse the kind of sweeping social changes that might be made. His need at the moment was for wider terms of reference.

The breach of the D notice had led to a top-level conference at number 10. It was a conference of some of the hardest men in the country—the editors of the nationals, press proprietors, a law lord, and it was presided over by the PM. He had taken personal charge of the affair the moment he heard of Evans' collapse. He was in no mood for nonsense, yet he was held back still by the knowledge that short of press censorship—and the D notice had failed to achieve that—there was little he could do to prevent the meeting's being reported. The knowledge checked him from being too irascible and high-handed. Such an approach, in any case, would not really have impressed this gathering. When he shook hands with Bill Hobbs, the editor responsible for the D notice breach, he did so with a look of paternalistic disappointment rather than anger. It gave Hobbs the feeling, world-hardened though he was, of being in the presence of a revered headmaster whom he had let down.

"I thought for a minute you were going to get the cane," said Jimmy Endells, Enid Markus' editor.

He was looking down at Hobbs, who was sipping a large Scotch and perspiring from every pore of his bald head.

"What the hell!" growled Hobbs with a shrug of his heavy shoulders and another sip of Scotch.

"We're all jealous," said Endells, "that's the top and bottom of it. That Reggie Deacon of yours deserves a medal."

"Think so?" said Hobbs, looking up at Endells.

He felt exposed. He still had doubts about his decision to publish. He was glad of Endells' shred of comfort.

"Of course," said Endells. "In your position there's not one of us that wouldn't have damned that D notice to hell. Just wish to God that Markus girl of mine could get through lavatory windows."

Yet for all that, Endells was glad it hadn't been a decision that he'd had to make. He knew that Hobbs' chairman had leaned on Hobbs very heavily, and he knew that in the PM's eyes Hobbs was little less than a traitor, despite the view of his fellow editors. And this attitude to Hobbs the PM succeeded in imposing on the meeting. It was an attitude that made everyone feel he had acted a little irresponsibly, and it produced a swing toward the PM's viewpoint that was not altogether rational. The meeting agreed with him that the assassination was something that could have the most ugly consequences. He told them that he'd put Monckton in charge of the case because he was convinced that the most stringent action was necessary to bring the person responsible to justice at the earliest possible moment. The longer that person was free, the more the rumors would fly. The more rumors, the more would a general suspicion spread. It would all lead to an increase in the feeling of national insecurity, and that could benefit no one—certainly not the immigrant population, against whom, he said, most suspicion would be directed.

The argument seemed to make sense. Sympathy continued to swing toward the PM's viewpoint, reinforced by the feeling that the

80

press had perhaps been too precipitate. A feeling that it might have been wiser if press men had paused to consider the implications of what they were doing before rushing after Hobbs through the security breach.

In consequence, almost all press coverage next morning was firmly behind the PM. Much of it was concerned with stories on Monckton and the way in which he proposed conducting the inquiry. Some of it was positively euphoric. One of the more "responsible" nationals had been researching Monckton's past, and came out with a two-page spread of his wartime investigations and of his later activities as head of the Dayton detachment, responsible for matters of special state security. The series of articles contained a good deal of personal information on Monckton that was either not generally known or had been forgotten over the years. His background was predictable—small preparatory school in Oxfordshire, lesser-known public school in Sussex, then Sandhurst. During the war—predictably again—he had seen service with the Provost branch. Yet together with these mundane facts, most in any case in *Who's Who,* there were others that suggested a man of some culture. He was widely traveled. He spoke fluent Urdu, Arabic and German, passable French and some words of Italian. Apparently at one time he had given his favorite authors as T. E. Lawrence, Doughty, Freya Stark, Sir Richard Burton and Flecker. In the same early interview, and presumably in a rare moment of levity, he had named his favorite singer as Abdul Wahab, the Egyptian "pop" singer of the 1940s. His life was one of rigid self-discipline. He was a vegetarian, a nonsmoker and virtual teetotaler. His principal recreation was gardening, though "recreation" was not his own word. The puritan in him saw gardening as an "activity"; "recreation" suggested something altogether too frivolous.

Other papers made other points. Some confined themselves to covering Monckton's life in pictures. There were shots of his cottage on the northern edge of the New Forest, and shots of him with his sleeves rolled up working in the garden. There were pictures of his dog, a square-faced boxer. There was a wartime shot of him taken against a background of ruined Cologne. One of the more "popular" papers dug up the story of his brush with the American consul in Frankfurt, when he had referred to the States as "that upstart colony of blacks and Indians." It was a story that fitted the paper's own anti-American bias, and it was treated in a favorable, slightly swashbuckling light. One of the more interesting stories appeared under the heading: MONCKTON: WHY NO KNIGHTHOOD? It was a point on which Monckton was particularly sensitive. The reason, though Monckton himself only dimly realized it, was that he was political dynamite. In a sense, he had always been a pawn in the hands of men in the real seats of power. Because of his methods, never widely known but always known to those in power, no one dared risk aligning himself and his party too closely with Monckton. It was a risk that even Churchill thought too dangerous. By those who knew him well Monckton was profoundly disliked, despite his ability and his undoubted usefulness.

So the pendulum swung, and it swung to excess in praise of Monckton. And yet the overall picture of the man that emerged, despite the praise for deeds past, despite the chatty little pieces about his gardening activities and his devotion to his dog, was somehow sour. It was a picture of an arid puritan, an extreme rightwing authoritarian, an establishmentarian, an elitist, a traditionalist. His belief in the God-given superiority of the British ruling class fitted him more for the eighteenth or nineteenth centuries than for the twentieth. Given a certain benevolence, a certain paternalism, he might have made an outstanding viceroy in some wide territory east of Suez before the First World War. But no such qualities emerged from all the mass of press stories that appeared that morning.

Evans, propped up with pillows and still in a condition of postoperational daze, glanced at the coverage with dismay. He put his hand out for the phone, but there wasn't one.

Briggs, the leader of the Opposition, was sitting in his study at home, still in his dressing gown. At his right, on the desk in front of him, all the morning papers were piled. He tore his way through four of them, tossed them aside, and then with his right forearm swept the remainder onto the floor. He saw at once what had happened. With that kind of press support there would be no holding Monckton. It would take some shifting, would that body of opinion. How could the press come out with that kind of support one day and withdraw it the next? It damn well couldn't. It daren't publish doubts for a week. By then—God alone knew. That bastard Kitchin must be well pleased with himself!

Sir John Kitchin, the Prime Minister, was quite well pleased.

It was after five o'clock when Taylor left the office and went home. The evening was hot. The town felt baked and desiccated. A sense of oppression hung over the streets.

Beryl Taylor was sitting in the kitchen. Adrienne was on her knee. Jimmy was pushing a toy car across the tabletop. When Taylor came into the room, Jimmy got off the chair on which he was kneeling, ran to Taylor and put his arms round his legs. Taylor picked him up.

"Got a car!" said Jimmy. "Got a car!"

"Well," said Taylor. "So you have. Did Mummy buy that for you?"

"Granny bought it," said Jimmy.

"Did she?" said Taylor.

He looked down at his wife. She didn't look at him.

"What did she want?" he said.

"I asked her to come," said Beryl Taylor.

"Did you?"

"If I can't ask my own mother to come and see me!"

"That's all right."

"After what happened."

"What did happen?" said Taylor.

He put Jimmy down on the floor.

"It doesn't matter. It's done with now."

"What was it?" said Taylor.

"Just—Annie Jeffries."

"Not her again!"

"A remark she made," said Beryl Taylor. "About Jimmy."

"Jimmy?"

"About his—you know."

"You can't take any notice of what a woman like that says. She'd say anything," said Taylor.

"It upset me—referring to that."

"You're too sensitive."

"Perhaps," said Beryl Taylor.

Taylor had changed into civvies. He sat in the living room with the report from Inspector Ted Marston on his knee. Beside him were statements from the British Rail police and local taxi companies. No records were available as yet of movements by bus, and car movements were impossible to check. The information was nonetheless considerable. He began a rough elimination, comparing home addresses on Marston's list with stations of origin of travelers who had arrived by train.

At six-fifteen the phone rang. It was Marston. He said, "I'm in the Black Bull. Can you get down? George Freeman had a chap staying with him. He's not on our list."

The Black Bull stood in the marketplace, a rambling timber-framed sixteenth-century building with low ceilings, oak beams and uneven floors. It was packed on market days and almost empty the rest of the week. George Freeman had had the tenancy for thirty-eight years.

Taylor pushed open the bar door. Ted Marston stood at the bar talking across it to Freeman. Both were in their shirt sleeves. Marston was the only customer.

"Look, Mr. Taylor," said Freeman, drawing a glass of beer and putting it down in front of Taylor, "I didn't know I was doing wrong. I've a spare room—"

"What do we know about him, Ted?" said Taylor.

"About sixty-five, small, thin—glasses," said Marston. "He was sitting over there."

He nodded to a corner table.

"You saw him?" said Taylor.

"Well, it didn't mean anything. I never connected him—"

"How long did he stay, George?"

"Two nights. He came in about seven on Friday. Left on Sunday afternoon."

"How did he come?"

"One of Jack Ellis' cars brought him from the station."

"How much luggage?"

"Just the one case," said Freeman.

"How big?" said Taylor.

"Well," said Freeman. He drew the outline of a large case in the air with his hands.

"Did you carry it up for him?"

"No," said Freeman. "He took it himself."

"Did it look heavy?" said Taylor.

"So-so, I suppose," said Freeman. "He was only a small chap. I've told Ted—Ted saw him. He had a stick."

"I didn't see a stick," said Marston.

"He was sitting down," said Freeman. "He used it when he walked."

"Some—deformity?' said Taylor.

Not a deformity," said Freeman. "No. But something about his leg or his foot when he walked. He might have broken it at some time. As if he couldn't put all his weight on it."

"What name did he give?" said Taylor.

"Brown—John Brown," said Freeman.

Freeman's bald head was perspiring. His neck was red.

"God almighty!" said Taylor.

"I never thought anything of it at the time. It sounded like the kind of name he would have. He looked like a John Brown."

"What address did he give?" said Taylor.

"He didn't."

"What did he put in the visitors' book?"

"I haven't got a visitors' book," said Freeman. "I don't take visitors as a rule—just to help out."

"You could get yourself into trouble, George," said Taylor.

"But I'm not registered. I don't take visitors—not as a rule."

"But he'd heard of you, hadn't he? He wasn't just going down the street, knocking on every door, asking them to give him a room. You said one of Ellis' cars drove him straight here from the station. He must have known you had a room."

"Well, he came straight here because he'd booked," said Freeman.

"Booked? Beforehand?"

"Yes. He came in about three weeks ago and booked."

"Then you'd seen him before?"

"Haven't I said so? About three weeks ago. Somebody must have told him."

"Who?"

"He never said. I didn't ask him. I didn't know there was going to be all this fuss about him, did I? If I'd thought that I wouldn't have taken him."

"Where was he staying then—three weeks ago?"

"How should I know? I didn't know he was staying anywhere. He just came in and asked if he could book the room."

"Where did you record the booking?" said Taylor.

"Where I usually do," said Freeman. He turned and tapped a

large commercial calendar. The appropriate days had been marked with a cross.

"And that's the only record? No correspondence—you didn't get him to sign anything?"

"That's the only record. That's all I need to know."

"How much did you charge him?" said Taylor.

Freeman put his hands on the bar and stood up straight. Standing on the raised platform behind the bar, he was seven or eight inches taller than Taylor. "Now look here, Chief Inspector—"

"Never mind," said Taylor. "We can get it from your tax returns."

"Twenty-seven and six," said Freeman. "Fifty-five bob for the two nights."

"Did he pay by check?"

"Cash—he paid when he made the booking."

"In advance?"

"Yes."

Taylor turned to Marston. "Did you talk to him, Ted?"

"No," said Marston. "We may have nodded."

"Did he talk about anything much, George?" said Taylor.

"No. He was pretty quiet. Just went out in the daytime, then sat there for half an hour. Then went up to the room."

"What about his speech? Any particular characteristics? Any accent?"

"He wasn't from round here," said Freeman. "Somewhere south, I would have thought."

"London?"

"No, not London. Not cockney," said Freeman.

"Southwest—Bristol, Somerset?"

"No, not Bristol. I've a brother in Bristol."

"You'd recognize it again if you heard it?"

"I think so," said Freeman. "Yes. I might."

Taylor picked up the glass of beer. He touched Marston on the arm and walked over to a corner by the door.

"I'd get yourself a visitors' book if I were you, George," said Taylor.

Freeman took two small glasses from a rack above his head, then turned and poured brandy into them. He walked over to Taylor and put the glasses on the table.

"It's only pin money, Mr. Taylor," he said. "You don't have to verify it with the tax office, do you?"

"Not now you've told me, George. That's all I wanted to know."

Freeman nodded and turned away. "Any time, Mr. Taylor," he said.

"Listen, Ted," said Taylor. "I'm dropping. I've got to get to bed. But get him to make a full statement before you leave him. Then I want to know where this little chap stayed three weeks ago and how long he stayed there. Then there's this discrepancy—he left here on Sunday but he had to be back within five miles of the hall on Tuesday night to detonate that thing. Where did he spend Sunday night, Monday and Monday night? Somebody must know. You can't keep anything quiet in this place. And didn't Leeds University do some dialect survey or other? See if they've any records you can borrow. See if George can pin down that accent."

Leaders of provincial immigrant groups—particularly those in the west Midlands—saw the press coverage given to Monckton with mounting horror. They saw precisely what Briggs had seen, the possibility of public opinion turning openly against them at a time when they had been desperately trying to hold it. Among many things they feared, one assumed priority. As long as they had shown that a policy of tolerance and even appeasement worked, their more militant elements were checked. But let Monckton take some discriminatory action against them, and many of them would refuse to be held. It could lead to the most terrifying consequences.

Meetings of immigrant groups were called for that afternoon and evening, in places as far apart as Glasgow, Belfast and Southampton. In the meantime, agreement was reached by phone among the group leaders that no action of any kind should be taken which would be likely to draw attention to the immigrant community.

John Turner took a quite different view. He was, in outward appearance, a pleasant, sensible, mild-mannered young man of twenty-four but beneath that exterior there was within a core of intransigence on certain issues. The press coverage of Monckton that morning was such an issue. He was chairman of the Immigrant Community Society of the London School of Economics. He conferred with Paul McGregor, the Society's secretary, and called an emergency meeting of the council.

Like many student organizations, it was a good deal better informed on Monckton than other members of the general public. McGregor himself was particularly skilled in leading fast research. He knew where to look for facts about Monckton that no paper had chosen to print. What he and his colleagues turned up did not please them or inspire their confidence. When the full council met, Turner and McGregor put to it a clear and well-documented case. Unlike the immigrant groups, anxious to shrink as far as possible from any kind of publicity, the council of the Immigrant Community Society decided that the situation called for some form of direct action. A massive protest of some kind. A strike, perhaps. A sit-in. Some sort of open demonstration that would get its views before the public in the most forcible way. The technical details of this decision were worried over for thirty-five or forty minutes before a precise plan of action emerged. That plan involved a march on the London premises that the Home Office had provided for Monckton. It was to be a peaceful march, designed simply to draw attention to the fact that certain sections of the community were not in sympathy with the image painted of Monckton by the press.

It was timed for five o'clock that afternoon. There were two reasons for this. In the first place, that was the earliest that they could expect an organized demonstration to be mounted. In the second place, five o'clock marked the beginning of the daily movement out of London. A demonstration at that hour could be relied on to cause the maximum of traffic confusion, and in consequence draw the maximum amount of publicity. It seemed certain that nationwide TV coverage would be given to such a demonstration on the five-fifty news.

A student meeting in the school was called for one o'clock. It carried the recommendations of the Immigrant Community Society without dissent. There was scarcely any need for John Turner to put briefly the points about Monckton that the press had not carried. In particular, the press had made no reference to Monckton's xenophobia, of which Paul McGregor produced recorded examples. The purpose of the demonstration, then, was to correct the imbalance in the picture of Monckton as it appeared in the press and to stress the fact that the appointment of such a man could only increase the sense of enmity between Britons and non-Britons, which was already a major issue in the country.

But there was more to the organization of such a demonstration than assembling a body of students at a certain place and time. If the demonstration was to have its maximum effect, then the press and the television stations would have to be briefed. This took longer than was expected. Each paper wanted confirmation of the announcement. Naturally, editors didn't want experienced journalists wasting their time on a hoax. Turner, as chairman of the organizing council, agreed to give a news conference at two-fifteen.

The first sign of official opposition to the demonstration came when

90

Paul McGregor told the police that it was to take place. The officer on the phone said he would have to take higher advice, but on the face of it he thought it unlikely that police permission would be given.

The police were a little unsure of the exact relationship between themselves and Monckton. He had Home Office powers to conduct the Powell inquiry and they knew from the reports from the north that within the framework of that inquiry he had authority over the police. The northeastern Inspector of Constabulary had given that ruling on Home Office instructions. In the case of demonstrations—issues of public order—Monckton had, of course, no such authority. But the fact that this particular demonstration was directed at Monckton himself made the police position less clear-cut. Monckton, they felt, should at least be informed.

Monckton saw the implications of the situation. He could argue that this demonstration, directed not at him personally but at the position in which the PM had placed him, was central to the Powell affair. It challenged the right of the PM and the government to conduct a major investigation in the way that seemed to them most effective. It had to be stopped—"crushed" was the word that first suggested itself to him. Now was the time for authority to reassert itself, the opportunity to say, "Enough—no more!" Characteristically, Monckton did not raise the matter with the police or the Home Office, but took it instead to the PM.

The PM hesitated. He assessed the possible reactions of this colleague and that; the reaction of the House.

Monckton said, "With respect, sir, it's the very thing we wished to avoid—the use of the Powell assassination as an excuse for mass indiscipline and large-scale breaches of public order. It's not an attack on me, sir—God knows that's neither here nor there. What they're after is the authority vested in me by yourself. If there were time, Prime Minister, I'd advise waiting —perhaps taking other opinions. But they're holding a press conference in half an hour. After that it might be too late."

There was an emergency meeting of the executive committee of the council of the Immigrant Community Society to discuss the police refusal to grant permission for the demonstration. The executive committee took a predictable line—the right of any organization in a free society to nonviolent protest. There was little discussion. The meeting, injected now with a deep emotional determination, was unanimous.

John Turner, pale-faced and tense, said, "The demonstration— will take place as planned."

Enid had tried to sleep on the train south, wedging herself into a corner of the compartment. But sleep wasn't possible. One of her companions had bought a bottle of Scotch and when he had consumed half of it, he began to sing. He produced a pack of cards and insisted on playing poker with three of the others. Finally he was sick and had to be laid flat on the floor. He kept up an intermittent groaning during the rest of the journey. She took a taxi from King's Cross to the flat off Lancaster Gate, dropped her clothes on the floor and got into bed.

At ten-thirty next morning and again at eleven, the phone rang. On both occasions she turned, knitted the strident sounds into the fabric of her dreams and sank back into sleep. It rang again at one-thirty. Her eyes opened. She reached out a hand and picked up the receiver.

"Christ," said Jimmy Endells. "Thought you'd left the world, love. Trying to get hold of you all morning."

"I've been asleep," she said, still only half awake.

"Look, love. Soon as you can, let me have a memo on what you actually saw. You know—the Powell thing. How the police coped,

92

whether there was any panic. And Monckton—anything you've got on Monckton."

"All right."

"But for Christ's sake get out of that pit! There's a student press conference at the LSE in less than an hour. I want you there!"

The conference had started when Enid got there. The room was small. It smelled of tobacco smoke. Turner and McGregor sat behind a table in one corner of the room. A girl sat between them making notes. Turner was on his feet making a statement about the aims of the demonstration and why the Immigrant Community Society thought it necessary. He looked under considerable strain. Occasionally he glanced toward McGregor and McGregor nodded to him as if to give him support. Then, before anyone really expected it, he sat down. For a moment no one spoke. Then Reggie Deacon got up from the second row of press men.

"Can you let us have the route?" he said.

McGregor took up a piece of paper and read out the route. Deacon was jotting it down on a notepad.

"What about the timing?" asked someone else.

"How big's it likely to be? I mean—what kind of support do you expect?"

McGregor read out prepared answers.

Enid stood up.

"I missed the opening remarks," she said. "I'm sorry. I want to know what opposition you expect. Is it likely to be violent?"

Turner got up at once. His annoyance showed beneath his placid, drawn exterior.

"There'll be no violence," he said. "The Immigrant Community Society is an entirely nonviolent organization."

"But if there's opposition—if the police try to stop you. Can you guarantee the behavior of your members?"

"Of course," said Turner.

McGregor nodded.

The question seemed to have annoyed both of them.

Enid sat down. Turner remained standing. He looked belligerent, despite his words about nonviolence. When no one else spoke, he said, "Thank you for coming, ladies and gentlemen."

Everyone began to get up. Reggie Deacon pushed his way to the door. "Christ!" he said as he saw Enid. "Rush, rush, bloody rush!"

But the door opened before he reached it, and two policemen came into the room. Others were standing in the corridor outside. One of them leaned toward Reggie Deacon and said, "Excuse me, sir; Mr. Turner—Mr. McGregor?"

Deacon turned and pointed toward the table. "At the table," he said. He pushed past the man and out of the door.

The policeman walked down the middle of the room toward the table. The journalists stopped moving and turned back to the table.

"Mr. John Turner?" said the first policeman.

Turner said, "That's right—Turner."

The policeman turned to McGregor. "Mr. Paul McGregor?" he said.

McGregor nodded.

The policeman took papers from his pocket and looked at Turner. "I'm Constable Alderson," he said.

An older, gray-haired press man pulled a tattered notebook from his pocket and said to the second policeman, "What the hell's going on?"

The second policeman was very young. He was flustered by the group of journalists pressing forward toward him. He said, "We've warrants for their arrest. Keep back. Leave a gangway there."

"For Christ's sake!" said the gray-haired press man. "What charge?"

"Action likely to cause a breach of the peace," said the young policeman.

"What action's that?" said Enid, pushing her way toward the table with the others. "What have they done?"

"It'll come out in due course," said the young policeman. "Now look—if the rest of you wouldn't mind leaving. . . . "

His colleague was just delivering the formal caution to McGregor.

Later editions of the evening papers carried brief flashes about the intended demonstration. Still later ones carried news of the arrests. The edition on the streets a little before five o'clock carried the headline in red across the stop-press column: STUDENT DEMO: ON–OFF?

The arrest of John Turner, far from quelling the demonstration, had opened the way for more militant elements. As with so many earlier demonstrations in Britain, it collected to itself a mass of people quite unconnected with the Immigrant Community Society, people who were not even sure of the Society's aims, people with a vague sense of injustice, people with an undefined sense of frustration. Many were peaceful enough, but there were others who were not. And it was these more militant elements who began to dominate. Many of these elements were unconnected with the School itself. The press flashes had brought them in. A few succeeded in getting into the School, but most waited at the junction of Houghton Street and Aldwych to fall in with the procession as it moved toward the Strand. Inevitably, among the most militant of these outside elements, were thirty or forty of Westbrook's men under the leadership of Johnny de Margolis. They bunched together to start with. Many carried short sticks. Others had petrol bombs in webbing containers, held to their bodies underneath their shirts. Then de Margolis began to argue with the crowd around him and his colleagues began to infiltrate it. The original intention of the organizers of the demonstration had been to march along the

Strand westward as far as Trafalgar Square, then south down Whitehall and east along Horse Guards Avenue to the Embankment. There the demonstration would picket Monckton's headquarters for half an hour before returning along the Embankment and up Lancaster Place. But de Margolis was arguing that the two arrests changed the whole nature of the situation. How the devil could the demonstration be peaceful? he argued. The police had shown that they were prepared to use their powers to smash it by arresting the leaders, and they had to be answered with force. "What else does this society understand? Smash it! Burn it! Let's get this man Monckton and make an example of him!" There were frantic cries from his supporters, now scattered through a large body of the crowd, and as they shouted, the fever they generated spread.

De Margolis could see that the police were apprehensive. He could see the slight unsureness of some of their faces. They were in an impossible position and de Margolis knew it. The increased shouts of the crowd and its increasing size only increased the unsureness of the police.

Assistant Chief Constable Matthews—an ox of a man who in his day had regularly been seen in the ABA heavyweight finals—knew the cause of the apprehension well enough. He felt that he and his men were no better than tools in Monckton's cause. It was on Monckton's orders that Turner and McGregor had been arrested, not on police orders. And it was Monckton who had refused permission for the demonstration to take place, not the police. Yet it was Matthews and his men who had to control a situation that was none of their making. It was the police who had to face the jeers, and possibly the brickbats, of the crowd, not Monckton. It did not improve relations between Monckton's faction and the established forces of order.

Past experience had convinced Matthews that a demonstration robbed of its moderate leaders did not become more moderate. It

simply cleared the way for immoderate leaders to assert themselves. It seemed to him best, under the unfortunate circumstances,
to try to nip the thing in the bud, to frustrate it before it had
actually got under way. Ideally, he would have liked to seal off the
two exits from Houghton Street, where, by four-thirty in the afternoon, the demonstrators were assembling with their placards and
banners. Matthews' men in fact managed to do this without difficulty at the exit into Clare Market, where they placed light alloy
barricades across the street. But it was impossible at the exit into
Aldwych because of the jam of militant outsiders who had already
collected there. Every attempt Matthews made at this point to get
barricades and men into position was repulsed by the milling
crowd. And each unsuccessful attempt drained the lighthearted-
ness and good humor out of the crowd. Many people had simply
gathered, on reading the press reports and hearing the stories of the
impending demonstrations on radio, to see the spectacle of students
marching. But in time, and under mounting pressure from de
Margolis and his supporters, it became impossible for anyone to
remain a sightseer. Everyone became involved. The resistance to
the police attempts at containing them changed from counterpush-
ing and jostling, through angry shouting as one or two people
began to be hurt, to a fierce determination to thwart the intention
of the police at all costs. It became, as it were, a matter of principle.
And naturally, as the crowd became more stubborn, the attempts
of the police to contain it grew in strength. A natural courtesy on
both sides changed inevitably to a determination on the part of
each side to break the resistance of the other. By four-forty-five, the
crowd had spread across Aldwych and had begun to force its way
toward the junction with Kingsway. A little before five, the Kingsway junction had been crossed and all traffic from north London
making for the river crossing at Waterloo Bridge via Kingsway had
come to a standstill. The air grew blue with exhaust fumes from
waiting vehicles. Irritated shouts rang out from motorists. The

blast of horns sounded far up the street. In a matter of minutes, traffic building up behind the jam had blocked Euston Road at its junction with Upper Woburn Place. All movement in that part of central London came to a stop.

Perched on the high balcony of a building at the junction of Kingsway and Aldwych, Reggie Deacon looked down on the scene. Since his escape from the northern school hall and the phoning in of his story, he had become something of a celebrity. Whatever the official attitude to the breach of the D notice might be, Reggie Deacon's own part in it was thought by his colleagues to be nothing less than a first-class blow for the freedom of the press. When news of the demonstration first reached Bill Hobbs, there hadn't been a moment's hesitation in his mind as to who should cover it.

"Send Reggie," said Hobbs. "He's the specialist in this kind of thing."

Such was the speed with which Reggie Deacon's reputation was built. And yet he wasn't at all that kind of person. Temperamentally he wasn't at all like that. He was, if anything, rather timid. And physically, the idea of his inconspicuously insinuating his great amorphous bulk into a mob of demonstrators was ridiculous. When he found the crowd spilling across Aldwych, he walked back into the Strand. He took the next side street back into Aldwych, and found that he was ahead of both crowd and police. He stood for a while watching the scene, peering not so much over the top of his glasses as around them, as if there were only certain parts of the lenses that brought the scene into focus for him. He might have stood for the rest of the late afternoon, leaning his back against a wall and peering, if the crowd hadn't begun to move forward against the police. At that moment Reggie Deacon turned and went into the first doorway he came to. He climbed the stairs and when he hadn't the breath to climb further he opened a door, confused two office girls with his press card, and went out on the balcony. When he looked down, all traffic in sight had come to a standstill. A blue smoke haze rose from the street below. The crowd had closed the road and the junction with Kingsway, and was already forcing the police line down the western arm of Aldwych. When he screwed up his eyes a little and peered through the right parts of his lenses, he could make out the great figure of Assistant Chief Constable Matthews with a loudspeaker to his mouth.

Matthews knew that his men had contained the crowd in the eastern arm of Aldwych. But he knew as well that this was not because of any numerical or tactical police superiority there, but simply that that was not the way the crowd intended to move. But along the western arm, where Matthews was in direct control, his men were being forced to give ground. He was controlling them through the loudspeaker, in his deep, calm voice. "Easy, lads; steady there, Murphy. Let 'em carry you. Don't rush it." The voice boomed in the confined street, over the tick of car engines. Matthews was far too experienced to risk any further attempt by his outnumbered forces to meet the crowd head-on. He didn't want men damaged unnecessarily. He began to withdraw his men steadily toward the western end of Aldwych to its junction with the Strand. Policemen began slowly to move backward through the jam of traffic. They still maintained a loose contact with the crowd, since previous experience had shown that to withdraw quickly and leave a gap between the front line of police and the crowd inevitably resulted in a sudden surge forward on the part of the crowd. This surge forward excited those behind. The surge became a trot and then a run. And the impetus that such a movement generated was impossible to stop.

Matthews' intention was to keep the advance of the crowd down to a walk. He could do this if his men moved backward slowly, keeping contact with the crowd. At the same time he gave instructions for alloy barriers to be erected at the Strand junction. His men were to withdraw to the barriers, duck under them and stand. In that position, with the backing of mounted men and water cannon, he was confident that the crowd could be contained.

On the face of it, it was a reasonable plan. It might well have succeeded in containing the whole demonstration within Aldwych until it had cooled. After that, it would simply have been a question of dispersing it as peacefully as possible. But there were two factors working against it. Because of the buildup of traffic down Kingsway, motorists were trying to find other ways across the river. Many going south were turning right through the Covent Garden area, then pushing south down Bow Street and Wellington Street. They hit the Strand at many different points between Aldwych and Trafalgar Square, and as they did so they brought the traffic in the Strand to a standstill. And so, despite the orders of police outriders, and the clatter of fire-engine bells, the water cannon were unable to get into position. They were simply brought to a standstill by the volume of traffic. The same was true of the mounted detachment that Matthews thought he had available. It had been held in readiness in the Covent Garden market area since the first announcement of the demonstration. Now it couldn't be brought into action. Horses became wedged in by cars. Some mounted the pavement in an attempt to bypass the traffic, and then found at the first crossroads that the way ahead was completely blocked. After ten minutes' hopeless struggle, the detachment had to be withdrawn.

Matthews heard of both these holdups by radio. He still thought, provided foot reinforcements could reach him in time, that he might be able to hold the crowd at the barricades. It was then that he heard of the second difficulty. A radio message from Clare Market told him that the main demonstration was only beginning to move out of Houghton Street into Aldwych. He knew what that meant. The fresh forces would move into the present crowd like a ram, forcing it forward from behind, moving it ahead whether it wished to advance or not. And that, he thought, he couldn't hold.

He was in touch with Monckton by radio and Monckton's order was characteristic: "Hold them at all costs!" Matthews rubbed his forehead and face with a handkerchief. He gave a little smile. What kind of a man was this, he thought—this Monckton? What sort of forces did he think Matthews had in that street? He doubted whether even tear gas would hold them, but he had men standing by to use it.

Reggie Deacon, high on the office balcony, could see all laid out below him the total confusion of traffic and the steady withdrawal of the police toward the Strand barricades. He could sense that whatever reinforcements the police brought up, it was doubtful whether they would be able to hold that surging mass. And then, looking again to his left, he saw the main demonstration pour out of Houghton Street. It lunged, like some uncontrollable wave of bright summer dresses and white and colored shirts, into the Aldwych shambles. The crowd ahead of it, as far as the line of steadily retreating police, seemed to sense its impact before its physical pressure reached them. The pressure ran like a shock wave from the back of the crowd to the front. There was a momentary pause, and then the full energy of the ram broke on the backs of the forward sections of the crowd, and they were thrust at the retreating line of police. They were thrown against stationary cars. Some fell underfoot. The police withdrawal quickened. Deacon could hear the boom of the loudspeaker, keeping them together, keeping them calm, preserving discipline. The jammed traffic was breaking up some of the force of the crowd's advance. People couldn't get through in an unbroken phalanx, except along the pavements. Men climbed on the cars and hopped from roof to roof. A few motorists tried to get out of their vehicles to stop the damage. Those who managed it had arms trapped in slammed doors, or, facing the oncoming crowd, were knocked backward beneath the flailing feet. Both pavements were jammed with the advancing, running figures of the crowd.

Then, on the southern pavement, Deacon saw the police line break. Men in blue shirt sleeves and dark helmets suddenly turned and ran before the clamoring crowd advancing on them. And as Deacon peered across at them, pounding their way toward their comrades behind the barricades, he heard the crack-crack of rifle fire, and then, some thirty yards behind the front ranks of the crowd, dense smoke puffed up in rising clouds. The middle of the crowd checked for a moment. "Gas!" Deacon heard somebody shout. Others took up the cry. "Gas! Tear gas! Shield your bloody eyes!" But far behind, fresh demonstrators pushed with increasing vigor. Men who had stopped when the tear gas first hit them were thrust forward again. Once moved, they plunged on to get clear of the choking, blinding fumes. They ran into the backs of those ahead, forcing them in their turn toward the barricades. Motorists made renewed attempts to get clear of their cars, which were filling with fumes. Most were driven back or found it impossible to get the doors open. Deacon saw one man climb on top of his vehicle through the sun roof and run forward over the rooftops of other cars, a handkerchief held over his nose and mouth. Women in the crowd began to scream as they found themselves trapped and enveloped in the rising gas. They smashed at the windows of cars in the hope of getting clear of it. The gas began to reach Deacon, clutching the metal handrail of the balcony. Exhaust fumes and tear gas produced together an atmosphere that he found unbreathable. Panic broke out in the center of the crowd. People began to claw one another out of the way. They fought to get clear of the center of the road, across to the pavements and into the shops and offices. They streamed through the swinging doors of a hotel and up the steps of an office building. On the south side of the road, they tried to fight their way through the barricades that sealed off the exits to the Strand. But there weren't sufficient bolt holes from the street to make any significant difference. The main body of the demonstrators still surged forward.

Deacon, his handkerchief over his mouth and nose and tears streaming down his face, turned from the balcony and blundered back into the office behind.

Despite Monckton's orders—"Damn the bloody madman!" Matthews was muttering to himself—the crowd couldn't be held. Matthews could see what was going to happen if he didn't relieve the pressure. More tear gas would only increase the panic. If there had been some easy exit from the street, he would have used it. But there wasn't. There was nowhere the crowd could be driven. It was trapped, like gladiators in an arena. To have continued to pump tear gas into such a situation would have been to precipitate a general hysteria and the possibility of untold violence. He had to let the pressure escape. And the only escape route possible was forward into the Strand. He ordered the removal of the barriers and the temporary withdrawal of the police. In a moment, the crowd had broken clear of the confines of Aldwych and swept into the Strand. Matthews stood aside and watched it surge past him.

The physical release produced a reciprocal emotional one. Some of the tension disappeared. Some of the militancy drained away. The tremendous unity of purpose that had existed five minutes earlier had gone. As much as anything, it was the physical conditions that prevented it from reforming. If there had been some clear area in which the physical contact could have been reestablished, then Matthews might have had a very dangerous situation on his hands. But there wasn't. The Strand was packed with traffic—cars, buses, trucks, waited with engines ticking over, jammed so close to one another in places that it was impossible for a man on foot to get between them. Only the pavements were clear of traffic, though they certainly carried their crush of pedestrians, hurrying from the central offices of the West End toward the bridges and the stations. And so it was to the pavements on either side of the Strand that the demonstrators took. Regrettably, perhaps, the experience that many of the less determined demonstrators had had in Aldwych made them only too anxious to withdraw from the affair as soon as possible. Their chance came with the movement into the Strand. Many of them turned left, toward the east; others ran over the road, bouncing against the wings of stationary cars, stepping on hoods, and into the open gates of King's College and Somerset House. It meant that those who took to the pavements of the Strand and fought their way westward were the militant elements in the demonstration. It meant that although the demonstration had been considerably reduced in sheer numbers, it had lost the leavening effect of the moderates. What was left of the demonstration, pushing and fighting its way along the pavements westward, was extremely militant.

On the southern pavement, Johnny de Margolis was ramming at oncoming pedestrians with his shoulders. They were the shoulders of a rugby player—square, hunched and irresistible. People fell off them like leaves. Behind him came Ken Braddington, Don Tremuris and Digger Long, all of them members of the British Union of Activists. They drove forward in a phalanx, managing a steady trot most of the time, since people ahead of them stepped rapidly out of their way—into doorways or off the edge of the pavement and into the road. They were one of many little groups bunched on the pavements, jogging forward together, yet no longer part of a larger, organized demonstration.

All the groups that clattered down the pavements of the Strand had this in common: they were militants. They were not so much concerned with the issue that had brought the whole thing into being—the specific issue of Monckton and the rights of the individual in a democratic Western society—as with the issues of social organization itself. Yet within each group views of individuals differed widely. De Margolis dreamed of a rigid, elitist social structure, in which he himself would be very close to the pinnacle of power. He thought of those who ran with him as no more than tools in an inevitable process. Others, who would have been profoundly shocked if they had known the real motivation that pushed de Margolis on ahead of them, thought of themselves, a little curiously perhaps, as "Liberal extremists." Typical of a third group, and perhaps the largest, was Mike Riches. He was short, square and compact. His head was shaved and he had a fair, close-cropped beard. Riches and his associates did not believe in any social organization. It was not a new nihilism. It was built on a quite positive belief that all social structures diminish the individual human beings they contain. They were not so much opposed to the discrimination of one social group against another—a system that de Margolis regarded as inevitable because it was "in the nature of things"—as to the way in which, they felt, any society must inevitably discriminate against the individual man. It was an issue they had thrashed out through dark nights in sparsely furnished bed-sitters in Earl's Court and Paddington. It was an issue that had cost many of them their places at University College, King's and Queen Mary's, because it had taken up time that those establishments felt should have been spent in coming to grips with the principles of linguistics, comparative theology or the physics of sound. Riches regarded himself as a professional revolutionary, doing the minimum work necessary to keep body and soul together, and spending as much time as he could discussing "fundamental problems" and acting on the conclusions that those discussions brought him to. He and his associates had been described in the press as "thugs," "dropouts" and "anarchists," but no one had ever suggested that they were not serious. "Seriousness" was in many ways their real crime against the society into which they had been born.

Yet all these disparate individuals ran together, clattering, elbowing, pushing, westward down the Strand, for at bottom they were united by one common belief—that violence was the only political tool available to them by which they might radically change the social situation in which they found themselves. For

Riches, violence was "the final communicative act of a man in the last stages of what the Catholics call 'despair.' "

De Margolis turned out of the Strand. He knew that now the main weight of the demonstration had been broken, the police could stop them at the entrance to Trafalgar Square. There were not enough of them to break through. He ran down Savoy Street, south to the Embankment. The others turned with him, and behind them other groups followed. The traffic along the Embankment was still moving, though its pace was no more than a crawl. They kept to the north pavement, a hundred or so of them jogging along in bunches of ten or twelve.

The block occupied by Monckton lay beyond the Embankment gardens. De Margolis slowed to a gentle trot. Ahead he could see the blue uniforms of twenty or thirty policemen, beginning to move away from the entrance to the block, across the gardens toward the Embankment. He wanted the others to catch up with him. He wanted to be able to go at them and break through the cordon in a solid mass of opposition. The mass tightened behind him. He could feel other young men close up to his shoulders, moving into spaces behind him. He could feel them solidifying. Some had the petrol bombs. Others carried short sticks and long cylindrical drawing rulers which looked like black truncheons. He knew that if the main mass could engage the police, some of the bombers might get in close enough to launch their missiles against the entrance hall.

The police sensed the seriousness of the threat. It was not the first time they had met it. They drew their truncheons and tightened their formation. It was not an occasion when they might use verbal persuasion. They knew that de Margolis would run with his supporters right into their midst. If they didn't break the thing up at once, they would be run into the ground. Ten yards from the line of police, de Margolis drew a length of steel rod from inside his jacket and pointed it before him like a thrusting sword. It was pointing at the face of the nearest policeman, and behind it was the whole impetus of de Margolis' body. The policeman that de Margolis had selected as his immediate target stood with his feet apart, his head held a little lowered so as to increase the protection given to his head by his helmet. His truncheon, the strap looped over his thumb, was held two feet in front of his body as if it were a knife or a short sword. His left hand, palm open, was held ready to parry the weapon de Margolis held out in front of him. As de Margolis made his thrust at the face, the young policeman swayed three inches to his right, like a boxer riding a punch, and snapped down on de Margolis' right wrist with his truncheon. De Margolis dropped his weapon. The wrist fell to one side. The policeman seized the outstretched arm, took a step with his left foot and pulled de Margolis past him. And as de Margolis lost his balance and fell forward, the truncheon caught him a crack on the side of his head that brought him to his knees. He fell forward into the second line of police, rolled onto his right shoulder and lay still.

Then the main body broke upon the police. They fell back under the immediate impact, then held. It was a matter of survival under that thresh of short wooden staves and lengths of chain. They parried, they dodged, they cut right and left with truncheons. Members of both forces fell, holding heads and bleeding noses, clutching at broken wrists and collarbones. But the attack served its immediate purpose. Five or six bombers got around or through the police line, lit the tarred fuses of their bottles as they ran, and tossed them into the entrance hall of the building. Blazing liquid gushed over the tiled floor and under inner doors. It splashed up the woodwork. It set alight the fitted carpet in the inner entrance. Air was sucked into the building over the top of the blazing liquid, drawing smoke and flames inside. Curtains at one of the inner windows caught alight. The police line wheeled and retired toward the building, cutting off the line of advance of the demonstrators to the entrance. They fought up the steps, standing shoulder to shoulder, cutting down and across with their truncheons.

Only when the first police got inside the building and began to stamp and beat at the flames with boots and jackets did the attackers pause. Still knit tight together, they began to back away, two of them carrying the unconscious body of Johnny de Margolis. Finally, when it was obvious the police priority was to deal with the fire rather than pursue them, they withdrew across the gardens to the Embankment and began to run south.

Taylor knew nothing of the demonstration. He caught the 3:33 from York in a state of intense irritation with his wife. For God's sake, he thought, if she couldn't show an interest in what he was doing, at least she could keep quiet. It could mean more than promotion. It could mean some special mention, if Monckton really had that kind of power. Or why didn't she leave? Why didn't they call it a day? Why didn't she just get up and walk out? It wasn't the children—she couldn't say they were holding her.

There was no sign of a break in the weather. The train was full of northern holidaymakers going south. Outside, cattle bunched together in the shade of trees. A newspaper placard on Peterborough station read: HOTTEST WIMBLEDON ON RECORD.

Police stood in shirt sleeves at the King's Cross barriers, apparently not looking at anything or anyone. Taylor passed a family of holidaymakers standing in the middle of the platform with a pile of cases and rucksacks. A little boy sat on one of the cases with his thumb in his mouth. They were waiting for a porter. As far as Taylor could see there were no porters.

Outside a car was waiting for Taylor. The driver was sitting with the door open, his feet on the pavement. He opened the rear door and said to Taylor, "Christ knows if we'll get through, sir. The whole bloody town's gone mad." He was a big man, dressed in lightweight slacks and an open-necked shirt. He was in his late forties. An ex-wrestler, thought Taylor.

The car moved into Euston Road. Traffic was moving again.

"Thank Christ for that," said the driver, turning westward. "Jammed solid twenty minutes ago. I had to come in from the north. Looks as if the Colonel's got it sorted out."

"Colonel Monckton?" said Taylor. "It's a police matter."

"Not any more," said the driver. "That's what they're saying. The Colonel's in charge now—that's the story. You an ex-Army man, sir?"

"I'm a policeman," said Taylor.

"Are you, by Christ?" said the driver. "You know Colonel Monckton well?"

"Not well," said Taylor.

"I was with him in the war. RSM. He'll sort the bastards out."

Police cars were parked down Whitehall. A fire engine stood outside the riverside headquarters. Firemen were rolling up hoses. The steps and entrance ran with water. A dozen policeman stood outside, truncheons hanging from wrist straps. A bell rang and an ambulance drew away from the pavement.

The woodwork inside the entrance hall was still smoking. Taylor took the lift. A man with rolled-up shirt sleeves stood in the corridor. He had a length of wood in his hand. He came up to Taylor and stood squarely in front of him.

"Who are you?" he said.

"Chief Inspector Taylor," said Taylor. "I'm expected."

"Got some identification?"

Taylor showed his identity card.

The man seemed unimpressed. He nodded and said, "First on the left."

Monckton was standing at the open French window, looking down over the rails of the balcony at the scene in the street below. On his desk was a Smith & Wesson service revolver. He turned when Taylor closed the door and looked at him for a moment.

"Car there on time?" said Monckton, coming into the room.

"Yes, sir," said Taylor.

"Any trouble in the streets?"

"None, sir."

"You know what's happened?"

"The driver was telling me, sir. The demonstration."

"It's what I predicted," said Monckton. "The vacuum—all the scum of the country's rushing to fill it up."

"The police, sir," said Taylor. "I gather the police—"

"Never mind about the police," said Monckton. "They'll do their job."

"And what about my own position, sir?"

"You're my link with the northern investigation, Taylor," said Monckton. "I want to be kept fully informed."

"Surely, sir, if I was on the spot . . . ?"

"Presumably your subordinates are competent to handle the—minutiae?"

"Of course, sir."

"Well, then!"

Monckton sat down behind the desk. He took up the Smith & Wesson and put it in a drawer. "Go on, man. What's the position up there?"

"We've a possible suspect, sir. He left the town forty-eight hours before the explosion. They're doing an Identi-Kit on him. That'll be circulated—"

Monckton took up a pencil and pulled a pad of paper toward him. At the top of the paper he wrote: "PM," and beneath that: "1. Need for overall coordinator. 2. Attack on self demonstrates inability of police to handle large-scale public disorder."

"—distinctive accent, sir," Taylor was saying. "We can narrow the geographical area when I've got the report on the listening tests."

Monckton had lost interest in the activities of the northern police. He had what he wanted—access through Taylor to the development of the police inquiry. If an arrest was imminent, *he* would announce it, not the police. Through Taylor he retained control of that situation. His preoccupation now was with those situations which at present he did not control.

The later TV coverage that evening, and press reports next morning, carried only passing references to the arrest of John Turner and Paul McGregor. What was given prominence was the attack on Monckton's headquarters. "Violent elements are abroad," announced one paper, "elements to whom attacks on authority and private property are second nature." "Where a disease of this kind is found in the body social," ran the leader in another paper, "it is necessary to exorcise it ruthlessly before it spreads to other parts of the organism." This pompous moral tone was the one that predominated. One of the more popular papers said: "One thing is certain. This is no ordinary situation. When thousands rampage through the streets of London, something extraordinary is happening. Extraordinary events call for extraordinary measures. Colonel Monckton is empowered to investigate the most terrifying political assassination of the century. If the police cannot protect *him* from anarchist mobs, how secure are the rest of us?"

There was a loss of confidence in the police. It spread through London during the morning. Sir Alan Potter, Police Division, asked to see the Prime Minister. He had opposed the arrest of Turner and McGregor. All reports on the Immigrant Community Society that Potter had seen indicated that it was a moderate organization run by moderates. The removal of moderate leaders could only leave the leadership open to the militants. And so it had turned out.

The Prime Minister had Monckton's memo on his desk. His recommendations did not seem unjustified in view of the tone that

Fleet Street was taking. He had sounded out a selection of close colleagues and it seemed he would be able to carry them. Briggs would, of course, mount as much opposition as he could. It was like him to put political opportunism before the needs of the country. But if it came to a division, as of course it would, the Prime Minister knew which way it would·go. He spoke to the Chief Whip of his intentions.

Sir Alan Potter had never had the full confidence of the Prime Minister. Perhaps it was because of his comparative youth. Perhaps his intellectual background had something to do with it. He said, "I think, Prime Minister, that in order to restore confidence in ourselves, we must know Colonel Monckton's exact terms of reference."

"I'm making an announcement in the House this afternoon," said the PM.

"The longer the police are unsure about their position, the longer it'll take to reestablish their confidence," said Potter. "Press comment has been grossly unjust."

"The police have no need to worry," said the PM. "No one doubts their devotion. But there is doubt about whether they're being deployed as effectively as they might be. This is an extraordinary business, Potter—extraordinary. If further public unrest develops, it might call for military intervention. You'd foreseen that, of course? It's not exclusively a police matter. It's possibly without precedent, even in the thirties. If the whole structure of public order came into question, some overall coordinator would be required to protect it. Someone in a position to marshal all our resources, not simply the police."

Later in the morning the PM carried a cabinet meeting against some violent opposition.

"I care about the party as much as any man," he said. "But it's not the party that concerns me now. It's the future of parliamentary democracy. If the government falls on this issue, what's to replace it? Briggs can't form a government. Who else is there? Disunity's understandable on issues where less is at stake than national survival. On that we can't compromise. We must be strong. We must be united. We must govern. . . ."

Phones rang in offices and homes throughout London. The lobbying, the threats of party discipline, went on throughout lunch and into the early afternoon. When the PM announced the appointment of Monckton to coordinate the forces of public order through the Greater London area, he had already secured the votes he needed. Briggs and a dozen others made bitter, impassioned speeches in the name of parliamentary democracy, but nothing changed the result of the division. The government majority had been cut from 182 to 39, but it was still a majority.

"Christ!" said Briggs. "Nothing panics authority so much as violence in the streets of London."

At seven in the evening, the PM accepted Sir Alan Potter's resignation.

Two rooms had been booked for Taylor in the annex to a Bayswater hotel. The hotel had been built as a large private house facing the park. A side entrance gave access to a cobbled yard with outbuildings and stables. Taylor's rooms were above the main stable block, independent of the main hotel. He had access to them through the yard, as well as through the hotel main entrance.

By nine in the evening Taylor had unpacked his case, hung up his clothes and put a file of papers on the writing desk in the corner by the window. From the window he could just see the park. A small group of children were playing with a ball. Two policemen walked along Bayswater Road in the direction of Marble Arch.

He rang Inspector Ted Marston.

"You were right," said Marston. "John Brown—on the twenty-eighth and twenty-ninth of last month he took a room with the Garsides. Much the same description that George Freeman gave us—short, thin, glasses. And the stick—something with a leg. Said he was writing a book on regional architecture. Took a lot of photos apparently."

"How did he pay?"

"Cash again. No writing, no address, didn't say where he came from. Didn't talk much at all. He ate at the Chinese place, but they don't really remember him. Anyway we've put out an Identi-Kit, but I wouldn't recognize him from it."

"What about the accent?"

"We've been on that this evening. Not easy getting any real agreement. Probably somewhere in East Anglia—say somewhere Spalding-Hitchin-Colchester-Cromer."

"But not London?"

"Not London. And I've had a report from BR police. A ticket was handed in here on the twenty-eighth of last month, issued in King's Lynn. And on Friday someone came in from Peterborough. They're both in the area."

"Did anyone see him—porters, ticket collector?"

"Nobody."

"What about Sunday and Monday?" said Taylor. "Where was he then?"

"Nothing yet. He didn't stay in town and nobody seems to have seen him. We'll check the village pubs tomorrow."

"And the car-hire firms?" said Taylor.

"He didn't hire a car. Not from anyone round here," said Marston. "He might have borrowed one privately."

"I'll ring you tomorrow," said Taylor.

"You want me to look in on your family?" said Marston.

"Hm? Yes—thanks."

Taylor went to the reception desk and bought an "A to Z" of

London. He asked for a road map of East Anglia. The receptionist shook her head. She pointed into the entrance hall. On the wall was a map of the British Isles showing the location of other hotels in the group. He outlined the square of country that Marston had mentioned. It looked vast on the wall map. Somewhere in there, thought Taylor—assuming the man hadn't moved and taken himself and his accent to some different part of the country. But there was the encouraging information from the BR police. All circumstantial, of course, but encouraging.

Taylor went through the glass doors and into the street. He turned toward Notting Hill Gate. Traffic hummed, moving westward toward Shepherd's Bush or east into the West End. The air was full of exhaust fumes. Across the road couples walked into the park. High above, light feathers of cloud were tinged with pink. A police car, its blue light flashing, moved eastward. Four policemen stood outside the tube station at Notting Hill Gate. Taylor walked past them, then turned and walked back toward the hotel. He took in few of the external images. John Brown, he was thinking. Retired, with all the time in the world on his hands. Living alone. Alone, certainly not part of a group. He did this by himself, all by himself. Thought it up, made the device, researched the site, planted it and triggered it off. Quite a man. Persistent, thorough, determined, organized, skilled. But why? Mad? He must be. Did he know Powell? Had he even met him? Probably not. Almost certainly not. A political motivation? No, not a man like John Brown. What political purpose did it serve? Some more basic protest, possibly. Something more complex, something philosophical —something a madman might dream up. And that name—John Brown. Why that? It argued a carelessness that fitted in with nothing else that Taylor knew about the man. Or it argued an arrogance that defied society to catch him. A kind of public nose-thumbing. And yet a conviction that despite that he was immune from detection. Perhaps there were other nose-thumbings in public, thought Taylor, other clues that carelessness or arrogance had made him leave. That journalist, he thought, that woman with the fair hair and the silver clip in her hair. What was her name?

He went into the public call box in the hotel entrance and rang her paper. She wasn't there. No, they couldn't give him her home number. It wasn't their policy. Not over the phone.

"Then *you* ring her," said Taylor. "Tell her it's Chief Inspector Taylor. I'm on the Powell case. I'll ring back in five minutes."

"Oh, I see," said the operator. "No, I'll get her to ring you."

Taylor went to reception. "There'll be a phone call for me," he said. "Put it through to the room, will you?"

He went through the door at the end of the hall, across the yard and into the annex. The phone rang as he closed the door.

"Well—" said Enid Markus. "I didn't know you were down here."

"Do you think we might meet?" said Taylor. "I don't want to say anything on the phone. It goes through the hotel switchboard."

"That's a Bayswater number, isn't it? Can you come here?"

She gave him an address.

"Is it far? I mean, can I walk or should I get a taxi?"

"Oh, walk. Ten minutes, that's all."

It was a small block of flats at the back of Lancaster Gate. The glass door at the entrance was locked. He pressed a button. Beside it there was no name, simply the number of the flat. A voice said, "Yes?" through the small speaker above the column of black push-buttons. "Taylor," he said. "Third floor," she said. "There's a lift on your right." There was a click in the door lock and he opened the door.

She was standing outside the lift waiting for him. She was wearing a floral maxi-dress.

"Must be easier to get into Holloway," said Taylor. "Two-way speakers, automatic door locks."

"It's different from the provinces," she said.

"So it is," said Taylor.

It was larger than he had expected, with a living room and a dining room and a kitchen beyond that. The window of the living room looked out onto two other buildings, and between them he could see the park. There were bookcases in alcoves. Magazines were stacked on the shelves and in the rack that stood by the television set. On the walls were pictures of Montmartre and Shepherd Market. A decorated camel saddle stood in one corner, the leather embossed with Arabic letters.

"Nice place," said Taylor.

"It's convenient," she said. "Let me get you a drink."

"You got a beer?"

He sat down on a studio couch.

She went into the kitchen and came back with two cans of Long Life and two glasses on a tray. She put the tray on a small table. Taylor opened the cans and poured out the beer. She sat down beside him on the couch.

"Cheers," she said.

"Cheers," said Taylor.

"Well, now," she said. "What was it?"

"It's a favor," said Taylor.

"Me do you a favor? Why?"

"It might help me."

"What I meant was—"

"I know what you meant," said Taylor. "But I can't tell you anything. You know that."

"Not now, no. But later—"

"Maybe," said Taylor.

"Only maybe?"

"Only maybe. When it's over it won't be up to me. There'll be a formal statement or something. I can't give you any guarantees."

"But you'll bear me in mind?"

"I'll bear you in mind," said Taylor.

She thought for a moment. She took another sip of beer. Then she said, "All right. What is it?"

"I want to see clippings on Powell."

"But why me? Why come to me?"

"You've reported his speeches. You know where that kind of material is," said Taylor. "Then again—I know you."

"Like hell you know me," she said.

"Well?"

"What kind of clippings?" she said.

"Not what he said—I know that. But pieces about him—articles, letters to papers, gossip."

She got up, bent over the little table and poured the rest of the beer into her glass. Then she turned and looked at him.

"I've my own file in the office," she said. "But I'm not just going to hand it over."

"A bargain, you mean? No, I can't."

"The police must have a file," she said. "Why not ask them?"

"I can't," said Taylor. "They'll think I'm trespassing—a policeman from the provinces."

"Then why don't you go over my head? Why don't you ask Jimmy Endells for it? It's official, isn't it?"

"You know damn well why. He'll want to know what for and wherefore and what I have in mind."

"You don't have to tell him," she said.

"Like hell I don't. Then he starts inventing reasons."

"Well?"

"For God's sake sit down," said Taylor. "It's distracting having you waving about like a flag in that dress. Anyway, what do you want to know?"

"I just want to be kept in the picture. I mean, it was my story. You could say I had a corner on Powell. Now it's the end of an era."

The lights were out in Daniel Westbrook's little antique shop. A policeman passed, walking slowly toward the central market of Covent Garden. To him the place looked closed and empty. In the back room the committee of the British Union of Activitists was in session. Seven men sat around the table on hard, straight-backed chairs. A single bare bulb hung from the ceiling. Despite the night heat and the smoke in the room, the window was closed and the heavy velvet curtains drawn. On the table was a map showing the approach roads to the All England Tennis Club at Wimbledon.

No one spoke. The committee members looked at the map. They traced approach roads with the tips of fingers, as if impressing them on their minds. They got up from the table and walked to some other point around its perimeter, as if trying to visualize the scene from other angles.

At last Westbrook looked up at them.

"Well?" he said. There was tension and excitement in his voice.

They nodded to him in turn. At first sight, they appeared to have little in common. One had the broken nose of a boxer and a thickset, powerful body. Another was smaller and quite bald. He had a scar running from the center of his skull, across his forehead and down his right cheek. He looked as if he had been hit by a machete. A third was tall and distinguished looking. He could have passed in the street as a professional man in the top income bracket. All were well dressed. They wore lightweight suits, the jackets unbuttoned because of the heat in the room. One dabbed at his broad forehead with a large white handkerchief. All were intent on the project. All listened when Westbrook spoke.

Westbrook unfolded another map and laid it over the top of the first. It was a plan of the club premises themselves. It showed the courts and the seating arrangements for the spectators. It showed the disposition of the dressing rooms, the bars, the showers. It showed the accommodation for club members, officials and distinguished visitors.

Again members of the committee leaned over the table, pointing at various features, turning heads a little to one side to read the print that identified the various rooms and buildings.

At last Westbrook tapped the plan with a thin index finger. "That's the target," he said. "The center court. Our aim must be the creation of the maximum confusion and panic. We must draw attention to the fact that law and order has broken down. We must show that even the most sacrosanct ground in the country is not above violence and confusion. We must demonstrate that no one is safe. Only then will people be convinced that unless the British Union of Activists is given the power and mandate it needs, anarchy will sweep us all to destruction."

Some of his supporters did not quite follow his line of argument, though they knew exactly what was expected of them in terms of action. It was enough for Westbrook. His political theories were his own. It didn't matter that others might not follow them. What mattered was that they could carry them into practice. He turned to each man around the table. Each in turn nodded.

"And remember Johnny de Margolis," cried Westbrook, lifting a pointed finger high in the air. "He died without ever regaining consciousness—clubbed down in action by the forces of this decadent society. Remember him! He shall be honored in the new society. He shall be the first of our heroes. Let that be the battle cry— Remember de Margolis!"

Monckton lost no time in exercising his new powers. He increased his quarters by taking over the entire building. He brought in men of his own choice, many of them ex-Army men who had worked with him during the war or as part of the Dayton detachment. He recruited a personal bodyguard on the grounds that his own life had been threatened. He insisted on the immediate suspension of immigration, at least into the Greater London area, and he interviewed the leaders of the metropolitan immigrant communities.

His definition of the word "immigrant," to judge from his actions, was somewhat elastic. He interviewed, for example, leaders of the north London Jewish community, whose forebears had been in the country for generations, while ignoring the small community of South Africans in Hampstead. Two East German students who had shot their way out of jail near Dresden, hijacked a plane and flown it to Gatwick were refused political asylum on Monckton's insistence and handed over to the staff of the Russian Embassy. By contrast, a retired American officer, once the center of the investigation into the notorious Mekong massacre, moved unimpeded into central London and took up permanent residence with his family in Highgate.

What began to emerge was not an inconsistency in Monckton, but an extreme right-wing view of the kind of action that the situation demanded. Even his personal interpretation of the word "situation" was infinitely wider than the already very wide powers that the PM had agreed to. His vision did not restrict the situation to the assassination of Enoch Powell and the nationwide unrest that it had triggered off. He saw deeper causes behind it. He saw a country losing its shape and coherence, a country in desperate need of discipline. He saw mass immigration as a principal cause of that lack of coherence—"this injection of foreign bodies" as he called it. Two things were needed; the reimposition of discipline by a strong central authority, and "national purification" through repatriation, to recreate the sense of "national identity." On the second of these two issues there was a certain semantic confusion in his mind, as his actions showed. His vision was not so much of *national* purification and *national* identity, as of *racial* purification and *racial* identity. Both issues demanded the "the strong man." In Monckton's view, no such man existed in the formal seats of government.

What London needed, thought Monckton, what the whole country needed, was to see the situation as clearly as he did himself. It still did not *believe* in any fundamental danger. This was a passing crisis, no more. What was needed was not less disorder but more. A little public bloodletting that would leave the country in no doubt about the real issues. Wasn't it the pattern of British history? What had pulled the country together after the loose liberalism and appeasement of the thirties? Not Spain, not the little jab of Cable Street—Dunkirk! Only with that massive disaster did the nation draw itself up, and prepare itself for the great feats of the battle of Britain and of Alamein.

The early editions of the London evening papers carried the headlines: "Monckton supports state funeral of Powell" and "Powell funeral for London?" Monckton had leaked the story through one of his close supporters. When the press rang him to know where he stood on the issue, he wasn't available. An aide said he thought Colonel Monckton would not be opposed to it. Monckton was tossing out ground bait, as it were, to test the reaction. He chose that course, rather than approaching the PM with a formal suggestion, because he felt sure of public support. That support would make it more difficult for the PM to refuse the suggestion, and Monckton saw a public funeral in the streets of London as producing the mass outcry that was necessary to bring the nation face to face with the facts.

Briggs was incensed when he read the first stories and the apparently favorable public reaction to them. He rang Downing Street. The PM was in an emergency cabinet meeting. He might be free in an hour. Briggs was in a state of growing despair. During the past few days he had fought every proposal the PM had made to the House, with the support of a united Opposition and a good deal of active sympathy from some members of the government back benches. Yet nothing had come of it. Each round had been lost. So much, he began to think, for the parliamentary process. He got in his car and drove to St. George's Hospital.

Evans looked pale and infinitely depressed, lying back on the pile of pillows under his head and shoulders. The evening papers lay on the floor where had dropped them.

"Look, Freddy," said Briggs. "You can influence him. You're the only one. As far as the rest of your colleagues go . . . ! Damnation—if I hold the phone can you ring him? Is there something we can do?"

With infinite care, Evans began to push back the bed coverings and ease himself toward the edge of the bed.

"For God's sake!" cried Briggs, putting a hand on Evans' shoulder. "You'll kill yourself!"

He rang for a nurse. She came in, argued with Evans, then went out. In a moment she was back with a doctor. They stood on either side of Evans' bed, holding his shoulders.

"Don't you realize, man," said the doctor, "that you're stitched up like a repaired teddy bear? If you move you'll fall apart!"

"What do you think this is?" muttered Evans, holding the bulky dressing tight to his stomach and still trying to slide toward the edge of the bed. "A bloody prison camp?"

"If you don't lie still," said the doctor, still restraining Evans, "I can't be responsible."

"Who asked you to be responsible?" said Evans. "As long as I'm conscious *I'm* responsible."

The doctor turned to Briggs. "For God's sake do something," he said. "He'll kill himself."

"Wait," said Briggs. "I'll get the PM."

Evans was panting and perspiring. His energy had gone. He couldn't make the edge of the bed. He lay back on the pillows and gave a little nod toward Briggs.

Briggs picked up the phone. Half an hour later the Prime Minister came into the little private room. He looked down at Evans, lying back on the white pillows, his face drawn, his skin a pale yellow.

"Some sort of relapse?" said the Prime Minister. "Sorry to hear about it, Freddy."

"Relapse be damned!" growled Briggs. "If you let Monckton go ahead with this public funeral idea, you'll kill your own colleague. Look at him—we had to hold him down to stop him coming to you himself!"

"Prime Minister," said Evans, "not this. By God, if you give this to Monckton I'll come to the House and speak against you. I'll resign my office and I'll resign from the party. They can bring the TV cameras to my bedside and I'll tell the country why I've done it!"

Evans voice was little more than a whisper.

"For God's sake, man," shouted Briggs to the PM. "Who's to know? Who's going to tell what went on in this room? Can't you see the man's ill? Can't you see you'll kill him if you don't compromise on this?"

"Compromise!" said the PM, turning on Briggs. "What compromise is this you're talking about? I've no intention of acting on this stupid rumor. Colonel Monckton's of the same opinion."

"Then how—?" cried Briggs.

"Damn you, man!" snapped the PM. "Can you do nothing but carp? Have you nothing constructive to offer? I was on the phone to Monckton twenty minutes ago. He said nothing at all to the press. Some underling on his staff might have made a comment—totally unauthorized. More likely the press invented it."

Taylor sat in the small room that Monckton had provided for him on the top floor of the riverside headquarters. In rooms on either side of him men worked. He could hear the ring of phones and the clatter of typewriters. He heard whispered conversations on the landing outside and the opening and closing of doors. The purpose behind the increasing activity in the building became more and more obscure to him. He was aware that Monckton had something a good deal more important in his mind than just the solution of a particular crime. This accounted for the general activity from which Taylor was excluded, though what exactly that wider purpose was he didn't know.

Axel, Monckton's personal assistant, rang Taylor in the late afternoon. Taylor went downstairs. There was a man with an armband standing outside Monckton's door with a pick handle. He barred the door as Taylor approached.

"For God's sake," said Taylor. "I've an appointment with him. The PA's just rung through."

"I'll check," said the man.

He opened the door three or four inches and spoke to someone inside. He nodded and opened the door wide for Taylor to pass.

Inside the room, Axel sat behind a desk. He was a square-built middle-aged man with a graying toothbrush moustache.

"What's the goon for?" said Taylor.

"Obvious, isn't it?" said Axel. "If anyone got at Colonel Monckton, who'd replace him?"

"Who's going to get at him?" said Taylor.

"If we knew that," said Axel, "the precautions wouldn't be necessary."

"He wants to see me?" said Taylor.

He looked around the room. The furniture had been repositioned.

"He's moved into the inner room," said Axel, pointing toward the door on his right. "More security that way."

"What do I do?" said Taylor. "Wait or go through?"

"I'll ring him," said Axel.

He picked up a phone and pressed a lever on the small internal switchboard on the desk.

"He's here, sir—Taylor," said Axel.

"Chief Inspector Taylor," said Taylor.

Damn these little upstart bureaucrats, he thought.

Axel said, "Just knock—then you can go in."

"Obliged to you," said Taylor.

He opened the door into the inner room and walked in. Monckton looked up from the desk. He watched Taylor come into the room and close the door behind him and stand there in front of the desk. After a moment Taylor saluted and Monckton said, "Sit down."

Monckton was wearing the uniform of a full colonel. He had three rows of ribbons on his chest. When he pushed back his chair toward the window, Taylor saw that there was a revolver in the holster at his belt. The pale eyes, when they looked at Taylor, seemed a little more distant, a shade further removed from reality. The whole man seemed a little unreal. It might have been partly that he sat between Taylor and the window, so that his outline was in sharp silhouette and only reflected light fell on his features. When he spoke the impression of unreality faded, for his speech was as incisive as ever.

"I want you in Wolverhampton, Taylor," said Monckton. "First thing in the morning."

"Wolverhampton, sir?" said Taylor.

He wondered what had happened that no one had told him about. He felt his grasp on the case slipping. If Monckton wouldn't keep him informed . . .

"The funeral," said Monckton. "I want you there as a liaison with the local police."

"What am I to do?"

"Nothing. They're expecting you. Just be there."

"But—"

"Must I spell it out, Taylor? Initiative—that's what they told me you had. I need a personal representative there. I need a presence. I want them to know that every aspect of this business is my concern. I don't want the local police thinking they can operate with any kind of autonomy because they're in Wolverhampton and I'm here. Whatever concerns Powell concerns me. You wouldn't argue that a man's own funeral is no concern of his, would you?"

"No, sir," said Taylor.

"Then be there. Let them know you're there. That's all."

He gave a dismissive wave of the hand and said, "Let me know when you get back."

Taylor took an official car to his rooms in Bayswater. A group of armed police patrolled Trafalgar Square. Two armed policemen stood in the foyer of the hotel when he arrived. They saluted. One of them said, "We've checked the approach, sir. Best place would be outside in the courtyard."

"What are you talking about?" said Taylor.

"Been detailed to keep a watch on your rooms, sir."

"What the hell for?"

"In case anyone tries to get to you, sir."

"Where did this order come from?"

"Division, sir—but originally from Colonel Monckton's office, I believe."

Taylor rang Bertram Warner. When he looked down from the window into the courtyard, he could see the two policemen standing with their backs to the entrance to the annex.

"Sir," said Taylor. "Do you know what's happening? Do you know what he's doing?"

"There's nothing you can do, Mr. Taylor," said Warner. "Not at the moment."

"But you know what they're going to think in Wolverhampton? They won't be sure that his authority doesn't extend up there."

"Some of them maybe," said Warner. "Not the Chief. He knows well enough what his own authority is."

"But you can see the way it's moving, sir?"

"I can see," said Warner.

Taylor rang Enid Markus. A girl's voice said, "She's out."

Taylor said, "Give me the editor, will you?"

"I'm afraid he's out," said the girl.

"Well, any message?" said Taylor. "Did she leave any message for me?"

"I don't think so. I don't remember—"

"Well, could you please look? I mean, I don't want to cause you any trouble or interfere with whatever it was that you were doing—"

"All right, all right!"

Taylor could hear her calling to someone at the other side of the office. "For God's sake!" said Taylor. In the courtyard below the window, the two policemen had moved a little nearer the double gates opening into the street. They were facing the main hotel building, looking up as if checking the roofline.

"She's in Northampton," said the girl.

"All right," said Taylor. "She's in Northampton."

"That's all."

"No message—nothing?"

"No message," said the girl's voice.

She put the receiver down as she spoke.

It was nine o'clock when Enid Markus rang Taylor. He had a briefcase on the bed into which he had put a toothbrush, brush and comb and pair of pajamas. He was waiting for them to tell him the taxi had arrived. He stood in front of the mirror making a final adjustment to his tie. He wore slacks and a dark linen jacket. He picked up the phone as it rang. It took him a moment to realize it was Enid, not the desk telling him about the taxi.

"Noel—Noel Taylor?" she said "Enid Markus."

"But God, I've been—"

"Did you get the message?"

"No message—no."

"Oh, God! I left it with them at reception."

"Here?" said Taylor.

"In the hotel. You didn't get it?"

"Nothing. And nothing from your paper either. You've a moron on the switchboard. She knew you'd gone to Northampton, but that's all she did know. She was right, I suppose? You are in Northampton?"

"Kettering."

"How long?"

"I'll be back in the morning. I've got all I need. I rang about the file I promised. It's at home. What about ten tomorrow morning?"

"I'm just leaving. I'm in Wolverhampton for the day. If I come round tomorrow evening—straight from the station?"

"Why not? Fine. Any time after seven."

The sky reddened in the west. High wisps of golden cloud darkened and finally disappeared. Through the train windows Taylor could see the first stars. It was quite dark when they reached Wolverhampton. Yet outside the station the feel of the town was not a night feel. It was not the feel of a town settling into sleep and quietude. Beneath the dark blanket of sky was an incessant activity, and behind it a sense of apprehension. Throughout the night, as Taylor lay only half asleep in the iron bed of the boardinghouse, there were the sounds of movement from outside: the hum of vehicles, the beating of iron on iron, the tramp of feet. At seven in the morning, when Taylor finally abandoned the idea of sleep and got up and dressed, a dozen policemen were standing on the corner opposite the window of his room. When he left the boardinghouse, a little after eight, he found that metal stakes had been driven into some of the pavements and sections of the town had been roped off.

A temporary police HQ had been set up in the Blackwell Arms at the back of Darlington Street. Inside the bar a police sergeant sat at a trestle table. He lifted his head and looked at Taylor for a moment, then he said, "What do you want?"

"Chief Inspector Taylor," said Taylor. "Colonel Monckton's office. I sent a signal. Chief Superintendent Ewart's expecting me."

The sergeant got up. "I'm sorry, sir," he said. "In the civvies— I didn't know." He took up a folder and opened it and ran his finger down a list inside. Then he looked up and his expression had changed. He said, "Colonel Monckton's office—*that* Chief Inspector Taylor?"

"That's right," said Taylor.

"I see," said the sergeant. "Perhaps if I could see your identification card, sir."

Taylor passed him the card and he took some moments scrutinizing it. He scribbled on a pad of paper, looked at his watch and made a note of the time. Then he handed the card back to Taylor. "He's in the back, sir," he said, leading the way out of the bar.

Chief Superintendent Ewart was in his late forties. His face had that leathery quality that comes of years spent out of doors. He didn't get up from the table. He didn't put out a hand to Taylor. He took a gulp of tea from a large mug, then he said, "We're quite capable of handling this ourselves, Taylor."

"Of course, sir," said Taylor.

"Then why have they sent you here?"

"Colonel Monckton wants to keep himself informed, sir."

"The usual channels aren't good enough for him, aren't they?"

"I think it's firsthand information he's after, sir."

"We could have given him that—if that's what he wants. You're a policeman, Taylor—how would you take to being spied on by some outsider?"

"He is in charge of the case, sir."

"Not here he's not. Not yet. Don't think we don't know his position in London—but that's not here. This is a funeral. Nothing to do with the case. We're quite competent to handle it ourselves. Whatever it is you propose to do, just keep out of our way."

"Sorry it annoys you, sir," said Taylor.

"Damn right it annoys me. As if we didn't know our own job. As if we needed some London intervention to help us handle our own affairs."

"I see, sir."

Ewart seemed to relent. He said, "Don't take it personally, Taylor. It's not you. I don't envy you. But the idea!"

The precautions were reasonable, as far as Taylor could see, and they were probably necessary. Yet they served inevitably to increase the tension. Taylor could feel it building throughout the morning as coachloads of mourners began to pour into the city and make their way toward the center. Cars and coaches were packed into every available space on the periphery of the center. Names on the coaches seemed to represent every town in the area—Cannock, Lichfield, Tamworth, Walsall, Dudley, Birmingham. Thousands more came in by train. In the streets film camera units were setting up their equipment. As Taylor passed one such group, standing on the pavement in Lichfield Street, he heard German being spoken. It brought home to him the significance of the movement with which he was caught up. For better or worse, the whole of Europe—perhaps the whole of the Western world—saw the event as the focal point of something that was happening in Britain, something they had not seen before, something that could change it out of all recognition.

By early afternoon, Wolverhampton had become two cities. There was the city through which the cortege moved, almost entirely silent. Only the inhabitants of the streets directly affected were allowed to line the route, sealed off from the rest of the town by barricades. People leaned from upstairs windows. Many of them were crying. A few had dressed formally in black as a sign of respect for the dead man. From a few houses, little Union Jacks flew at half mast. The atmosphere was somber in the extreme.

By contrast, there was the city beyond, the city in which Taylor stood, the city of mass mourners and a hundred thousand visitors. All were moved by the event. The massed feeling was greater than the feeling of any individual. It hung oppressively in the sunny air. It pressed down. It weighed down those who already felt a personal sorrow, and it impressed a sorrow and a sense of loss on those who had felt nothing personally. People stood along the pavements in the town center, staring at empty streets. They stood quite still, giving no trouble of any kind to the forces of authority. They felt the loss without protest or resistance. There was a massed unison of feeling, a sense of being moved by some great and tragic event. They could only respond, since no action seemed great enough to match their feelings.

They stood in silence—many in tears—from two to three in the afternoon. Though few saw the actual ceremony, the whole country knew that by three o'clock it would be over. And as three o'clock struck, clock chimes echoing over the silent streets, there grew a counteremotion. Taylor, standing in a shop doorway at the western end of Darlington Street, felt it like a physical presence. Something he might have put out his hand and touched. Crowds on the pavements shuffled as if shedding some net in which they had been held. People turned to one another, as if amazed to realize how they had been behaving, so quietly, so peacefully, so—obediently. They looked strangely shocked by the realization. A violent counterforce began to build in them.

"He's gone! Gone!" a woman in front of Taylor began to cry aloud.

"The bastards!" shouted a tall, heavy-jowled man standing at the curb on Taylor's left.

A cry rang out. It echoed across the still street. It ran right and left. Others took it up. An animal cry without the articulate words of human speech. Simply a cry—a great gasp of fury. A cry of savagery. A countercatharsis, as it were, responding to the sense of tragedy. But not a cleansing, rather a clearing away of barriers, a freeing of everything that had been inhibiting action. Waves of physical movement ran through the crowds on either pavement. Policemen began to grasp hands to form a continuous human chain against it, sensing the power behind it and what it might do. The movement rocked against the line of police. It was rhythmic. The police swayed into the road and then back onto the pavement, but each time the movement grew, until at last it couldn't be controlled.

Taylor got back into the shop doorway, and when the movement finally broke and the police line snapped, he was able to protect himself from flying fists and elbows fighting to get clear, to get out of the crowd, to get into the street and run. In a moment, all resistance to the crowd had broken. It surged forward off the pavement and into the empty street beyond. It hesitated. People stared from right to left.

"Let's get the bastards!" screamed a man opposite. He had climbed a foot or two up a lamppost to see over the crowd's heads.

The crowd hesitated. It bunched together, it swung around, it growled, it began to find direction, and finally, with what sounded like a baying howl, it broke westward toward Tettenhall Road.

There had been understandable attempts by the police to seal off parts of the Whitmore Reans district. Chief Superintendent Ewart had forward sections of his force out in front of the barricades, but most of them he held behind the protection of the tubular steel. He was listening to reports reaching him from other sections of the town over his personal radio. There was nothing encouraging in them. Even without the radio, he could hear the distant grumble of the crowds, though ahead of him the street was deserted except for his own advanced patrols. His men stood together behind the barricade, staring ahead down the street. He could feel their apprehension. He could understand it. They had no relish for what might happen. Most of them, he knew, felt disgust at what was taking place, though there were others whose feelings were caught up with those of the crowd they couldn't as yet see. Yet all had an understanding of the motives behind the situation—the sense of personal loss, the loss of a champion, the loss of a man whom thousands felt had spoken up for them when they were unable to speak for themselves. A man who had focused national attention on what to them was the real problem, the problem of personal definition. Someone they felt had answered the question: What does it mean to be a Briton in the middle of the twentieth century?

Behind Ewart stood Sandy Robo, tall, dark-skinned, a little curly black beard covering the lower part of his face. He stood with his arms folded. He was watching the street ahead, with a look of uncomprehending bitterness in his eyes.

"This your England, Mr. Ewart?" he called to Ewart. "This the milk-and-honey place they told us about in the Bible classes when we was kids back home?"

Robo had come from Barbados two years before, with his wife and two daughters. Despite his bitter comments to Ewart, he was not so naïve as to have believed so completely the image of Britain given in his school textbooks. Nonetheless, his feeling of total isolation from the community he had come to had been something of a surprise. He had fallen back on the companionship of his fellow immigrants more heavily than he had expected, and when the anti-immigrant feeling had grown among the white community of Britain, he had formed a local immigrant organization out of sheer self-defense. In connection with this organization, he had met Ewart on many previous occasions, and the two men had a relationship of mutual respect though never actual friendship. During the preceding few months, Robo's increasing sense of bitterness in any case prevented such a thing as friendship between himself and any white man.

Robo looked around at his fellow members of the colored community. They weren't speaking. They stood with arms folded, or hands in pockets. They stood in shirt sleeves or lightweight jackets because of the hot summer's day. They stared at the backs of the line of police, and beyond them across the barricade. There was an air of incomprehension about them, as if some dream had been shattered and they couldn't understand why. They looked at once helpless and defiant, as they listened to the growing clamor from the town center. Was it like this with the Israelites, Robo was wondering, when, having struggled out of the slavery of Egypt, they looked down not on the promised land but on the deserts of southern Palestine? Behind Robo, further down the street, others stood in doorways, leaning against the brickwork in that characteristic posture that has the appearance of total relaxation, the appearance of muscular limpness. Still more leaned on the sills of upstairs windows, looking down toward the barricades, listening apprehensively to the growing howl of the approaching crowd.

Ewart was listening to the radio. His expression was grim. He nodded. He put up a finger and beckoned to a sergeant. He leaned a little toward the man and gave some order. The order was muttered along the line of police. They drew their truncheons and took up positions of readiness, their feet a little apart, their bodies square to the front. They looked like a row of actors posing for some Hollywood spectacular. Their nervousness increased. Some tapped their truncheons into the palms of their free hands. One or two pulled at the peaks of their helmets to increase the protection to temples and foreheads. Ewart knew that only discipline held them there, not any taste for what was now to come.

Then suddenly the dull, still distant clamor broke into the far end of the street some hundred yards ahead of the barricade. Two policemen, then a third, ran round the corner. Two had lost their helmets. One had the unbuttoned sleeves of his shirt flapping at his forearms. They ran down the middle of the street toward the barricade without a glance behind them. One raised his arms and shouted something to those ahead, but his words were lost in the general howl behind him. The first of the pursuers ran into the street, ten or fifteen of them. They were younger men, men in their mid-twenties. Behind them came others, then still more. They began to fill the end of the street, fighting, elbowing one another to reach the front. Some were women, waving their arms above their heads and shouting as they ran.

Ewart walked behind his men. They were standing quite still. He could see the beads of perspiration on necks and foreheads. He could see the whiteness of their knuckles as they gripped their truncheons. They looked straight ahead across the barricade, at the oncoming mass of people.

"All right, lads," he said. "Hold your ground till you get the order."

Ewart looked behind him to see the reactions of those in the street. Robo was still standing with his arms folded. The look of bitterness in his eyes shocked Ewart, though he understood its cause. To some extent he sympathized with it. He had known Robo for almost two years, and he had seen the steady change in him. Others looked blankly uncomprehending, as if they couldn't bring themselves to believe what was staring them in the face. It was as if they were at last beginning to see through some colossal hoax, a hoax perpetuated by generations of missionaries and school text-books. The myth of a Britain that had never existed, the Britain that had forced Jesus on them and compelled their own gods to abdicate.

Behind them, others were beginning to act. They were coming out of their homes with sticks and pokers, prepared to make a stand. Ewart knew well enough what they were thinking. Robo had told him often enough. Had they crossed five or six thousand miles of ocean to be pushed out of their homes into the street? Were they to be forcibly repatriated, as Monckton was vigorously advocating, having been lured here by the tales told to their fathers by missionaries and administrators and educationists of a land flowing with milk and honey? Well, they might be—but by the Christian God they wouldn't go meekly! Gentle Jesus was a fine idea as long as it worked. But if it didn't, there were older ideas, more primitive and more telling.

The crowd, seeing the barricade some fifty yards ahead, began to slow its advance. It began to bunch together, shoulder to shoulder, to form a human ram that would scatter the barricade and the defenders. Ewart called to them through a loudspeaker. It didn't halt their progress. Two gunners fired CS gas grenades into their midst, but not in sufficient concentration to stop them. On they came, tightening their formation, hunching shoulders, gripping wooden staves and iron railings they'd picked up on the way.

The first line fell on Ewart's forward sections, who went down under it. The crowd walked over them. The occupants of the street hurled missiles—stones, bricks and empty milk bottles. It was all without effect. They lunged with clothes props across the top of the barricade, but the weight of countermissiles drove them back. Length by length the tubular steel barricade was picked to pieces and the howling crowd was through, swarming over the main body of the police. Men began to smash the windows of the first houses. They whirled boomerangs of glass at the defenders. Some broke down front doors and ransacked the houses behind. Others trampled underfoot the family treasures brought from Barbados and Trinidad—photographs of parents, a carved box given as a wedding present, a crude watercolor of St. Michael's cathedral in Bridgetown. Where there was opposition, it was beaten down. When the locked front door of Sandy Robo's house was finally smashed in, his wife and two girls were clubbed to death, and he, out in the street beating six young men off a fallen comrade, knew nothing of it. Further up the street they began the burning, piling up clothes and papers and furniture in the middle of ground-floor rooms and setting it alight. Smoke and flames began to billow from upstairs rooms on both sides of the street.

Yet they were nice people. Ewart knew some of them and they were all nice people. Douglas Whitcher, a toolmaker in a press-works, said in court the next day, "I don't know what came over me. I've never been in court before in my life. It was some kind of thing that got hold of you. I was so upset by the funeral. Something happened to all of us and we had to go with it." It was he who had struck down Mrs. Robo, though he swore he never touched the girls. He was a nice man. All his friends swore he was a nice man. His wife and son swore he was a nice man. His employer swore he was a nice man. He was undeniably a nice man. And yet—

Taylor stood alone in the street. It was empty. The roaring crowd had gone. He could hear rumbles from other parts of the city, but there was no noise in the street. Litter lay on the pavements and across the road. The afternoon heat created mirages above the road surface in the distance.

Taylor turned into a café. It was empty. A long, bare, narrow room with little tables set for tea. Inside, he could still hear the bells of the police cars. An ambulance drove past the window, its blue light flashing. He could imagine the mess, though he had managed to keep clear of it himself. The smashed windows, the bricks and broken bottles strewn over the roads. The country, he thought, had gone mad. No sense of purpose any longer. Nowhere to go. No identification with anything. A massive blindness, somehow. And all the time a massive bursting vitality beneath the surface, trying to get out into some creative channel that didn't exist any more. It must have existed at some time, he thought, otherwise we'd never have got anywhere. There had been a greatness about the place once. A sense of knowing where you fitted in and where most usefully you could direct your energy. Now what did you do? Offer your services to VSO or Oxfam, or put on your steel-capped boots and kick your neighbor in the teeth? Both made some kind of sense, but neither was wholly satisfying. There must be other ways, ways in which the bubbling vigor, the inventiveness, could be harnessed. But society had run out of ideas. It had hardened and fossilized. It couldn't meet the new demands. It had been with us too long.

Still no one came. He tapped on the table with the bowl of a spoon. He called. At last he got up and went through the swinging door into the kitchen. A great pan of potatoes simmered on the stove. But there was no one there. It was deserted. They had all gone—into the streets, perhaps. Home, maybe. He came out of the kitchen. Six or seven men in their late twenties came in from the street. They had lengths of wood in their hands. They looked around. One of them kicked over a table.

"Come on, you little Chinky bastard!" shouted one of them.

When he saw Taylor he said, "Where's that little bastard? You seen him?"

"There's nobody here," said Taylor.

"Foo Queue! Hoo Flung Dung! Whatever your bloody name is!" he shouted again, lifting his head as if he expected someone to reply from the room above. "Let's bloody have you, you cheeky little Chink!"

"I said there's nobody here," said Taylor. He stood between them and the door into the kitchen.

"And who the hell are you?"

"I'm a police officer."

"So?"

"Don't you think you'd better leave before you do any more damage?"

"Leave? We've just bloody got here. Christ, you want to see 'em the other side of West Park. Niggers—Pakistanis—Wops—blood all over the place!"

He knocked aside another table and came up to Taylor.

"Now look," he said. "I've nothing against the fuzz. So just step aside."

Taylor didn't move. He got his hands ready to parry any blow. His balance came forward automatically to rest over the balls of his feet.

"I'm going through there," said the man. He was shorter than Taylor by an inch or two, but his shoulders were broad and his neck was thick. Taylor could see his reddening scalp beneath the close-cropped reddish hair. He stood tapping the length of wood into the palm of his left hand.

"There's nothing in there," said Taylor. "Everybody's gone. Now why don't you just go home? There's been enough trouble already."

Perhaps it was something in the way that Taylor spoke—a certain paternalism that came from his police experience. Whatever it was, it seemed to touch the man on some sensitive spot. He looked at Taylor for a moment and then struck at the side of his head with the wood. Taylor hadn't really been expecting it, not at that moment. He'd thought the argument had a stage or two more to develop before that. He flung up his left arm and took much of the force of the blow on the outside of his forearm, though not all. The stick still gave him a crack on the head that disturbed his vision, and before it had cleared they were at him. One of them got behind him and began punching him in the kidneys and in the back of the neck. He began to feel himself going down. His knees wouldn't support him any longer. It may have been the crack on the head or the fist in the back of the neck, he didn't know. But as he fell forward he saw the toe of the boot coming up toward his face. He felt only the force of the blow. The pain, if there was any, seemed numb and distant as if it was happening through an anesthetic. He felt the force of the blow lift his body up again and carry it backward. Then nothing. Nothing at all, simply a swimming grayness which became darker and darker.

He looked at his watch. When at last it came into focus, he saw that it was twenty past six. There were two faces above him. They looked foreign. Chinese. Very old faces with yellow skin like parchment. Very wrinkled faces, very concerned.

"Where am I?" he said, lifting up his head. It had been lying on something soft.

When he lifted his head it ached and ached. It pounded as if his heart lay locked inside his skull. Every beat shook him and shook his vision. He put up a hand to his head. It felt uneven to the touch, not at all as he remembered his head. When he looked at his hand, it had smears of dark congealing blood across it. His head had been bleeding. He'd cut his head.

The little man above him who looked like a Chinese said, "Please —you want a doctor now?"

"No," said Taylor. He would have shaken his head. It would have taken less out of him than speaking. But he didn't want to move it.

"We found you. We just found you here," the woman was saying.

She kept looking toward the door. She was very agitated.

"How long?" said Taylor.

"Fifteen, twenty minutes," said the man.

The woman added quickly, "No ambulance—my husband said no ambulance."

"If they had found you here like this," said the man. "They are killing foreigners! If they had come in and seen you on the floor in my eating place—!"

"Of course," said Taylor.

They were probably right, he thought. Anybody might have jumped to the wrong conclusion. With things as they were outside, perhaps it was as well. He lifted himself on an elbow. He saw that they had put a cushion under his head. It was soaked in blood. Round him the café was in ruins. Not a table stood undamaged.

Lights and switches had been ripped from the walls. A blown-up photograph of the harbor at Kowloon had had bottles of ketchup and chutney thrown at it. No doubt it was the same in the kitchen. He thought they were very decent to put a cushion under his head.

"Give me a hand," he said.

They put hands under his armpits and helped him to his feet. He felt terrible. The room spun. He couldn't tell whether the noise of bells and sirens was inside or outside his head. They were still concerned for him. Not simply concerned to get rid of him, but concerned for him and for his condition. Very decent people.

He went into the kitchen. He was right—it was in a hell of a mess. Water was running over the floor from the pipe at the back of a sink, where the tap had been wrenched off. He put his hands under the flow and bathed his head. By the feel of it the blow had been across the left cheekbone and temple. He found part of a broken mirror and looked at himself. His face was a mess. The man got him a clean towel. He bathed his face again. It looked a little better. A little blood was still oozing from the wound. The cold water made him feel a little better, a little less dazed, though the pain still drummed through his forehead.

"Thanks," he said.

"What is going to happen to us?" said the woman.

"I don't know," said Taylor. It was the truth. He didn't know. "Get in touch with the police. Tell them what happened." He wrote his name and address on the edge of a newspaper and gave it to the man. "Tell them if they want any more information they can get in touch with me."

Outside, it was still very warm. Hard shadows fell across the street. Litter and glass lay on the pavement. Police were lifting a man from the gutter. He walked for ten minutes, not sure whether he was going in the right direction. In the distance the fire bells still rang intermittently. The atmosphere was full of spent energy.

It was almost dark. Enid Markus was at the open window of the living room looking toward the park through the gap between the two buildings. It was still hot without being oppressive. She had a glass of tonic in her hand. The ice cubes chinked as she moved. Beyond the buildings were the lights and cars of Bayswater Road, then the curving line of bluish lights across the park. On the far side of the park she could see the distant glimmer of Kensington Gore.

The news had been alarming. She had seen the film from Wolverhampton on TV at five-fifty. The radio reports were even more incredible. Someone talked about a "bloodbath." Noel Taylor hadn't rung and he hadn't turned up at the flat. She had the file on the bureau in the next room. She'd been through it and marked some pieces that might be useful to Taylor. She'd done it to fill in time. She couldn't stand waiting. She had to be doing something. But now she'd given him up. It was after midnight.

She was in bed when the bell rang. She got up and put on a dressing gown. The bell rang again. A long ring that clattered through the quiet rooms.

"Taylor," he said through the little speaker by the door.

She pressed the button that released the catch on the downstairs door. She unlatched the door of the flat then went into the kitchen and plugged in the electric kettle. When she got back to the flat door he still hadn't appeared. She opened the door and looked onto the landing. He was leaning against the wall outside the open lift. She couldn't make out his face clearly in the dim landing light.

"What's wrong?" she said.

He didn't move. She crossed the landing to him. He had a handkerchief up to his face. There was blood on it and on his hand. She put an arm round him and led him to the open door of the flat.

"For God's sake!" she said. "What happened?"

As Evans' physical condition improved, so did his fury increase. The growing conflict between himself and the PM was in essence one of interpretation. To the PM, the chaos of Wolverhampton was further proof of the need to support Monckton, who had made it clear that in his view the assassination was merely a symptom of a much deeper unrest. To Evans, Monckton was the major cause of that unrest. This basic difference in viewpoints added a further strain to the relationship between Evans and the PM. The memos that Evans sent remained unanswered. The PM drew into that aloofness which he had always used as a refuge.

Briggs, on the other hand, was a regular visitor to Evans' bedside. When Evans, in a moment of impotent fury, drafted a letter of resignation to the PM, it was Briggs who persuaded him not to send it. An astonishing position, with the leader of the Opposition sitting at Evans' bedside arguing that to resign would only isolate the PM further.

"You've got to keep him where he's susceptible to outside pressures," said Briggs. "And let's face it, Freddy, as long as you're there you've a chance of putting a brake on the bloody old goat. No one else can. You did it over the funeral—whatever he believes. You can get to him."

Others began to have doubts about the wholehearted support Monckton had been officially receiving, and Jimmy Endells was not the only editor who confronted his proprietor with the problem.

"We've got to lay off, Jack," he said. "We've fanned this thing far enough. We've built Monckton up and now he's ruling us. We've got to cool it."

"How?"

"Take him off the front page for a bit. Lessen his space. Cut the enthusiasm. Find some other story—something safe, something uplifting."

"What other story?"

"Look, it's the men's finals. Wimbledon. If we drum it up a bit, give it some background treatment, it'll distract attention for an hour or two. Surely to God—the most English event on earth, the British on their best behavior. Let's give it a try. Where's the harm?"

Wimbledon had had the best weather for years. For the entire period, not a minute's play had been lost through rain. Not once had there been an appeal against the light. The crowds attending the men's final were bronzed. They sat in shirt sleeves and light dresses on the terraces of the center court. Some of the men wore straw hats; others had laid handkerchiefs over their heads as a protection against the fierce sun. The temperature in the shade was in the high eighties. On the court, where there was no protection from the heat and no breath of wind, it was over the hundred mark. No one really envied the players. Whatever happened, they were in for a grim and grueling trial.

It wasn't the final that people expected. Tim Fawcett, the American, had been heavily tipped to win before the championship got under way, but he slipped on the turf in his first match and strained his back. He survived for four days, never reaching the form that had made him famous, and finally went out to Burgess of Australia.

Eric Burgess began the championships as an unknown. But as the days ran on, game following game, victory following victory, he sprang into national prominence. The image he projected seemed quite un-Australian. He had been destined at one time for a career as a professional ballet dancer. Then at eighteen—four years earlier—he had discovered a natural tennis ability. But many of his movements still seemed to belong more to the theater than to the tennis court. There was a flow and fluency about the way he moved on court that almost suggested previous rehearsals. And this physical ease was reflected, too, in an ease of personality. He was a man of quite exceptional charm, both on and off the court. He seemed never to mind the autograph hunters or the cameramen or the journalists, who sought him out increasingly as the championship progressed. In front of the TV cameras he still looked quite at ease. There was a sense of enjoyment about everything he did. The crowd warmed to him. TV coverage was rejigged so that each of his games was broadcast. Toward the middle of the second week, he had become quite the most popular player in the championship. Spectators delighted in his showmanship, his panache, his sense of the dramatic. Perhaps most of all they enjoyed his chivalrous behavior to all his opponents. His assurance, as he fought his way through opponents—Americans, Italians and his own countrymen—increased with his progress.

His opponent in the final was in complete contrast. Harry Monsy was an American Negro of twenty-seven. It was his third appearance at Wimbledon, though the first in which he had got past the quarter finals. There was a determination about his play that didn't commend him to British spectators; a quality of ruthlessness that they thought more appropriate to professional boxing. It showed, too, in his handling of journalists and in his TV interviews. His face was quite immobile. He never smiled on court. He never smiled in front of the cameras. He would sit facing a TV interviewer, a little squat and thickset, giving the interviewer nothing, making him work for every monosyllabic answer. He was never a popular man. In some circles he was profoundly disliked.

Enid Markus sat on the back row of one of the side terraces. She wore a simple blue dress, with short sleeves and a square neckline. Jimmy Endells had said to her, "Honey, there's no one else. You'll have to go. Never mind the tennis—take the human angles. What they're wearing, where they've come from, why the hell they go at all." And so she'd left Taylor still asleep on the studio couch and gone. But Jimmy Endells had forgotten to inform the press officer, and when she got there the press seats were full. They might squeeze her onto the back row, high above the action, but it would be a squeeze.

Reggie Deacon said to her in the bar, "Christ, they couldn't demonstrate here—the English holy of holies. I don't believe all these bloody rumors. Like pissing in Westminster Abbey."

It began as it always had, as if nothing that happened in the world outside could impinge on its enduring normality. The perfect day, the high fashions, the polite gossip. A gay, party atmosphere on the face of it. An impeccable British institution, part of the enduring image that Britain had of herself. That image of liberal fairmindedness in which a nation is free to indulge when it sits unassailably on top of the midden. Yet an image that no more reflected the real nature of the British than any other national image reflects the true nature of those seeking to project it. More really a target than an image—more something to aim at, more an idealized view of what the British might have been like in an ideal world than what they were in fact like. Not altogether an unworthy target, Enid Markus was thinking, if it had been even remotely attainable. But it wasn't any more, even if it ever had been.

Eric Burgess walked onto the court in white tennis shirt and shorts. He carried three rackets with him. He was smiling. The spectators gave him a warm, civilized reception. He turned very slightly from one terrace to the other, still smiling, acknowledging the measured applause. He walked to the umpire's chair, put down two of the rackets and took the third out of its press. He loosened his shoulders and ran a hand over his dark hair. He looked toward the sun, then up at a flag to check the strength of any wind. The flag hung limply down the pole. Finally he looked back toward the players' entrance. Still there was no sign of Monsy. Burgess began to tap the strings of his racket against the ball of his left thumb. Finally he looked upward and said something to the umpire. The umpire shook his head.

The spectators became restive. One or two of the younger members, still insufficiently schooled in the Wimbledon tradition, tried to establish a slow handclap. But it died for lack of general support. The excited chatter that had followed Burgess' appearance subsided. A sullenness settled on the spectators.

Burgess began to lose his sense of ease. He could feel the growing tension in the crowd, the growing irritation. He felt partly responsible for it. It was the most crucial match in the world for him and it was getting off on the wrong foot. That assurance he'd felt as he left his dressing room was slipping out of his grasp, and assurance was his major asset.

And at last Monsy appeared, a squat unsympathetic figure carrying two rackets, walking slowly across to the umpire's chair, his head pushed forward, legs bowed like a jockey's. The crowd breathed its relief. People moved again, though no one clapped. The woman in front of Enid turned to her companion and said, "Well!"

People began to turn toward the distinguished visitors' box. Those near the box were clapping. A woman in pale pink was waving from the box. The sporadic clapping grew into a general applause. The figure in pink waved again, then sat down. The applause began to fade. Burgess and Monsy walked down the court, stood for a moment looking up at the box, then bowed. There was something about Monsy's bow that didn't please the crowd. The mechanical, stiff little movement of the head seemed more an act of defiance than of courtesy. Burgess could feel the growing crowd hostility. It wasn't the antipathy toward Monsy itself that drained his confidence, but rather the quality of it. A quality somehow alien to the spirit of the game.

In the first game, Burgess struggled within himself to restore the sense of ease. "Relax!" he kept saying to himself. But relaxation wouldn't come in answer to a command. It required a sense of buoyant assurance that he couldn't infuse into himself. He was aware of the lack of fluency in his movements, and he knew Monsy could sense that lack. He could feel the crowd's disappointment. He knew that he stood for them not so much as a tennis player but as their representative against this arrogant opponent.

It was a fight, that first game, but Burgess took it. He took it more through sheer determination than through skill. Still the fluency wouldn't come. He took the next game and the next, but each by a diminishing margin. It wasn't Monsy that affected him but the crowd. He didn't like the position they'd put him in. He wasn't built to be a bastion on their behalf against the changing influences of the outside world. "Look," he wanted to say, "I'm a tennis player. Don't make me into what I'm not."

Monsy took each minor defeat without a flicker on his face. He showed no pleasure at any small victory that he achieved. He showed nothing in either expression or general movement that gave an onlooker the least idea of what emotions or thoughts might be taking place inside him. He seemed less than human—an expressionless automaton moved as it were by computer.

Burgess took the first set 7–5. The spectators clapped mechanically. Neither they nor Burgess felt the score to be significant. It indicated no break in Monsy's dogged ability, nor any sign of an innate superiority in Burgess. Burgess stood at the umpire's chair, rubbing his face and neck with a towel. His whole posture showed a lack of ease. He picked up another racket, took it out of its press and rapped the strings across the ball of his left thumb. He tried a stroke with it, and then again took up his position on court.

Someone called out, "Come on, Eric!"

People turned to see where the call had come from. Burgess looked round for a moment. Monsy threw up the ball and served. The game ran to 40–15. Monsy grew steadily in power. Burgess put up a hand to hold the play for a moment, took out a handkerchief and wiped his hand and forearm. The crowd could feel the energy draining out of him. Its mood was not one of sympathy for him, but of anger against Monsy. He gave them nothing, this unattractive black figure. He had no rapport with them. He ignored them. When he served Burgess hesitated, moved too late and missed.

An arrogance grew in Monsy, something the crowd could sense without being able to pin down to a particular gesture or facial expression. He moved about the court with mounting sureness, chopping a ball just over the net, lobbing within an inch of the base line, deliberately exposing Burgess' weaknesses. It seemed to Enid that Monsy was after more than victory; he wanted the public demolition of Burgess and all he stood for in the spectators' eyes. He was proving some kind of superiority that had nothing to do with tennis. She remembered what Hoffa, the American labor leader, had once said in an interview: "I say to the Negroes, why don't you build yourselves a city?" Monsy was building his city, publicly and at the expense of Burgess and the crowd. Both the spectators and Burgess knew it. The spectators at least began to hate him for it.

Burgess rallied. He forced a glimmer of confidence back into his play by an act of will. But Monsy was not to be dominated. He had no need for acts of will. He knew he was superior. He knew that in the end he would crush this man with the rhythmic movement and easy smile. He drove, he smashed, and Burgess failed. The crowd's disappointment was palpable. Its dislike of Monsy led to open remarks. A gray-haired man on Enid's left sat with arms folded as if physically holding himself in check. His face was red, his jawline set rigid. She could feel the woman on her right, sitting almost locked back in her seat. She wasn't moving. She seemed not to be watching the play. She was stiff and tense. She muttered to herself, "Get him, get him."

The heat drained the crowd's patience. They watched Burgess humiliated in the third set, the massed tension building and building. Still Monsy drove on like a machine. Feeling turned against both players; against Burgess for failing to live up to the ideal of his supporters, and against Monsy for demolishing that ideal. But still the tension held, tightening with every stroke.

No one had any doubts that the fourth set would be the last. There was nothing that Burgess could pull out of himself now that could prevent total defeat. And so it was. At love–30 Burgess served a double fault. Still no one reacted; no one groaned. He crossed the court wiping his forehead with a sweatband on his right wrist. He turned and made the final serve of the match. Monsy swayed to his right and returned the ball an inch above the net. Burgess checked, moved again, and managed to return. It was short. It brought Monsy up to the net. He chopped the ball with his backhand. Burgess ran. He stretched over to his left and lifted the ball in a high lob over Monsy's head. Monsy lifted his head, watching the flight of the ball, moving steadily backward, lifting his racket as he went. The ball began to drop. Monsy continued backward. Then he stopped and hit the ball. Burgess was eight or nine yards out of position. He was broken. He made no attempt to get across court to the ball. It landed five inches inside the base line and shot away toward a judge in the rear. It was over. A total humiliating killing. Burgess had been as completely crushed before the public and the TV cameras as any finalist in the history of Wimbledon. The crowd felt the humiliation personally. If it had been a football crowd, it would have swarmed onto the field. Since it wasn't, it sat. But it glowered, it fumed, it hated Monsy.

Burgess, a smile of total dejection on his face, came to the net. He put a hand across. It was simply a conventional gesture. It wasn't backed by any genuine regard for the superior play of his opponent. Such a regard could hardly have been expected. And Monsy refused to take the outstretched hand. He stood for a moment looking at it, then walked away toward the umpire's chair. It was too much. A man stood up on the far terrace and shouted, "You black pig!" The tension that had built through the hot afternoon shattered. Whole sections of the crowd began to cry out. When Monsy showed no reaction, it incensed them. They got to their feet and pressed forward toward the court. Police began to shout at them but they were already kicking down the low wooden fencing and beginning to run onto the grass.

Four of Westbrook's men pushed forward. They got through the broken fencing and onto the court. One of them ran straight at

Monsy. He took a long-bladed knife from his pocket and when he reached Monsy he seized him by the shoulder and ran the knife into his body. Monsy said nothing. He didn't cry out. The expression on his face didn't change. He continued to look at the assassin for a moment, then dropped his racket, put a hand to the place where he'd been wounded and fell to the ground. Burgess tried to hold the man, but was knocked down by a blow from the man's left forearm. And only Burgess and the umpire, trapped in his chair, could see exactly what had happened. The umpire began to call through his microphone for the police. They were already getting over the barriers and crossing the court. The crowd was on its feet. It didn't know what had happened, only that the tension had burst. People began to climb over the seats in front of them. They trod on one another in an attempt to do something, to launch themselves into action, though against what they were unsure. But they had to go forward. They had to move. Some mass feeling was impelling them. Some of them who had seen Burgess reel back and fall thought he had been struck by Monsy. Now that they were on the move at last, it was Monsy they wanted. They wanted to get their hands on him. They wanted to beat him until the humiliation had gone out of them. For they knew that somehow the humiliation hadn't been so much Burgess' as their own. They were humiliated. They had been scorned and derided. It was them that Monsy had driven so ignominiously into the ground.

Monsy's attacker began to run toward the far exit. "Stop that man!" the umpire was calling through his microphone. "Stop that man!" yelled the loudspeakers, loud enough to be heard over the increasing clamor of the crowd. Three policemen were after him when Westbrook's other men began to release smoke bombs and containers of CS gas. In a moment the crowd went hysterical. The smoke and gas checked its forward movement over the barriers and onto the court, yet it did nothing to lull the violent feelings that had driven them forward off the terraces. They turned on one another.

They began to lash out with fists and feet at anything that stood in the way of their escape from the gas. But they were trapped. The place was shaped like some old-time arena. They couldn't get out of it and there was nowhere for the gas and smoke to escape. No wind, only the fierce heat of the afternoon sun blazing down on the scene. The smoke rolled and hung, moved only slowly and sluggishly by the movement of the crowd through it. And in the smoke hung the gas. It flamed in the eyes and clawed at the membranes of the respiratory tract. People gasped and screamed and held their throats. Some put handkerchiefs over their mouths, but it penetrated through them.

Enid was above the main confusion. Below her the crowd milled. It moved in waves, this way and that, at one moment sure of its direction, and at the next hopelessly confused. Police were trying to direct sections of the crowd toward the exits, but there it jammed together into a clawing mass, trying to get clear, narrowing and narrowing to get through the openings.

The terraces were almost empty, except where some injured person sat recovering from a blow on the head or waiting for medical attention to a broken wrist. The surface of the court had been churned by the passage of a thousand feet. The net lay on the grass where it had fallen when the wire broke under the pressure of the swirling crowd. The smoke had begun to clear, and with it the gas. With the exits wide open, some slight movement of air was carrying it away. Police were still ushering the last members of the crowd out of the exits. A group of them were holding two men with their arms twisted high up their backs. And at last the arena emptied. Burgess had tried to lift Monsy to his feet but had failed. When they put Monsy on a stretcher, Burgess let himself be helped off the court. Eyes were burning. A policeman, his helmet on the ground in front of him, was sitting bent double, coughing and coughing.

The reactions of the Wimbledon crowd were mirrored in the reactions of the millions who saw the match on TV. An impotent fury grew that demanded action. Yet what was the target of that action to be? On what were people to vent their fury? They couldn't get at Monsy through a TV set. In any case, it was only some electronic image of him they'd seen, not Monsy himself. Then a doubt grew: was it Monsy they really wanted to get their hands on? Wasn't it perhaps something beyond Monsy—Wimbledon itself, or the system that Wimbledon represented? Wasn't it really this: Wimbledon projected a London-based middle-class Anglo-Saxon image that Monsy had derided. People had clung to the old image too long. Now it was desecrated they wanted to smash the facade. They turned to other images to give a shape to their actions.

The breakaway Scottish Action Group mounted demonstrations in Glasgow, supported by a mass of unofficial strikers from the shipyards. The aim was immediate independence for Scotland. The position of the Welsh under Geraint Edwards was similar. Wild demonstrations took place in Cardiff. The long and bitter strike of miners in the South Wales coalfield, still without the backing of the NUM, dragged on. The cause seemed trivial to those outside the industry, but those inside knew that the root cause was something other. A loss of identity and personal significance. The miners, who had spent weeks waiting for some move from the Coal Board or from their official or unofficial leaders, were only too glad of an opportunity to give expression to their feelings in Geraint Edwards' massive demonstration. But here at least some individual intervention was possible. Against the PM's advice and the advice of the security services, the Prince of Wales drove to Cardiff and made a speech of pacification. It served its immediate purpose. It confined the series of demonstrations that Geraint Edwards had planned to peaceful marches and peaceful speeches. It brought official support for the strike from the NUM, though it could do no more than temporarily calm the deeper discontent that lay beneath the situation. But it brought a member of the royal family to the forefront of a political situation in a way that caused the PM acute embarrassment. It had broken a rigid tradition that had held throughout the twentieth century. Any breach of tradition was offensive to the PM, but in this case he found the implications alarming. If political action was possible by one member of the royal family, wasn't it possible by others? How far, the PM seriously wondered, might control of government move out of his hands and back into those of the crown? He saw the speech by the Prince, and the popular support it aroused, as something ominous.

Monckton was in the basement of the building he had taken over. The room was bare except for a table and a single chair. On the chair sat a man, his arms and legs bound. His hair was matted with blood. Blood ran down his face. His jaw hung down as if it had been broken. A brilliant light from the ceiling hung a little way above him, shining down on his battered face. Two men stood behind him, supporting him by the shoulders to prevent him from slipping to the floor. Monckton stood facing him, a draftsman's cylindrical ruler in his hand. He put the end of the ruler under the man's chin and lifted it up. It rose an inch or two then slid off the ruler and lolled downward again. The man was one of the two that the police had taken at Wimbledon. There was no doubt that they had been involved in releasing the gas and smoke. But the man in the chair hadn't talked. He hadn't give his name or his address or the name of his accomplice. He hadn't said a word from the moment when Monckton had started shouting at him to the moment when the last blow had cracked the side of his face. He had sat all the time in silence, giving no more than an occasional grunt of pain. He was a professional. When he first slid into unconsciousness, Monckton had had him revived with water. Later the syringe had been necessary. But now it was no use. He could beat him and revive him and beat him again, but he would get nothing out of him. He was an uncommon type of detainee, but nonetheless he existed.

Monckton looked up from the beaten face and spoke to one of the men behind the chair.

"Bring the other in," he said.

The guard left the room and returned in a moment with the unconscious man's colleague. Monckton looked at him as he came into the light. He felt more hopeful. He took the man by the hair while the guard still held his arm high up his back.

"Look at him," said Monckton, pointing with the ruler to the unconscious man in the chair.

The man looked. Although Monckton could hold his head, he couldn't prevent the man from lowering his eyes. The man couldn't look at his colleague. Tears filled his eyes.

"Lift his head," said Monckton.

One of the guards took hold of the unconscious man's hair and lifted his head upward.

"Look at him now!" snapped Monckton.

There was not only savagery in his voice. There was a certain satisfaction.

"Take him out," said Monckton.

One of the guards put his hands under the unconscious man's armpits and dragged him clear of the chair and through the open door. The other helped Monckton to push the new arrival into the chair.

"I want you to look at me all the time," Monckton said to him. "I don't want your eyes to leave mine. Every time they do, I shall beat you."

The man looked at Monckton. His eyes began to water because of the intensity of the light shining into them. He blinked and Monckton cut him with the heavy ruler across the top of the arm. The man cried out.

"My eyes," said Monckton. "Always my eyes."

156

The man again looked at Monckton, again his eyes watered and he closed them for a moment. Again Monckton struck him and again he cried out.

He was a young man in his late teens. He was in a state of great fear and nervousness. Monckton had met them before, young idealists. He'd show the guards how to crack such a man.

"Name!" he shouted suddenly.

The young man jumped in the chair, his eyes still on Monckton, who stood in the shadows just beyond the beam of light.

"Hargreaves," he said quickly, wincing in anticipation of the blow from the ruler.

"And Christian name, Hargreaves?" said Monckton.

His voice was suddenly soft and gentle, as if he wanted to protect the young man from actions that were causing him pain.

"Michael," said the young man.

"And where do you live, Michael?"

"Exell Street—thirty," said the young man.

"Who with?"

"By myself."

"And what's your job?"

"I'm a student."

"Are you?" said Monckton.

His voice was still soft, but there was a quality of menace in it, as if he was about to spring at any moment. The youth reacted to it at once. He tried to lean forward a little, but the guards held him with his back against the chair. He licked his lips. Perspiration from his forehead was running into his eyes.

"Yes," said the young man. "A student."

"You're a liar," said Monckton, the menace in his voice growing. "You're a professional revolutionary. You're an anarchist. You want the overthrow of the forces of law and order. You belong to some organization."

The young man continued to look at him. The pupils of his eyes were surrounded by the whites. He was fighting to protect himself and yet not reveal anything—an impossible dual task, since the two aims were irreconcilable. If he talked, then he might just save himself from damage at Monckton's hands. If he refused to talk, then he would be reduced to the mess that had been his comrade.

Monckton knew the conflict from long experience. He knew how it would end. Those who never cracked never faced the conflict. For them this apparent choice between personal safety and silence never arose. For them there was only one way in which an interrogation could go. Monckton knew that where the possibility of personal safety had entered a man's mind, that possibility would triumph. The man would talk. Hargreaves would talk. It was simply a matter of squeezing him a little further.

Monckton said, "It's not a matter of your telling us anything we don't know. You saw the man we've just taken out. Do you think he let himself be beaten like that without saying anything? We know as much as we need to know about you and your organization. All we want is further confirmation. If you give it to me you'll be able to walk out of this room. If you don't we'll still have the information we want, but you'll never walk again."

To stress the point, he cracked the young man across his left kneecap with the heavy ruler. He cried out and put his hands over his knee. Monckton rapped him on the side of the head and cried, "Look at me, Michael!"

It went on for five or six minutes, the taunting, the quiet voice which occasionally burst into frenzied shouting, the carefully timed raps with the ruler. All the time the two guards held him back in the chair and he did his best to keep his eyes on Monckton to avoid further punishment. But tears were streaming down his cheeks; his head, his upper arms, his legs ached. And when Monckton said at last, "Now! The address!" he muttered the street and number of Daniel Westbrook's shop. He cried out those details of Westbrook's organization that were known to him. He told

Monckton what the intention had been behind the Wimbledon attack. He told him what the British Union of Activists had hoped to achieve by it.

Daniel Westbrook had followed the Wimbledon attack on TV. He had seen the chaos and the confusion. He had felt the hatred the affair had engendered before the transmission closed down. On the face of it it had been a complete success. A triumph. He made a dozen phone calls, giving his orders for the next stage of the plan to be put into action. His men moved into the streets to follow up the success of Wimbledon. He thought that he could muster behind him a good deal of the shock that millions must be feeling by what they had seen on TV and heard already on the radio. He knew that public horror would have mounted to such a pitch that it would be screaming for something to be done, some strong measure to reimpose order on a situation that had got quite out of hand. It would want a strong man with a few clear-cut aims. A man who could impose his will and take the reins of government in his hands. He could hear the country calling out for him.

His units sprang into action throughout the capital. They had banners prepared. They had slogans. They had leaflets to hand out, printed in bold type, announcing the half dozen simple aims. They had speakers bellowing through megaphones at the street corners, whipping up feeling against the softness of a government that could allow these things to happen. Strangely, perhaps, many of the aims of the organization were identical with those that prompted Monckton himself. Only the means were different. And the means were different only because Monckton already had a certain power, whereas Daniel Westbrook at that moment had none.

So the crowds began to assemble in a dozen different places. They were harangued and bullied, flattered and cajoled. They began to call out their support, prompted by Westbrook's men among them. They cheered. They waved the leaflets in their hands and chanted the simple slogans that seemed to them to contain the essential truths that would resolve their difficulties. The crowds grew. The speakers harangued them. They spread out from the street corners and the open spaces until they closed the streets themselves. Dozens became hundreds and hundreds thousands. And then they turned toward central London. They came from the north, from Kilburn and Willesden, down Kilburn High Road and Maida Vale. They came from the east by way of Pentonville and to Euston Road, and from the west along Bayswater Road, Park Lane and Piccadilly. They cheered, they sang, they chanted slogans that had caught their imagination. They smashed shop windows to keep up their spirits. They stopped the traffic and kicked in the windows of stationary cars. At times the drivers got out and joined them. They were damn well going to show that they'd had enough. They were the silent majority and if it came to it they'd put a match to Westminster.

Taylor looked up at the pale lilac ceiling. He thought he was still asleep. It seemed like a dream, as if he were lying on the seabed and looking upward through fathoms of bluish water. He put a hand to his face and found it bandaged. When he touched the bandage, his face hurt. He knew he was awake then. He sat up. He felt sick. The room smelled of perfume. He could see the bookshelves in the alcove, and beyond that the opening into the dining room. Then he remembered where he was.

He got up and walked toward the bathroom. When he got inside he put his hands on the wall and leaned his head forward. He thought he might faint. The pain didn't trouble him but the dizziness and the sense of unreality that gave everything the quality of a dream made him unsteady. He turned and looked in the mirror. His forehead and cheek were bandaged. When he began to take off the bandage he could see the discoloration beneath. The pain came when he opened his jaws wide or turned his head quickly or put any pressure on the gauze dressing. He bathed the dressing with warm water and when he lifted it off blood began to ooze from the laceration beneath. The wound itself wasn't deep. It looked as if the boot had ripped and split the flesh rather than penetrated it. The cut inside his mouth, where the flesh of the cheek had been driven onto the teeth, felt more impressive than the outside wound.

He bathed his face and looked for a new dressing. He tried to lift his upper lip with his finger and thumb to look at the cut inside, but it was too painful. He could feel the edges of broken teeth and taste the blood in his mouth, and he lowered the lip again. He went back into the living room and took up the phone, but when he put the receiver to his ear he couldn't remember who it was he wanted. The receiver fell out of his hand and dropped onto the carpet and as he bent to pick it up his head began to spin and he found himself falling past the table and onto the floor. He crawled to the studio couch and pulled himself up on it. When he lay back he was already slipping into sleep.

When he woke again, Enid was standing by the couch and leaning over him. Her face was just a few inches above him. He put up a hand and touched her cheek. She said, "For God's sake, what have you been doing? What did you take the bandage off for?"

He remembered that the bandage was in the bathroom. He'd put on the new dressing but forgotten the bandage.

In the distance some great crowd seemed to be cheering. Someone was blowing a bugle—a long, raucous fart of a noise. He said, "What's that?"

"The town's gone mad," she said.

It seemed a quite matter-of-fact statement to him.

"I see," he said. Then he remembered what he'd come back for —last night, was it? the night before? He said, "The file? Did you get it?"

"It's here," she said. "On the chair."

He put out a hand toward the chair, but she took hold of the hand and laid it firmly back on the couch. "Later," she said. "Look at it later."

"You're beautiful," he said. "You know that? Beautiful."

But as he spoke his eyes closed and the muscles of his face relaxed.

Crowd reinforcements were waiting in Trafalgar Square, goaded by Westbrook's lieutenants. They were waiting for the main force coming from the north of the city down the Haymarket and Charing Cross Road. Some advanced groups broke into Whitehall and began to run south. Police moved into the road ahead of them. Other groups ran through Admiralty Arch and south through the park, making for the western end of Downing Street.

The PM was pale. Even from his study he could hear the distant hum of demonstrators. He walked into the corridor. The building itself was silent but in the distance the hum had become a roar. From a first-floor window he looked down into the street outside. At the eastern end the police had put up wire. Groups of them were now running toward it. Some were armed. Others had truncheons in their hands. The PM stood and watched, his hands clasped tightly together behind his back, his tall angular body bent forward. There had never been a situation like it and it was beyond his grasp. Even during the General Strike and the internal troubles of the thirties, no government had faced scenes like those taking place in central London at that moment. The cabinet was split down the middle on the issue and on the course of action that should be taken. The problem was his. It was all of it on his shoulders. Perhaps if there'd been more sharing from the start, perhaps if he'd taken more of them into his confidence and spread the responsibility. Too late for that now. There had only been

Evans, and Evans was out of the battle. Was he right to pick such a man as his deputy—a man with a basic physical weakness?

The police in the street had begun to beat back a group coming from the park. Two of them broke through. A windowpane to the left of the PM shattered and petrol from a smashed bottle ran over the floor. In a moment it was alight and flames ran across the floor and up the wall behind him. He stood aghast. It seemed to him that the most sacred political edifice in the world had been defiled. It was beyond his comprehension. If he could explain to them what they were doing, if they realized the barbarity of their actions. He hesitated. He turned to the window. He could hear dimly the shouts from below. He called out, "Beckett!" Then the glass of a second pane showered about his head and a half brick struck him on the temple. He put out a hand to grasp the back of a chair, missed, and fell full length across the carpet.

Beckett, the principal member of the permanent staff at number 10, ran in. He took hold of the PM's bony ankles and pulled him out into the corridor. The flames had singed his hair and moustache. The skin of his hands was blistered. His clothing had begun to smolder. Beckett took off his own jacket and beat at the flames until they began to subside. Finally he rolled up the smoldering square of carpet and flung it through the broken window. Outside in the street it burst into flames again. A policeman pulled it clear of the pavement and left it to burn.

At that moment the situation turned on Beckett's action. He might have phoned Monckton when he discovered the unconscious body of the PM. He might have phoned for an ambulance and so made public the PM's condition. Instead he carried the PM into a bedroom and bathed the wound on his head. Then he rang Evans. Evans grasped the loose reins of power.

To Reggie Deacon, the whole thing looked like a more massive continuation of the scenes in the Aldwych, from which he felt his nervous system was only just recovering. "I'm one of life's rabbits," he used to say of himself, and certainly his instinct for self-preservation was highly developed. He got himself up the steps of the National Gallery, and stood with his back firmly against a pillar. By turning his head a little to the right, he could peer over the square. The great open space continued to fill. People were pouring into it down St. Martin's Lane and Cockspur Street. At the southern corners they crammed forward under the banners of Westbrook's lieutenants, from the Strand and through Admiralty Arch. Loudspeakers boomed insistent, hypnotic slogans. The feeling swirled like a whirlpool, round and round the packed square, gaining speed and momentum. Even the ripple of mass movement took a circular motion. Looking down on it, with people now crushing him against the parapet, Reggie Deacon thought the movement looked like some massive weight being swung around on the end of a chain, some massive centrifugal movement. And when the anchor point of the chain was released, the whole giant weight would plunge off at a tangent with monumental force.

And at last it began to move. The first crowds began to burst into Whitehall, running, chanting, shouting the slogans that induced a self-hypnosis, and Reggie Deacon was caught up, pulled clear of the parapet and the protection of the pillar, flung down the steps and into the road. The bag of sandwiches he had been carrying fell out of his grasp. His feet left the ground. He was floating, carried helpless on some irresistible wave, round the square toward the entrance to Whitehall. He fought. He cried out. But nothing could get him clear of it. He ran, he was buffeted, he was lifted by the human wave and forced into the confined channel of Whitehall.

Assistant Chief Constable Matthews was more hopeful this time. Aldwych had shown him what he was up against. Men were no match for this kind of hysterical savagery. He wouldn't put his men right up against them until he'd done something to break the first charge. He had CS gas launchers in position in buildings on either side of the street. Barricades and wire lay across the approach roads to the House itself. Barricades closed Whitehall at the level of the Whitehall Theatre.

Yet against the weight of rampaging humanity, whipped to frenzy by the deafening slogans pouring out of the loudspeakers, Matthews' prepared positions fell like paper walls. The gas and smoke had some momentary effect, but the breeze blowing from the river carried much of it away before it could settle into an effective barrier. The Whitehall barricades were overrun, the baton charges thrust aside. All opposition only increased the determination of the crowd to reach its objective—the occupation of the House of Commons. It thrust forward, advancing over its fallen front line. It rammed between the walls of the buildings on either side of the wide street. It hurled whatever it could get its hands on. Men picked up fallen batons and used them against the line of police as it retired steadily southward. They seized what they could from kicked-in shop windows and hurled whatever came to hand at the police in front of them. Reggie Deacon, now carried over to the east side of the street, got his hands on the corner of a doorway. He grasped the stonework. He got his nails into it and clung. People fell into him and rolled past, and at last his grip broke. Again he was on the move, crushed against the sides of the buildings, turned and carried backward, swirled again toward the middle of the street. The gas began to choke him. Tears streamed from his eyes. He took out a handkerchief and as he pushed it upward toward his eyes, he knocked his glasses off. He groped for them but they fell from his grasp onto the road, to be ground to pieces by the trampling feet behind. Without them he was all but blind. His resistance broke. He let himself be carried forward without knowing where the movement was taking him, his small, fleshy hands over his face.

At last, Matthews could hear the first armored units rumbling into position behind him.

"Steady, lads," Matthews was calling through a loudspeaker. "Easy, lads. Few more yards."

Behind him infantry were advancing with the armor, carrying rifles and fixed bayonets. A few more yards and he could pull his men clear. Still they were coming, and his line of men began to sag. He stepped forward himself, and as he did so the line broke and a section of the crowd was through. Someone dragged the loudspeaker out of Matthews' hand. Matthews punched him in the face and he dropped to his knees. Matthews had his truncheon in his hand. His men were falling on either side of him. He stood, a giant of a man, striking at heads and shoulders as people clawed at him, trying to pull him down, trampling over the bodies of his fallen men.

Another was coming, an amorphous pudding of a man, howling out loud, pudgy hands covering his face. Matthews struck him with all his tremendous power, square on the forehead. The man stopped dead. He rocked for a moment, backward on his heels, then sagged in a shapeless heap to the road. Matthews, still fighting backward toward the security of the armor, never knew who it was he'd hit. Reggie Deacon, blind without his glasses, never saw the face of his killer.

Matthews withdrew behind the first advancing infantry units, and ran toward the nearest armored vehicle. A young lieutenant was standing up in it, his head and shoulders clear of the bodywork.

"Matthews—Assistant Chief Constable. Thank God you've come!"

"Lieutenant Jobling. They've got to be stopped, you know! I've orders to stop them!"

The idea seemed to frighten him. Matthews wondered if he'd ever seen action before.

"Get on with it!" cried Matthews. "You've had it if they close with you!"

166

"Get clear! Get your men out of the way!" shouted Jobling.

He knew he had to open fire. Even the infantry weren't holding them. The whole street ahead of him was crammed with frenzied people as far as he could see, all pressing irresistibly forward. If the armor was supposed to hold the crowd and stop it from reaching the seat of government, then he must do more than simply stand there. He gave the order for a burst of light automatic fire to be directed over the heads of the demonstrators. The gunner fired. Windows on first floors of buildings shattered and glass dropped down on the heads of the crowd. The noise burst down the street. For a moment it had some effect. There was a temporary check to the advance. But still those people in Trafalgar Square were too distant from the action to realize what the noise meant. They continued to push and lean and shout. And again the movement advanced. The gunner fired again. Again the check and the renewed advance. A few of the demonstrators had got beyond the bayonets and the armor and were beginning to pull away the wire at the entrance to Downing Street.

Lieutenant Jobling adjusted his orders. The guns of the leading armored vehicles were lowered. The front rank of the crowd parted where the guns threatened them. Jobling saw the problem quite clearly. The front ranks would break if the pressure from behind could be taken off them. He selected four areas of the crowd ahead of him, the crowd that was packed from pavement to pavement and ran back out of his vision into Trafalgar Square. They were areas in different parts of the street. If confusion could be caused there, he could break up the crowd into five separate units and so weaken the pressure on the whole. His gunners fired a single short burst. People fell in the four areas. The realization dawned on them at last that the opposition ahead could not be crushed by sheer weight of numbers. In a dozen parts of the crowd, people turned and began to fight to get out of the street. They turned to the obvious exits —Horse Guards Avenue, Whitehall Place, Horse Guards Parade

—and ran clear. The movement relieved the pressure on the front ranks. They turned at last and began to retreat up the street. As they did so, the armor and the infantry followed, running through the fallen.

Daniel Westbrook was elated. It seemed the end of all his subterranean endeavors. London was on the march for him, and where London marched the rest of Britain would follow. He had given his last orders. He had had his reports back from his lieutenants in the streets. He had heard of the massing in Trafalgar Square. He knew that thousands were moving down Whitehall. It was enough. Nothing, he thought, could resist them. The dream, conceived sketchily so long ago, was blossoming into reality. Jerusalem was being built, though not the Jerusalem of the Hebrews—God forbid! The new Jerusalem of Britain, purged, cleansed and made pure.

He shut down the radio receiver and prepared to move. He put on a black battle jacket and took up a briefcase. In the battle jacket's inner pocket he put a Browning Hipower.

There was a long ring at the bell of the shop. He stopped. Who the devil could that be? Fletcher? Quirk? They were all involved in the march on the House. Everyone was involved in it. Some late customer, who couldn't read the "Closed" notice?

He went into the shop. A man in a light-colored jacket and trilby smiled at him through the glass. The man was pointing to the lock on the door. He wanted to come in. Westbrook went up to the door and pointed to the notice.

"Closed," said Westbrook.

"I know," said the man. "It's not about the shop. It's about—you know."

"What?" said Westbrook.

He put his hand inside the battle jacket and took hold of the butt of the Browning.

"I don't want to bawl it across the street," said the man.

He looked quickly up and down the street as if he was anxious not to be seen.

Westbrook opened the door. The man had seen Westbrook's hand slip into his jacket and as he walked in he struck Westbrook full in the stomach with his fist, then, as his head came forward, he hit him a chop with a cosh on the back of the neck and Westbrook dropped to his knees.

Two others walked into the shop from the street. They took hold of Westbrook, pulled him to his feet and walked him out to a waiting car. When the car had driven away, the first man began to look round the shop and in the back room. Almost everything he touched was incriminating. There were bundles of inflammatory pamphlets bound with strips of gummed paper. There were firearms and banners and armbands with the letters BUA on them. And in a heavy wooden box under the back window there were explosives. He was Monckton's man and he knew what he was looking for.

Taylor was kneeling on the floor of the flat, piles of clippings spread in a wide arc in front of him. He had found what he was looking for. From the correspondence columns of a West Norfolk parish magazine the clipping agency had cut the following letter:

Sir, I have recently been reading the reports of speeches made by Mr. Enoch Powell. Until certain recent events, I have had the greatest regard for Mr. Powell, but I find the following statement in the report of his speech at Trinity College, Dublin, on 13 November 1964: "To be happy it is not necessary to live in a *folie de grandeur;* to be successful it is not necessary to beat the statistical record of all comers. Happiness and success are likeliest to come to the nations which know themselves as they really are. . . ."

How can such a statement be reconciled with the cry of Nietzsche's Zarathustra: "My suffering and my fellow-suffering—what matter about them! Do I then strive after happiness? I strive after my *work!"?*

I have been one of Mr. Powell's most devoted disciples, but such a departure from the Nietzschean ideal, coupled with Mr. Powell's recent tragic action, fills me with a sense of desperate disillusion.

The letter was signed, "One Who Cares."

What man, thought Taylor, would sit down and write such a letter, carry it to the mailbox and presumably read it when it appeared in print? A man who had at least heard of Nietzsche and taken the trouble to look up a particular passage in a particular work. A man who was reading the printed reports of the speeches of Enoch Powell. And "Mr. Powell's recent tragic action"—what obscure reference was that? Again, why the comparison between Nietzsche and Powell—had Powell invited it? What kind of a man was he, this letter writer? A man alone, perhaps? A man with time on his hands for such things? A man separate from the world, yet one who let the world and all its teeming ideas and images come to him through the media of press, radio and TV? It brought Taylor back to the messianic idea that had occurred to him earlier. What were they up against—a lunatic, a philosopher, a social outcast, a recluse, a political renegade? A man, perhaps, with a limp?

Taylor rang the editor of the parish magazine, a Reverend R. Black. Over the phone he sounded spiky and waspish, with a thin whine of a voice. Yes, of course he knew the identity of the writer. He insisted on that from all his correspondents, as a token of good faith. But he could reveal it only in exceptional circumstances. What would be the position of letter writers wishing for some very good reason not to reveal their identity, if those writers could be readily identified by a phone call? And why had he published such a letter in a parish magazine? That depended, didn't it, on editorial policy? And his policy was to provide the widest possible forum for the discussion of any ideas that his parishioners wanted to air.

Taylor rang Monckton's office. Axel said, "He's engaged."

"I'll hold on," said Taylor.

"No point," said Axel. "He's too busy."

"What the hell are you talking about?" said Taylor. "Tell him I want to talk to him about the case. Tell him—"

"The case is over," said Axel. "He's talking to the press now."

Taylor put the phone down. He took a taxi to the Embankment. There were a dozen armed men outside Monckton's headquarters. They held him at the door and questioned him.

"For Christ's sake!" he stormed, handing a letter signed by Monckton to a guard. "Read the authority! You've seen me a dozen times before. Chief Inspector Taylor."

"Yes, I've seen you," said the guard. "Things have changed. New order."

"Can I get to my office or not?" said Taylor.

"All right," said the guard.

"The pass," said Taylor, holding out a hand. "The authority from Colonel Monckton."

"It'll be safe with me," said the guard, putting it into a pocket. "They're issuing new passes anyway."

Taylor ran up the stairs. The place was bursting with new men. All of them were armed. A man with a submachine gun stood outside Axel's door and wouldn't let Taylor through. He argued for a moment. He shouted, "Axel!" but no one opened the door. Then he turned and ran up to the next floor. He could ring Axel from his own room and get past that damned guard. But upstairs there were more men standing on the landing, leaning against the light-colored walls. He walked past them and put his hand on the handle of his door. As he did so, a man reached out and took him by the shoulder. "Where you going?" said the man. Two others joined the first man and stood on the other side of Taylor.

"All right," said Taylor, dropping his hand from the handle. "*You* tell *me*."

"Tell you what?"

"Why I'm prevented from going into my own office."

"It's not your office. That's Captain Davies' room."

"Since when?" said Taylor.

"Since last night. Since the Emergency Order."

"What Emergency Order?"

"Colonel Monckton's." The man took up a sheaf of papers from a table by the door. He said, "What's your name?"

"I'm Chief Inspector Taylor."

The man turned over the sheets of paper. "You're not on the list," he said. "You're not supposed to be in here at all."

"For God's sake!" said Taylor.

He opened the door and walked into the room. He didn't recognize it. The desk had been moved and four new filing cabinets stood against the opposite wall. The carpet had gone from the floor. A man in the uniform of a British Army captain looked up from behind a stack of documents. He was quite bald. He wore steel-rimmed spectacles resting just above the tip of his nose. He looked at Taylor over the top of the spectacles and said, "Well?"

"What's happening?" said Taylor. "What have you done to my office?"

"Your office?" said the captain.

"My office! I'm Chief Inspector Taylor—"

"I don't give a damn who you are. Get him out of here."

The men behind Taylor put hands on his shoulders and began to pull him backward.

"Yesterday—" said Taylor.

"Ah, yesterday," said the captain. "There've been changes since yesterday."

172

They pulled him to the stairs. "Out!" said one of them, pushing him down the first few steps.

On the floor below Taylor pushed his way toward Axel's door. Again his way was barred. Two men with submachine guns stood in front of him. He began to shout, "Axel! Axel! I want to see you!" The men began to push him backward toward the stairs. Still he shouted. His voice rang up and down the stairwell. At last Axel's door opened and Axel said, "All right! Bring him in."

"You're out," said Axel. "The Colonel doesn't need you any more. It's over—your part of it. It's solved. We've got the assassin. There's nothing more for you to do. What do we need a liaison with the police for when the police are ours? Now out— out."

"Monckton!" shouted Taylor. "Monckton!"

He took a step to pass Axel and get to the inner door, but the two guards seized him from behind and pulled him back onto the landing.

"Out!" cried Axel. "Throw him out!"

They pushed him down the stairs and across the entrance hall. Armed men stood aside as he passed. The guards still held him, pushing him toward the main doors. Once through them, they thrust him forward into the street.

At the hotel the assistant manager was standing at the reception desk as if waiting for Taylor. He looked anxious. He looked as if some embarrassing situation had arisen that he was unsure how to handle. He went straight across the foyer to Taylor, an ingratiating smile on his face, tapping the tips of his fingers together. He said, "I'm most dreadfully sorry, sir. I really am most terribly sorry. We've had instructions from the police not to hold your rooms any further. It was absolutely official. There was nothing I could do."

"How long ago?" said Taylor.

"About an hour. I think they hoped to have a word with you. We had you paged, but—"

"I was out," said Taylor.

"I took the liberty, sir, of collecting your things." He turned to the clerk behind the reception desk. She reached down and picked up Taylor's case. "I really am most terribly—"

Taylor walked toward Lancaster Gate. He bought an evening paper. There was nothing in it. What was it Monckton had been telling the press?

Enid Markus was standing in the open doorway of the flat as he came out of the lift.

"Can you put me up?" he said.

"Haven't I been putting you up?" she said.

"What's happening?" he said.

"Monckton's called the press in. I don't know what for."

"He claims to have made an arrest—or he's got the police to do it for him. The man who killed Powell. But that's only the start of what he has in mind."

"What else?"

"You don't know Monckton," said Taylor.

But then no one really knew Monckton. Only two or three of the considerable body of armed men who now surrounded him had any idea what he had in mind. The first brief news flashes on TV gave only the bare announcement of the arrest. Not until later were there fuller stories. At five o'clock ITN announced an interview with Monckton to be shown in the early evening.

Monckton didn't interview well. Television was too exposed a medium for him. Even in color, his eyes revealed nothing of the human being behind them. He made pronouncements rather than answering the interviewer's questions. He gave the impression of being someone apart, someone who could see wider implications than could the viewers he was addressing. An impression of innate superiority that many found irritating. Taylor found it alarming.

Westbrook, according to Monckton, had confessed to the actual assassination. But Westbrook himself was nothing. The tip of an iceberg. The assassination itself was no more than a symptom of a massive collapse of the social framework. Hadn't the conventional forces of order shown their total inadequacy in Wolverhampton? Hadn't the same disaster only just been averted in London, when rioters had been turned back from the very doors of Parliament? And what had prevented it here? What else but the concentration of responsibility for public order in the hands of a strong man? What was needed for the future safety of the country was an extension of that responsibility to embrace the whole kingdom.

Much of the later comment sympathized with Monckton's general view. Individuals questioned his specific recommendation. Was it not politically dangerous to concentrate so much power in the hands of one man? But then hadn't there been the precedent of Churchill? No one could say that the outcome of that had been anything but glorious. And the general feeling in the country was that the liberal, permissive trend had gone too far. It was time for some stiffening process, some hardening of social discipline.

"Well?" said Enid.

"It never occurred to me," said Taylor. "He's gone mad. Those eyes—I've seen that look before. He's got to be stopped."

He got up and walked to the window. Traffic still moved steadily along Bayswater Road. Beyond, couples still walked in the park.

"How?" said Enid.

"He could be chopped down, I suppose. If someone could get to him."

"By you?"

"Perhaps."

He turned and walked toward the Powell file that lay open on the studio couch.

"No," he said. "Not by me. There's a more effective way. If I bring in the real assassin it'll cut the ground from under him."

"But—Westbrook?"

"How do I know? Some crazy political opportunist. Not much to choose between him and Monckton. But not the man who killed Powell. Quite a different character, that one."

"What'll you do?"

"I'll bring him in."

"All by yourself?" she said.

He looked at her. She was smiling at him as if he amused her.

"Yes," he said. "If that's what it comes to. All by myself."

There was a train going north in an hour. He could get off in Peterborough and take a taxi to King's Lynn.

"Will I see you again?" said Enid.

"Of course," said Taylor. "Yes, of course."

He thought it unlikely.

But even Taylor hadn't realized the grip that Monckton now had on London. Outside, the street was deserted, but at the tube station an Army picket stopped him. Didn't he know about the curfew? Didn't he know that no one was allowed on the streets at this time? No, he said, he hadn't heard about the curfew. Well, he knew now, didn't he? And if he didn't get off the street straightaway they'd have him inside.

He turned back toward the flat. He slipped down a side street and out at the other end. Someone shouted at him as he crossed Edgware Road. They began to run after him, two of them, with a clatter of boots ringing out across the deserted evening. But they didn't catch him. He got through the back streets. He could hear another group ahead of him. He stood in a doorway and let them march across the junction ahead. There were six of them, carrying short automatic weapons. It took him the best part of an hour to reach Tottenham Court Road and cross it toward the main University buildings. Sometimes he heard them approaching from his left or right. Then he had time to get out of their way. At other times he almost walked into a group of them standing with weapons ready on a corner or at the entrance to some building. Russell Square was the most difficult obstacle. It was so exposed. There was no cover. But he got across at last and up Herbrand Street and Marchmont Street, checking his direction from time to time on the maps in the "A to Z." His checks were frequent, since there was no one he could ask, no one except the prowling pickets of armed troops keeping the streets clear on Monckton's orders, and London was not a town he knew well. And so at last he got to Birkenhead Street and its junction with Euston Road. Across the open space ahead lay the station, and in front of it, covering all the main approaches, were the troops. He could have cried with frustration. He looked at the map. If he went back, if he crossed Gray's Inn Road and came at the place from the Pentonville Road side, he might approach it from some side entrance. He got through Collier Street and came at it through Railway Street. He got across York Way to the great bulk of the station itself. There was an entrance ahead. He ran toward it. It was closed and barred. Across it someone had written in chalk: SERVICE SUSPENDED TILL 7 A.M.

Enid was watching a late parliamentary report program when Taylor got back to the flat. A middle-aged man was talking about discipline and social responsibility.

"I can't get through," said Taylor, dropping his bag on the studio couch. "They've closed the stations. They're everywhere."

"Your Inspector Marston rang. He's got to get hold of you."

"What for?"

"The police don't talk to journalists. You should know that."

Taylor rang the northern police office.

"It's the CC, sir," said Marston. "He wants you back. Soon as you can manage it. He's been trying to get you most of the afternoon. Nobody at Colonel Monckton's place seems to have heard of you."

"The place is in a state of siege," said Taylor. "You can't move on the streets. Everything's at a standstill. They've closed the stations. Does he know what it's like down here?"

"I think he's got some idea. As soon as you can manage it—that's what he said."

"I'll try first thing in the morning," said Taylor. "I'll ring you when I know the train. Can you get a car to York?"

"I'll see there's one there. And look—I'm sorry, it's your wife."

"Beryl?"

"She's cleared off. She's taken the little girl with her but she's left the lad."

"Jimmy?"

"He's all right, I mean. He's staying with neighbors. Don't worry about him."

"Where's she gone?"

"Can't say yet. Probably not far. Probably back by the time you get here."

"For Christ's sake!" said Taylor.

He put the phone down and went into the kitchen. Enid was pouring coffee out of a stoneware jug.

"When are you going?" she said.

"In the morning."

"Do you have to go?"

"Yes, I have to go. I have to see the Chief Constable. I have to sort out my family."

"You can stay, you know—if you want," she said. "You can come back."

He bent and kissed her. "Thanks," he said.

Armed troops stood on the platforms. At the barrier they wanted to know who he was and where he was going. They wanted to see his identification card. But at last they let him on the train. It was the same on the journey. Troops were guarding signal boxes and bridges. Troops stood on the platforms of the stations they passed through.

The car was waiting. In half an hour Taylor was in Marston's room at Subdivision.

"The CC's coming over," said Marston. "About twenty minutes. And Dixon's just been in—wish you'd had a word with him. He's been on a door-to-door round the farms. The Pilkingtons down at Long Bank put up a Mr. Brown on Sunday and Monday. That's within the five-mile radius forensic mentioned. Said he was conducting some BBC reception tests. Mr. Pilkington said he had some radio stuff in a case. He's our man, you know. He left about ten on Tuesday morning."

"Where was he the rest of the day?"

"Stuck in some barn, do you think? He had a taxi from York waiting to pick him up near Upper Bank crossroads at eight-thirty. The secretary of the cab association's getting hold of the driver. He'll ring me back. But there's no doubt about it—the description we've got from the Pilkingtons is the same as we had from George Freeman."

"But no more?" said Taylor.

"No."

Taylor was looking out of the window. The place looked as if nothing could ever change it. A different world up here, he was thinking. He said, "What about the lad?"

"Jimmy's all right," said Marston. "Don't worry about him. He's with Mrs. Jeffries."

"Annie Jeffries?" said Taylor. "Well."

"You never know," said Marston.

"And Beryl?"

"She's gone to her mother's. The girl's with her. They're all right. Look fitter than you do, really—that head of yours has taken quite a crack."

"Have you seen her?"

"Dixon had a word with her. She's all right."

The Chief Constable met him at the desk. "Your room's free, Mr. Taylor?" he said.

"We can use that, sir," said Taylor.

"What happened to your face?" said Warner.

"The Wolverhampton business, sir. A boot, I think."

"Anything broken?"

"It's all right, sir."

"What's your position with Monckton?" said Warner, closing the door of the Chief Inspector's room behind him.

"I think I'm out, sir."

"You think?"

"I couldn't get to him, sir. I tried. I couldn't get past his personal assistant and the guards he has. But they took over my room and canceled the hotel booking. The PA told me they didn't need a police liaison any more."

"This came over the teletype yesterday," said Warner, taking a paper out of his pocket. "Better have a look at it."

Taylor took the paper. It read: "Re—Chief Inspector Noel Taylor on secondment. Services of this officer no longer required. Recall to normal duties. Authority Colonel Jeffrey Monckton, Coordinator Protection Public Order."

"I wish they'd told me, sir," said Taylor.

"Obviously didn't think it necessary. You'd served their purpose."

"Sir, if I could have two days. I know who I'm looking for. I think I know where he is."

"Who've you told about this?" said Warner.

"No one, sir."

"No one? Why not?"

"I tried to get to Monckton, sir. I couldn't get near."

Warner looked at him, then he took his pipe out of his pocket. "Look," he said. "I know you're ambitious. I know you're a damn good policeman. But you can't do everything yourself."

"No, sir."

"Come on. What is it you want?"

At first her mother wouldn't let Taylor in. She stood in the doorway, squat and determined. He didn't argue. He just stood and waited. Finally, when it was clear that he wouldn't go away, she gave in.

It was a small room with no pictures on the walls. A screen with a picture of an idealized rural scene stood in front of the fireplace. The wallpaper had patterns of large roses on it. Beryl sat in a stiff armchair and looked across at him.

"Hello, Beryl," he said, standing in the doorway.

"Hello, Noel," she said.

"How are you?" said Taylor.

"I'm all right," she said.

"How's Adrienne?"

"She's all right."

"And Jimmy?"

She looked very small, sitting in the stiff armchair, her hands and knees together as if to make herself more contained.

"I'm not coming back," she said.

"Course you're not going back," said her mother. "What's there to go back to? Insults—"

"Insults?" said Taylor.

"I thought I could give him a home," said Beryl. "It's no good. I can't."

"What's happened?"

"What do you think they've been saying?" said her mother. "What do you think she's had to put up with all by herself?"

"What have they been saying?"

"You don't know," said her mother. "You weren't here when she needed you. My little girl. They told her what they thought of her—harboring that little darkie. I told you it was wrong. I told you it was unnatural. I told you that however you bring them up you can't hide it. There's always this race thing that shows. It's not their color—I don't mind their color. But they're different. No matter what you say they're different. Don't say I didn't warn you. But would you listen—would you?"

She was standing very upright and puffing out her great breasts. She said, "You didn't have to listen to them—Mrs. Farrow, that Mrs. Jeffries!"

"Annie Jeffries?" said Taylor. "Jimmy's with her now. She took him in."

"I don't care where he is. He won't come back here. He won't come troubling my girl."

"I'm sorry," said Taylor, turning to Beryl. "I'm sorry for the kind of life you're going to lead. I'm sorry you're saddled to this —prejudiced cow for the rest of your life."

There it is, he thought. It's over. A marriage, after all. Not perhaps the ideal one. Not like the marriages of the cinema, with their trials and tribulations—good dramatic stuff—but ending always in some kind of calm and reconciliation. Ten years. Ten years of her life— his too—and a single episode can come and smash it. An episode that really didn't have anything to do with them. London—that's where the real battle was being fought. The backstairs battle. Power stopping at nothing to assert itself. Monckton, Westbrook —you couldn't tell them apart. What had that to do with life up here? And yet it had. Somehow the battle was woven into the fabric of the nation. Everyone was involved.

He stood on the doorstep of Mrs. Jeffries' terrace house and rang the bell. When she answered, she stood squarely in the doorway and looked up at him. She almost filled the opening with her large, shapeless body. She had curlers in the bottom rolls of her gray hair, and she wore a faded print apron. She was in her slippers.

"Oh, it's you, is it?" she said.

She spoke bluntly. She seemed almost belligerent.

"I came to see about Jimmy," said Taylor.

"Better come in," she said.

Inside the little hall he could smell cooking from the kitchen beyond. There was a china plaque on the wall to his right, with the words: "A Present from Scarborough."

"Come in the front room," she said.

She opened the door on the right and went in. It was a room in which nobody ever really lived. Perhaps they used it for an occasional Christmas party. Perhaps she put a fire in there every Sunday to keep it aired. It smelled unused and a little damp. There were net curtains at the window.

"Right," she said. "What've you heard?"

"I've just seen my wife," said Taylor.

"What's she say?"

"I believe Jimmy's with you?"

"In the kitchen."

"You've been looking after him?"

"Poor little sod," she said. "Somebody had to take him in. She left him with Gertie—you know, Gertie Redfern—and cleared off. Well, Gertie has a job to go to. She couldn't have him forever, and nobody knowing where Beryl had gone. So I took him in. It was either that or the street."

"It was very good of you," said Taylor. "Thanks."

"Good be damned," she said. "What else could I do? I mean,

183

he's a bairn, isn't he? Father and mother gone—I couldn't just leave him."

"Thanks anyway."

She looked up at him, her arms folded over her apron.

"What's happening then? I mean—what you going to do? She won't come back, you know. I know her sort. What are you going to do?"

"I'm not sure," he said.

"Look. It's no trouble to me. You got a job or something on, I know that. Leave him here till it's over. He'll be all right. I'll see he gets to that nursery school. He can go with mine. Then you can decide. Will you want to keep him?"

"Keep him? He's my son," said Taylor

"I just thought," she said. "He's in the kitchen, if you want a word with him. Go on—just walk through."

The news at one o'clock was subdued. Reports were brief and vague: The usual half-hour radio program had been cut to ten minutes and all background comment had been excluded. It seemed to Taylor that Monckton was beginning to get at the broadcasting media. His next move would be into the rest of the country —a geographical extension of the hold he already had on London. If Taylor was to take advantage of his present mobility, he must move at once. Two hours after he had reached the town, Marston saw him off again at York station.

It was late when Taylor reached King's Lynn. A man in plain clothes met him and took him to a police car outside the station. In the back was a thickset man in shirt sleeves. "Tate," he said. "Chief Super." The car pulled away.

"Had a word with your CC," said Tate. "Now listen—anything

you want. We don't want to interfere unless you want us. But if you do, don't hesitate. Got you into a bed and breakfast place out in Gaywood. It's not much but no one's going to bother you there. We won't go right up to it. Better if you do the last hundred yards on foot. A Mrs. Westbury—she doesn't know you're in the force. She thinks you sell insurance. No need to tell her anything anyway. Look in tomorrow. And if there's anything else—"

The room was small and the iron bed looked uninviting. On the washstand was a bowl with a large jug standing in it. The towel had frayed edges and had worn thin in the middle. From the window he could see the lights of the town. The place looked as if nothing had disturbed it in five centuries.

"I don't have a telephone," said Mrs. Westbury. "There's a box by the school. Won't they have gone to bed? It's near eleven-thirty."

From the call box Taylor rang the Reverend R. Black. There was no reply. He walked beyond the call box then turned, walked back and rang again. Still there was no answer. A car approached, passed him and turned the corner toward Castle Rising. He went back to the house and at midnight he was in bed. He lay wondering what Monckton's vision of a "reinvigorated Britain" would look like, and whether if it came to it he could bring himself to pull the trigger on the man.

The Reverend R. Black was very much as Taylor had pictured him. Thin, precise in his movements, in the forty to fifty age group. His voice whined at Taylor, as Taylor stood on the doorstep. He was, as it were, on his dignity, conscious of some vast responsibility that faced him as an editor.

"If I could just come in a minute, sir," said Taylor.

The Reverend R. Black looked down at Taylor, took a step backward and opened the door.

Inside, the place was large. It gave an impression of utter bareness. There wasn't a picture on a wall and in the large reception room there were only two Victorian chairs and a big claw-foot refectory table.

"I'm a police officer," said Taylor.

"You've already told me that," said the Reverend R. Black. "But I'd remind you that we live in a free society, not a police state."

Do we? thought Taylor. For how much longer?

The Reverend R. Black seemed to be making a deliberate effort not to be impressed.

"I could get official, documentary authority," said Taylor.

"I wish you would," said the Reverend R. Black. "I should be relieved of a heavy responsibility."

"But then, of course, the whole thing would have to be made official. As it is, I can have a quiet chat with this letter writer of yours, and nobody any the wiser. Preferable, isn't it, to having uniformed men arriving in a police car? If, of course, it's his well-being you're most concerned with?"

"And what else might it be?" said the Reverend R. Black.

"I've no idea," said Taylor. "I don't know anything about the pressures an editor faces."

The Reverend R. Black looked at Taylor with an expression of infinite distaste on his thin face.

"I shall want a signature, of course, clearing me of any responsibility," he said at last.

"Of course," said Taylor.

"Wait here."

He walked out of the room and across the bare hall. Taylor could hear him opening a drawer in some other room. At last he came back and handed Taylor a piece of paper. It was the original of the letter. Taylor took out a notebook and wrote down the name Colin Nelson, and after it an address in West Wilney.

186

"Thanks," he said.

"Just sign your name at the bottom of the letter," said the Reverend R. Black. "And your rank."

Taylor scrawled his name across the letter.

At the door Taylor said, "How do I get there?"

"Personal transport is the best way," said the Reverend R. Black, beginning to close the door. "Otherwise taxi."

"Perhaps I could use your phone?"

"You'll find a kiosk in the village."

"Christian bloody charity!" said Taylor.

West Wilney was set in heath and silver birch country. It consisted of a single street. There was a chapel and a sub-post office. There was a little country store and a petrol pump. Beyond that, there was little else. A few small holdings and one or two small farms lay behind the street and behind them the open heathland with its scrub, its silver birches, its bracken and coarse grass and heather. Even in his own area, rural though it was, Taylor couldn't have found anything to match the isolation of the place, no more than ten miles from the center of a thriving town.

"Whereabouts then?" said the taxi driver.

"Outside the store," said Taylor.

"The supermarket?"

"If that's what you call it," said Taylor.

"Shall I wait?"

"No," said Taylor. "I'll take your phone number. When I want to come back I'll ring."

The two women in the little store—four sets of shelves, a deep freeze and an adding machine—looked at him curiously.

He said, "Mr. Colin Nelson—wonder if you could tell me where he lives?"

Neither woman spoke. They looked at him. They looked at one

another. Then one said, "You a friend of Mr. Nelson's?"

"Well," said Taylor. "A friend of his asked me to look him up."

"I see," said the woman. "You might find him out. He likes walking. Doesn't get far, of course."

"You know Mr. Nelson?" said the other woman.

"No—just this friend of his."

"Well, you'll know him if you pass him. Very quiet. Keeps to himself. Doesn't mix."

"Is it far away?" said Taylor.

" 'Bout a mile. Straight up—down a lane on the right. It's easy to find."

"Thanks," said Taylor.

It was more than a mile. Beyond the village, the road curved away to the left. It began to dip gently into a wide plain, broken up by clumps of trees and areas of marsh. The land was covered in scrub and heather. It had never been cultivated or enclosed. It was half past ten in the morning with the sun high in the sky and a few heathland birds busy among the grasses. Again the road turned. There was nothing in sight along it, and when he looked back the village had disappeared from view behind a roll of the land. It was wild and isolated in the extreme.

He saw the lane the woman had spoken of, running away to a group of birches and pine on the right. It was hardly a lane, really no more than a track. Two lines of bare earth showed where the wheels of a car had run, and between them the grass grew in coarse clumps. He turned down it toward the trees. Some signs of an earlier cultivation appeared. Bushes of gorse and broom rambled on either side of the track as if at one time they had formed an approach to some habitation. Brambles weaved their way through and over them. Two large and shapeless lilac bushes thrust their branches into one another on the right. Rhododendron bushes grew darkly on the corner, and round it lay the house in a small clearing in the birch wood. It wasn't large—perhaps no more than three bedrooms—but it had a certain Victorian distinction. If it had been nearer the village, it might at one time have been a rectory. Now it looked faded and shabby, with paint peeling from the woodwork and the unchecked growth of virginia creeper masking the outlines of the windows.

Taylor looked at it for a moment. Nothing moved. It looked at first glance uninhabited. He went to the door and knocked. The sound echoed in the hall beyond. He waited. No one came. He knocked again. Still there was no answer. He stepped backward and looked up at the windows above. There were curtains beyond the fringe of the virginia creeper, but no sign of life. No one peered down at him. Nothing moved. He walked to the first ground-floor window and looked in. It was a study of some sort, with books lining the walls and paper on the table. It had been used recently but now it was empty. At the back of the house there were two or three outbuildings.

"Hello!" he called. "Mr. Nelson?"

No one replied. Perhaps they had been right, those two women, thought Taylor. Perhaps he had gone for his morning walk over the heath. He knocked at the back door and still there was no reply. He walked right around the house and then around again to the back. He tried the doors, but they were locked. But above the back door a small window with frosted glass was open. A lavatory, perhaps. He found a ladder in one of the outhouses and set it up against the wall. If he could have ten clear minutes in the house, he thought, it might be long enough to decide whether Nelson was Brown and Brown Nelson. Just ten minutes. It was worth the risk.

The window opened into the bathroom and beyond that was a landing. He tried the doors that opened off it. One was into the toilet and two others led into quite empty rooms. Behind the fourth was a furnished bedroom. The bed had been made. A folded towel lay across the back of a small upright chair. Everything was in its place. It was the room of an organized and tidy-minded person.

One or two paperbacks stood in a small bookcase on the wall, within easy reach of anyone lying in the bed. There was nothing whatever unusual about the place. It was a quite ordinary bedroom, and its appearance disappointed Taylor. He didn't know what he had expected to find, but the very ordinariness was depressing. Perhaps it was simply that after the risk he was taking, he had expected something more dramatic.

The downstairs rooms smelled of damp. In the hall at the bottom of the stairs, the paper was beginning to lift from the wall. He could see the area of damp rising in a great semicircle from the skirting board. He thought there must be rot at the back of the woodwork. The furniture in the sitting room was curiously old-fashioned. It all looked to be out of the nineteen thirties, as if it had been bought new and kept ever since. Nelson was perhaps more interested in other things than outward appearances. Only the study was different. A large mahogany table stood in the middle of the room, and drawn up to it was a massive Victorian carved chair. Here the atmosphere was different. Again the place was ordered. Even the scattered papers on the table had a certain order. There were drawings of mechanical devices and pages of handwritten manuscript. The place had a life about it, as if this was the hub of the house, this was where the important things went on.

The books that lined the room were an odd mixture. Works on color chemistry and the chemistry of food. Works on electrical and mechanical engineering. Some poetry—Shelley, two volumes of the works of Shakespeare, Wordsworth, Herrick. The impression they gave of the reader was of a man with wide general interest. But, apart from the scientific section, one other section gave the impression of specialization. The field was philosophy and political theory. The section was comprehensive. It ranged from Plato through Tom Paine to modern Fabian tracts. Engels, Marx, Lenin, Trotsky, Shaw were all represented, and beside them Mussolini's autobiography and *Mein Kampf.* There were biographies of Mao, Che and

190

Castro. There were works on the activities of guerrillas in Yugoslavia, Bolivia and Indonesia. There was a volume on the activities of the Stern Gang and other Zionist revolutionary movements during the forties. Copies of Mancellino's *Political Action* and *Street Fighting* stood next to a copy of *Deutschland Erwacht*. In a section apart were twenty-two volumes devoted to Nietzsche. At last Taylor felt some excitement moving in him.

He moved back to the table, and turned over the papers there. Nelson was working on some mechanical device that Taylor couldn't follow. On one of the drawings, all of which showed skill in draftsmanship, were the words "Trigger capsule." He looked up, trying to puzzle out the nature of the device that Nelson was designing, and as he did so he caught sight of a small framed photograph on the mantelpiece. It was a picture of Enoch Powell, bought perhaps from the newspaper in which it had first appeared. In front of it, blackened by age, were two crossed and withered laurel leaves.

It was enough for Taylor, but what court would it convince? He went through a filing cabinet and checked the contents of a cupboard. He pulled back a corner of the carpet and stamped with his foot to try to locate an entrance to the space below. There was nothing. The floor was quite firm, except along one outside wall where the rot was beginning to work its way inward. He moved to the stairs. He thought that in the attic ... but that foot of Nelson's. The attic would hardly be convenient. He went outside and took the ladder away from the window. He was thinking, as he took it back to the outbuilding, that if he could steal another five minutes before Nelson returned, he would have him. The place must be near. It must really be obvious. It must be convenient for Nelson to get in and out of. There was, as far as Nelson knew, no need for secrecy. His house could hardly have been more isolated. There was nothing to suggest to him that any suspicion had begun to fall on his activities. Then, as Taylor put the ladder back, he had it. The outbuilding had been a stable. The wooden sides of two of the stalls still remained. The place was full of empty boxes. There were a few empty wine bottles covered in thick and dusty cobwebs. But above the stabling was an old hayloft, and it was against the edge of this that the ladder had been resting. He climbed upward. The place was lit by glass tiles in the roof above, and it ran back some twenty feet. It was a well-equipped workshop, with a bench and a small lathe. There were electric drills, electric soldering irons and a range of hand tools. Along the end of the loft ran another wide bench, covered in chemical and electrical equipment. He pulled out a box from under the bench. It was full of small metal castings. A stout wooden box with a hinged lid contained forty or fifty sticks of explosive, and another had the word "Dets" written openly in chalk across the front of it. It contained six or seven little cardboard boxes, into each of which were packed a dozen detonators. In a long drawer below the bench was a Remington fitted with a telescopic sight and wrapped carefully in damp-resistant paper. Taylor closed the drawer. There wasn't a doubt in his mind that this was where the assassination had been planned. There wasn't a doubt that Nelson had carried it out himself.

Taylor closed the door of the outbuilding. He looked up at the bathroom window, still a little ajar as he had found it. He closed the back door and heard the latch click. Had he left things undisturbed in the study? If not, too bad. There wasn't time to do anything about it now. He walked straight into the trees at the back of the house and made his way through them. He walked along the back of the bushes of gorse and broom, ready to drop down if there was a sound ahead of him. But there was no sound, and no one came. At last he got back on the road. When he looked around there was nothing at all in sight. A few heath birds, a kestrel swinging past on the light breeze, but nothing else. He turned and began to walk back toward the village.

He turned the first of the curves in the road, and began to climb the gentle slope. In a moment the village street would appear. But as he looked toward it, a man came into view on the road ahead. He was just beginning to rise over the horizon. He walked with a stick and despite the weather he wore a light plastic raincoat buttoned down the front. His head was bare and he wore glasses. He was staring down at the surface of the road ahead of him. As Taylor approached, he noticed the man's limp. Was this Nelson? Was this really the man behind the whole thing? Had this thin little man, perhaps sixty-two or -three years old, been responsible for that explosion and the terrors that had followed it? This insignificant man with the limping left leg? Here he was on the road ahead. Taylor could have taken him in with one hand. He didn't look the kind of man to resist. Yet who knew what kind of man he was? Who would have thought to look at him that in that outbuilding he had enough explosive to knock the guts out of York Minster? Who was to say what arms he might be carrying under that plastic mac? No, thought Taylor. Let's do it properly. Let's bring Tate in on this. Too much at stake to make a mess of things now.

Nelson noticed Taylor when the two of them were less than ten yards apart. He looked up, then back at the road, then up again at Taylor. He gave a little nervous smile. His eyes seemed shy and perhaps a little apprehensive behind the glasses.

"Lovely day," said Taylor.

"Lovely," said Nelson, in the characteristic accent of the area. "Quite lovely."

And so they passed, Taylor and the man whose activities he had discovered, neither of them giving a clue to anyone who had seen them of the secrets both of them held.

The press and TV reports of the arrest of Daniel Westbrook had been unsensational, yet a vast sense of relief spread through the country at the news. With the relief came wild and highly vocal support for Monckton. Evans was under mounting pressure from most responsible quarters to remove the man. He knew the pressure was just and right. But he knew as well that in the present climate of public opinion no politician with any claim to sanity could have sacked Monckton and survived. The public wouldn't stand for it, nor would many members of the House. In the eyes of millions, the arrest of Westbrook for the Powell assassination vindicated everything Monckton was doing. Any official move against him would only erode Evans' remaining influence, and that at least must be preserved if the country was ever to return to normality.

"I want one small thing to play on," said Evans, looking up at Cleashaw and Potter from the bed that had been fitted up for him in one of the ground-floor rooms of number 10.

"What's that?" said Cleashaw.

"I'll recognize it," said Evans. "When it comes."

Tate got up from behind his desk as Taylor came into the office. He looked eager for something to break his normal routine.

"Well, Chief Inspector?" he said.

"There's no doubt about him, sir," said Taylor. "He's got arms in an outhouse there, and enough explosives to rip this town apart."

"Show me," said Tate, turning to a map on the wall.

Taylor traced the road to West Wilney and then the lane to the house. He tapped the place with his finger.

"Hm," said Tate. "How many men, do you think?"

"The two of us, sir. That's all. He won't offer any resistance."

"What about the firearms?"

"He doesn't intend them for us. He has bigger fish in mind."

A shadow of disappointment crossed Tate's face. "What kind of an approach?" he said.

194

"The house is hidden from the road by trees. We could get right up to it without being seen. There won't be any trouble."

"Right," said Tate, picking up a trilby from the hatstand by the door. "Better get moving, hadn't we?"

They took Tate's Cortina.

"Better than an official car," said Tate. "No use scaring him off."

It took twenty minutes, the way Tate drove, to reach West Wilney, and another two minutes to park the car in the cover of trees near the turning to the house.

"If he's got a gun he might just use it," said Tate. "Better stick to the trees."

They took the route through the shrubs that Taylor had taken earlier.

"How old did you say he was?" said Tate.

"Sixty," said Taylor. "Maybe a bit more."

"Hm," said Tate. "Unless he's armed, shouldn't give us much trouble. We'll know in a minute."

They stepped out of the bushes and across the drive to the house. Tate glanced at the upper windows and then rapped on the door. He stood with his hands clasped before him and his head held toward the door. He was listening for some sound inside. He nodded to Taylor after a moment. He could hear someone moving in the hall. The door opened and Nelson stood on the step.

"Mr. Nelson?" said Tate.

"Yes?"

"We're police officers. Wonder if we could have a word with you."

"Perhaps you'd come in," he said.

He led the way into the study. He walked round the table and put his hand out to the chairs, indicating that they should sit. Tate sat. Taylor stood by the door. Nelson never looked directly at either of them. Occasionally he seemed to catch sight of them out of the corner of an eye or over the top of his glasses. Most of the time he looked down at the desk or the floor.

Taylor said, "We're investigating the murder of Mr. Enoch Powell. We thought you might be able to help us."

"Murder?" said Nelson. He glanced over the top of his glasses. The word seemed to surprise him.

"You've heard about it?"

"I heard of his death," said Nelson.

"You knew it was murder?"

He tapped the floor with his stick. "No, I—is that how you think of it—murder? Is that how everyone thinks of it—a case of murder?"

"How do you think of it?" said Taylor.

"An execution. An act of execution," said Nelson.

Tate glanced at Taylor and raised an eyebrow. He said, "What's the difference, Mr. Nelson? You've lost me."

"Look here," said Taylor. "Why don't you sit down? That leg—"

Nelson looked down at his foot. It had a slight twist outward. Then he turned and sat down at the desk. In front of him were the sheets of drawings. He took up the top one and turned it over.

"In the days of capital punishment," said Nelson, "a man might kill a bank guard for gain. Murder. In retribution he was executed by society. You see a difference between the two acts?"

"Of course," said Tate.

"I'm not quite clear," said Taylor.

"Murder is motivated by personal gain. Behind execution there is a principle—justice, social well-being, retribution," said Nelson.

"And Mr. Powell wasn't murdered?" said Taylor.

"No," said Nelson.

"Then what was this principle you're talking about? What was it that made this 'execution' and not 'murder'?"

Nelson lifted his eyes from the blank paper in front of him and gave Taylor a quick glance. There was a secret smile behind his face, as if he thought Taylor incapable of grasping his ideas. He said, "You must understand, some men devote their lives to the pursuit of the great man—the natural leader. A man to whom they can give all their energies. A man they can follow without questioning his judgment. A man who will lead them—you know. Because they never feel themselves—particularly significant. But they can reach significance through him. Blind faith—a great quality. This man, this leader—of all the attempts to define him, Nietzsche's definition is the most satisfying."

"To you?" said Taylor.

Nelson glanced at him. His smile was one of mild superiority, as if he knew well enough what admission Taylor was trying to get him to make. He said, "You don't follow, do you?"

"Not entirely," said Taylor. It wasn't true: he was beginning to follow well enough.

"Enoch Powell *was* that man!" said Nelson. He looked at both of them, as if he were producing some revelation to a pair of children not quite bright enough to understand. "Enoch Powell was that leader—the Nietzschean ideal. If you followed him through all his complex arguments, if you followed in the direction he indicated, how could you be anything but a fanatical supporter?"

"But somewhere he failed?" said Taylor.

Nelson looked back at the paper on the desk. "Yes," he said. "He failed. When the final test came he failed. When the invitations came to step into the final seat of power, to don the mantle of supreme leadership—you remember them? A hundred thousand pounds—wasn't that the figure they mentioned to back him if he would take up the leadership? And he refused. The final leap, and he refused it! Can you imagine how they felt—his supporters? The sense of personal desolation! To give yourself totally to an ideal and then discover a flaw in it, a fallibility! No man can live with himself after that."

197

" 'Mr. Powell's recent tragic action,' " said Taylor. "That was it?"

Nelson nodded. He said, "It was an act of purification."

"How was it done?" said Taylor. "The bomb—how was it detonated?"

"That wouldn't be difficult," said Nelson. "Electronically—any competent electrical engineer. A device that would take radio commands from five or six miles away. Perhaps a two-way device."

"Were you there when it went off?" said Taylor. "Did you hear it?"

"Me?" said Nelson. "You're not thinking I did it?"

"I thought you might know who did."

"He's won in the end, hasn't he?" said Nelson. "Whoever did it, hasn't he cleared the way for the true leader? Hasn't he brought Colonel Monckton out of retirement and set him firmly in the saddle? Hasn't he won?"

"Perhaps he has," said Taylor.

"It had to come," said Nelson. "There had to be a social purification, a new discipline. Against this permissiveness, this free sex, this growing black cancer."

Taylor said, "Well, I think we've come to the right man, sir."

Tate got up. "Not much doubt about it," he said.

"I wonder if you'd mind coming back to the office with us, Mr. Nelson. If we just had a statement—perhaps a few more questions. . . ."

"Back to the office?" said Nelson. "I don't see what else I can say."

"The official forms are there," said Tate. "If we got it all down on one of those . . . "

"We've a car outside," said Taylor.

Tate had joined Taylor at the door. Nelson looked at them over the top of his glasses.

"You think I did it, don't you?" said Nelson.

"I think with your knowledge you can help us," said Taylor.

Nelson got up from the desk. He stood leaning on his stick. "I want to see my solicitor," he said.

"You can ring him from the office," said Tate.

Nelson nodded. He said, "All right. If I can just go to the toilet."

Taylor looked at Tate. "Why not?" said Tate.

Tate opened the door and Nelson walked through it. Nelson climbed the stairs slowly, with Tate a step or two behind him.

"I'll hang on to your stick," said Tate. "Leave the door unlocked."

Nelson nodded and closed the door behind him. Tate heard him lift the seat.

Taylor came quietly up the stairs. Tate tiptoed toward him.

"What do you think sir?" said Taylor.

"No doubt about it," said Tate. "He knew about the trigger mechanism. He knew it was two-way."

The lavatory cistern flushed and began to refill with a noisy sizzle of water.

"What's this Monckton fellow going to think?" said Tate. "Like to see his face when he hears of it. Going to knock him back, isn't it, when he finds the police can still do their own job better than an outsider."

Taylor could imagine what he'd think. It would certainly shake public confidence in Monckton.

"I'd like him up north as soon as possible, sir," said Taylor. "Could you provide a car?"

"Of course," said Tate. "You can take Hemmings and Peterson —young, keen. First class."

"What the hell's he doing in there?" said Taylor, looking across the landing. The water still sizzled into the cistern. "Mr. Nelson!" he called, crossing the landing and turning the doorknob. The door wouldn't open. "Christ, he's locked it!"

He put his shoulder to the door and the flimsy lock bent and broke. The place was empty. The window stood wide open.

"Round the back, sir!" said Taylor. "He's dropped down the roof."

There were scratch marks down the slates of the lean-to roof. Below them the wooden guttering was broken.

Tate said, "You can see where he dropped down." He bent and pointed to the shallow imprints made in the hard earth.

Taylor said, "Try the barn, sir. That's where he's got the stuff stored."

Before he reached the barn, Taylor could smell smoke. It was rising through the roof tiles.

"Christ, don't let him kill himself!" said Taylor. "It's no good if we don't get him alive."

Tate pulled at the barn door. It was barred from inside. He rammed it with his shoulder, but it held. As he backed away, looking for something to prize it open with, two shots burst outward through the woodwork.

Taylor leaned a long plank against the eaves. He began to climb toward the roof.

"Watch it," said Tate. "He's armed. And when you get a couple of tiles off, the air's going to send the whole thing up."

"Get a spade, can you, sir?" said Taylor. "When I'm in, can you get that door open?"

Taylor lifted off four tiles and dropped them behind him. Nelson, crouched inside with a service revolver, fired at him. The shot missed.

"Now!" shouted Taylor, and Tate began to lever the door open with a spade. The wooden bar inside cracked.

Smoke began to pour through the hole in the roof. Taylor could only feel the tiles as he pulled them clear. His eyes were streaming with tears. He smashed through two tile bars with his foot and dropped down into the hayloft. He could make out Nelson crouching down with his back to the workbench, the revolver held in both his hands. Between them was the fire that Nelson had started with a pile of paper, shavings and paraffin. The flames had already spread on one side of the loft to a container of ammunition. The cardboard was on fire and rounds were rolling onto the floor. Nelson fired. Again the shot missed and Taylor pushed through the flames and dragged him forward.

"You there?" called Tate, now at the top of the ladder leading up to the loft.

"Take him, can you, sir?" said Taylor. "I can't breathe."

Nelson fell headfirst toward the ladder and Tate caught hold of his clothing. He dragged him down the ladder and onto the earth floor of the barn.

"My leg!" Nelson was screaming. "It's on fire."

Nelson's clothes were smoldering. Tate picked up a sack and beat out the flames.

Ammunition in the hayloft was beginning to explode. Bullets whined off the tiles.

"For Christ's sake get out!" shouted Tate.

Taylor was seizing hold of drawers and apparatus and flinging them out through the hole in the roof.

"We've all the evidence we need!" cried Tate. "For Christ's sake get out!"

He pulled Nelson out into the open. He could see Taylor getting out of the hole in the roof, smoke and flames curling round him. Taylor got clear of the hole. He was coughing continuously. He got a foot on the plank and began to feel for the edge with a hand when something exploded inside the loft. The roof lifted. The side wall cracked and the building began to collapse at one end. The main roof beam sank, tiles fell inward and a roaring sheet of flame rose up through it. Taylor slid down the plank, then fell off on his back. He got to his knees, still coughing, and tried to grin at Tate.

"You bloody maniac," said Tate. "What are you after—promotion?"

Monckton had withdrawn from direct contact with the outside world. He ate and slept in his office. Axel protected him from all callers. Yet outside, his control of London remained firm. He had the authority of Coordinator of Public Security for the Greater London area, conferred on him by the PM, and he had the support of large sections of the country and some highly vocal elements in the House. He had, after all, produced an assassin. More than that, he had highlighted for many people the real nature of the social sickness of which the assassination of Enoch Powell was merely a symptom. To many responsible people, Monckton seemed the only man between them and social disaster. It was on the support of such people, and on the authority of the PM, that he relied. He was convinced that they would carry him inevitably into that position of power from which he could really heal the country's sickness. The glimpse of such power within his grasp gave him a sense of unquestioning self-assurance. Even when news of the PM's injury reached him, it did nothing to shake that self-assurance. He knew in himself that he was too firmly entrenched, too irreplaceable, to be unseated. Evans, of course, who had seized the reins of government with the temporary removal of the PM, would do his damnedest. Let him try, thought Monckton.

But Evans' reappearance made it impossible for Monckton to sit and await events. What would have been inevitable in Monckton's eyes if the PM had retained power required action with the return of Evans. He felt secure enough to take that action, to let the country make the inevitable decision itself. He intended now to present himself in person before the House and ask it for the powers that he had so obviously earned.

Even Axel paused and looked at him. Were the rumors true? thought Axel. Was he after all quite as balanced as he appeared?

News of Nelson's capture reached Evans at three in the afternoon. It was the "small thing" he had been waiting for. Yet now that he had it, he hesitated. He called in the police and Army commanders and asked for their views. Monckton could be dismissed, though no one believed he would go. Legal processes could at least insist on his ejection from the property he was occupying but they would take time. The publicity would complicate the situation. More important, what forces would be used in the ejection? Hardly those of the Greater London police, since even after Monckton's formal dismissal there would be inevitable confusion if they were suddenly to be used against their former chief. Yet time was pressing. Monckton epitomized all the reactionary forces in the country. The longer he remained in power, the more those forces would harden, for whatever the country's ideal image of itself might be, reaction was firmly establishing itself.

"To hell with formality," said Evans. "We want him out, don't we? Does anything else matter? Do we care how he goes? We'll bring in an outside force—that northern force that was handling it in the first place, what about that? Arm them. Give them military support. Put them into the place in the small hours. The town will wake up to a *fait accompli*. . . . "

Axel's doubts concerning the balance of Monckton's mind were based on only one side of the man, the messianic side, the side that had an unswerving belief in his ability to save society from what Monckton saw as a slide into anarchy. Axel overlooked the other sides. Evans made the same mistake. Though it was true that this side of Monckton had an unshakable confidence in itself, there were other sides characterized by extreme caution. Evans never appreciated the extent to which Monckton's opinions had infiltrated the thinking of some of Evans' own close associates, for example. Since to him Monckton was the most dangerous kind of elitist, he assumed that the police and Army commanders he had been addressing held the same view. But by late afternoon, Monckton knew the principal points that had been discussed at the meeting, and Evans' plans for his removal.

Whatever imbalance Axel had detected in Monckton seemed momentarily to correct itself. Instead of the precipitate action that Axel had expected, Monckton drew in the reins.

"So that's it, Axel," he said. "A show of force. I hardly expected such an opportunity."

"Opportunity?" said Axel.

"When they fail, what do you think the country will make of it?"

It was six in the evening when Nelson was formally charged with the murder of Enoch Powell. By six-fifteen, Warner had briefed his Chief Inspector.

"I want you to go, Mr. Taylor," said Warner. "You've been in it from the beginning. You know the building. You know Monckton. Take a man with you. They want only a token force. Hertfordshire are providing the main body. Pick them up in Welwyn."

"If I could take Dixon, sir?"

"Whoever you like," said Warner.

"And the car, sir. We might not get in through the stations."

Whatever Evans' intentions, Monckton's authority still held when Taylor reached the capital. The car and the bus carrying the police detachment from Welwyn were held up at a roadblock in Cricklewood. Taylor's authority, signed by Warner and countersigned by the Inspector of Constabulary, was scrutinized, checked, questioned. Phone calls passed from police car to HQ and from HQ to Monckton. Only when Monckton's office had given the necessary clearance could the convoy proceed.

"Hardly likely to be a surprise party," said Taylor.

"Did you expect to surprise him, sir?" said Dixon.

"No," said Taylor. "He's got this city by the throat. It'll take a death to release it."

Whitehall was deserted, or so it appeared as the car turned into it from Trafalgar Square. Then Dixon, looking in the mirror, said, "They're coming, sir."

Behind, a Rover 3-liter was edging between the car and the police bus, forcing the bus across the road into the other lane.

"I can turn round, sir," said Dixon.

"No you can't," said Taylor.

Two other cars had left side streets and were closing on them right and left.

"Steady," said Taylor. "Keep going. See if you can make this left turning."

The turning was closed by a tubular metal barrier. Four men stood at the barrier with submachine guns.

"It's up to them," said Dixon. He leaned back and put his hand on the butt of his revolver.

One of the cars drew level. The man in the front passenger seat waved them on. He had an automatic pistol in his hand. The car stayed level with them. They turned left into Bridge Street and left again along the Embankment. The police bus had disappeared.

"Where we going, sir?" said Dixon.

"Monckton's place," said Taylor.

"Anything we can do about it?"

"No."

The man in the car flagged them down. When they stopped, the man came over to them and said, "Out."

A semicircular wall of sandbags had been put up outside the building. The area inside the wall was packed with men. Some were in uniforms that seemed to Taylor oddly old-fashioned. All of them were armed. In front of the steps a light mortar had been set up, pointing down the road toward Westminster Bridge.

Axel was operating the little switchboard on the desk in front of him. He looked up when Taylor and Dixon came in. He said, "Did you really think you could manage it? After all the precautions he's taken?"

"I thought we might," said Taylor. "Somebody will."

"You know where to put them," said Axel, looking past Taylor to the guards in the doorway. "Check them for arms—knives. Then lock them in."

A guard pulled Dixon back onto the landing. Another seized Taylor by the elbows. Taylor stepped forward to free himself, clenched his fist and began to turn. But the voice stopped him, that harsh voice, Monckton's voice.

He was standing in the open doorway beyond Axel. He seemed even more gaunt than when Taylor had last seen him. The stoop was more pronounced. The look in the pale eyes was still more distant, as if focused on some spot beyond Taylor, infinitely far away.

"Did you think you could match me, Taylor?" said Monckton. "Did you think you could close the campaign with a handful of your police?"

"I thought so," said Taylor. "I still think so. If not me, then someone else."

"What arrogance," said Monckton. He said it quietly, though still with the rasp in his voice. And as he said it he came as near as Taylor had ever seen him to a smile of amusement.

"It's aged you, Monckton," said Taylor. "Whatever dream it is that you keep staring at, you won't live to see it. You lack the stamina."

If it had been the suggestion of a smile that Taylor had seen on Monckton's face, it had gone now. Monckton said, "Make a note of his name, Axel. Taylor—policeman. See it appears near the top of the list." He stood looking at Taylor for a moment, his eyes as distant as ever. Then he made a dismissive gesture with his right hand and the guards pulled Taylor toward the stairs.

Dixon was already in the room, standing with his face to the opposite wall, his hands raised, the palms flat on the wall. A guard ran his hands down Dixon's sides, then up the inside of his legs. They took Taylor's revolver and the penknife from his pocket. When he turned round from the wall, they had gone. He heard them lock the door behind them.

"That's it, is it, sir?" said Dixon.

"Perhaps," said Taylor.

It was the same room, the one they had first given him as an office. But the desk was gone, and the two chairs. The telephone had been removed. Only the metal filing cabinets remained. The window looked out on the back of the property. In the distance, beyond the main mass of the War Office building silhouetted against the moonlit sky, he could see Nelson's column. To the left, he could see lights in the palace at the far end of St. James's Park. He opened the window. Below was a drop of forty or fifty feet into darkness.

Dixon was tapping the internal walls with the end of a pencil. "Brick," he said. "We'd need a cold chisel, sir."

Taylor looked at the ceiling. It was of plain plaster, with a heavy plaster molding round the periphery. He pulled himself onto one of the filing cabinets. When he stood up, his head was within a foot of the ceiling.

"You got a penknife, Dixon? Nailfile?" he said.

"They took them, sir. Try the pencil."

"Won't get far with that," said Taylor.

But beneath the new skim surface, the plaster was old. It crumbled as he worked the pencil into it. It was more like dried sand than modern plaster, and he could see the bullock hairs that had been used to bind it. He turned the pencil like a small drill, so that it ground a hole up through the plaster. When an inch of the pencil had disappeared into the hole, it struck something more substantial. Taylor concluded that he had reached a lath structure to which the plaster was attached. He withdrew the pencil and began to bore a new hole. In ten minutes, by boring, prizing, and boring again, he had uncovered a square foot of laths. He found the weakest of them, pushed, twisted, and finally broke it upward. He could get his fingers through the hole, so that the next lath broke more easily. Now he could strike the remaining laths upward with the heel of his hand.

Dixon had taken off his jacket and laid it on the floor, so that any larger fragments of plaster that fell made almost no noise. He kept up a low mutter, as if conversing with Taylor. Not that the guard on the door was likely to be listening. The door was locked and escape from the window was impossible. But then, he thought, you never know.

At last, Taylor put the pencil in his pocket. He put up a thumb to Dixon and hauled himself up into the roof space. He disappeared into the darkness and when Dixon saw his face again, he was beckoning for Dixon to climb up after him.

It was pitch dark inside the roof space, except for the glow of light from the hole. There was no flooring, only the ceiling joists on which to perch.

"Let's get orientated," said Taylor. "Where do you make the landing?"

"Diagonally across, sir," said Dixon. "Shall I—"

"Hang on. That should be where the trap is. Wait here."

Dixon lost sight of him. He could hear an occasional scrape, over to his left, then no sound at all. He bent and looked down through the hole into the lighted room below. If the guard walked in, he thought, how long before they were discovered? Had they left the window open? He might think they'd got out that way. But that wouldn't delay him for long.

"I've got it," said Taylor.

Light from below outlined the edges of the trapdoor into the roof. Taylor felt the surface of it. With a handkerchief he dusted round the edges. He didn't want any dust to fall through when he lifted it. He bent down and put his ear on the trap. Finally he took hold of the wooden handle and lifted the trap an inch. Light shone into the roof space from below. Far away were the sounds of some human activity. Through the gap between the edge of the trap and its surrounding housing Taylor could see the landing. The door to the room was somewhere behind him. There was no sound from the landing itself. He lifted the trap wide open and let it rest on the joists behind. A smell of stale cooking rose into the roof space.

"Watch my feet," said Taylor.

He lay down across the joists so that his head and shoulders hung clear over the square hole. Dixon put his hands on Taylor's calves, and Taylor leaned forward through the hole. The room was behind them, round the corner of a corridor. The guard was hidden from view. The stairwell was in front and to the right. Night noises rose from the lower floors.

"I can't see anyone," said Taylor, getting to his feet.

"Shall I go down, sir?" said Dixon.

"What about the noise?"

"If I could hang onto the joists, then you could give me a hand. There'd only be a couple of feet to drop."

"If the guard comes for you, give yourself up. Don't fight. Get him under the hole, where I can drop on him. We need the gun."

Dixon took hold of the joists and lowered himself through the hole. When he was at arm's length, Taylor took hold of his hands. Taylor crooked his toes round a joist and gripped another with his free hand. The drop was less than six inches. Taylor hardly heard the sound as Dixon's feet touched the floor. Dixon stayed crouched for a moment, then he stepped to the wall and listened. Finally he went to the corridor entrance and looked around.

"Nobody, sir," he said.

Taylor got through the hole and lowered himself until Dixon had hold of his legs. When he touched the floor he said, "That fire extinguisher. Get it, will you?"

Dixon took the extinguisher off the wall. Taylor said, "You hear the voices?"

Dixon pointed to a door on the far side of the corridor.

"How many?" said Taylor, mouthing rather than speaking the words.

Dixon stood by the side of the door and listened. Then he put up three fingers. Taylor pointed to the extinguisher and Dixon passed it to him. He held it upside down with the plunger six inches from the floor. He nodded to Dixon and dropped the extinguisher on the floor. There was a moment's pause, then foam began to gush out of the nozzle. Dixon opened the door and Taylor ran into the room.

There were three of them. They were sitting round a small table playing cards. A submachine gun lay on the table at the side of one of the players. Taylor shot the jet of foam at his eyes. The man cried out, leaned backward on the chair and fell over against the wall. The others got to their feet. One reached round for his gun, propped against the wall at his side. The other reached for the extinguisher but was hit in the eyes by the foam before he could get his hands on it. Then Dixon had the submachine in his hands. Taylor kicked over the card table, knocking the second man off his feet and away from his gun, and as the first man began to get up Taylor hit him on the head with the extinguisher and he rolled unconscious into a corner of the room.

"On the floor!" said Dixon, moving the gun in an arc to cover the men.

Reluctantly, two of them lay face downward on the floor. The man in the corner didn't move. Taylor took hold of the telephone cable that ran round the skirting board to the door and pulled it clear of the staples, then he seized the hair of one of the guards and pulled his head backward. "The knife you took from me," he said.

"The drawer," said the man. "In the desk." His head was held so far back he couldn't close his jaw.

Taylor took the knife and his revolver from the drawer. He pushed the revolver into his waistband, then cut the telephone cable with the knife. With the cable he bound the three men, then gagged them with lengths of material torn from their clothes. He took the submachine gun from against the wall, cocked it, and walked out onto the landing.

"What now, sir?" said Dixon.

"Monckton," said Taylor. "His room's on the next floor."

He went to the stairs and took off his shoes, nodding to Dixon to do the same. They kept to the wall to avoid any creaking steps. Someone on the next landing was complaining about the quality of the coffee he had been given. At the turn of the stairs, Taylor stopped. Two men were sitting on the bottom step, their backs toward Taylor, mugs of steaming coffee in their hands. Their reactions were slow, as if the night took away their alertness. One paused, the mug of coffee almost at his lips. He listened. He began to turn his head as the suspicion that he was being watched slowly dawned on him. When he saw Taylor he began to get to his feet and lift his hands up.

"Just put down the mug," said Taylor.

At the sound of Taylor's voice, the other man turned. He put his mug on the step, then glanced toward the gun on the floor at his feet.

"Don't," said Taylor.

Dixon passed the two men. The landing was empty. He nodded to Taylor. Taylor stepped down and walked to the middle of the landing. He listened. The night was full of unidentifiable little noises. From below, someone began to run up the stairs. Dixon leaned over the stair rail. A guard turned the lower corner and began to run up toward him. Halfway up he lifted his head and saw

211

Dixon standing above him with the light behind. The guard stopped. He glanced behind him to see how far he was from cover, then, deciding the distance was too great, he dropped to the stairs, cocking his gun and lifting it to a firing position. Dixon slid behind the heavy newel post and opened fire. The guard rose from the steps, lost his balance and rolled backward down the stairs. The noise hammered through the building. The silence that followed it seemed to Taylor more stunning than the firing itself. The two guards on the stairs stood for a moment in total immobility, then one of them flung himself forward toward his gun and Taylor fired. Both guards fell, one forward onto the landing and the other backward onto the steps. He lay on the steps for a moment, then began to slide down toward the landing.

On the floor below someone was shouting orders. Doors opened and closed. There was the sound of a mass movement of men. Another man looked round the corner of the stairs and drew back when he saw Dixon. Taylor ran across the landing to Axel's door and kicked it open. A man who had been about to open it from inside was flung across the office into the side of a filing cabinet. Axel was getting up from his desk. Two men standing behind him began to raise their hands.

"Dixon!" called Taylor.

Dixon left the stairs and ran across the landing. As he reached Axel's door, a door on his left opened and a group of armed men were pushing to get out. Dixon fired at them and they began to fall backward into the room.

"Lock the door," said Taylor. "Don't let them move. Don't let anyone in."

He crossed to the inner door and opened it. The room was in darkness. When he put on the light, Monckton was sitting on the edge of a camp bed reaching for a gun. He was fully dressed except for his jacket. His pale eyes blinked in the strong light. He got to his feet. He seemed to be unsure where he was. He said, "Taylor

—if you come between me and the country's needs . . ." The words seemed to be the continuation of a dream he had been having.

Taylor picked up the phone from Monckton's desk and shouted through the open door, "Axel—get me a line to the Home Office."

"Shoot him!" Monckton was shouting.

"Don't let them through that door, Axel," said Taylor. "if they come in I'll kill him."

There were twenty minutes of confusion during which Taylor stood over Monckton with the submachine gun and Axel explained the situation to Monckton's personal forces. At first they wanted to storm the room, then they wanted to continue under some new leader. But Monckton had never allowed any deputy to develop and the discussion broke into factions, each proposing a different name for the new leadership. Finally, it dawned on the men that the thing was over, that surrender was the only way of saving anything. So at last detachments of provincial troops moved into the building, in support of the Welwyn police contingent. As dawn began to break over the city, Monckton, arrogant and savage even in defeat, was driven to the prison in Brixton.

Taylor was strapped to a chair and Monckton was questioning him about Jimmy. The pale eyes were only a few inches in front of his face. That rasping voice was saying, "How do you expect us to preserve the purity of the race when men in your position adopt little nigger boys?" His fists were clenched. He tried to get up, to get at Monckton, but Monckton was holding him down by the shoulders. He began to shout. He got an arm free and struck Monckton in the face and the face began to dissolve as he looked at it. Then he woke up and saw Dixon sitting on the end of the camp bed, nursing his jaw. He looked round the room. There was no one there but Dixon.

"God!" said Taylor.

"You've been asleep, sir. You've been dreaming," said Dixon.

"Did I hit you?"

"It's nothing," said Dixon. "I wasn't expecting it."

"I thought—"

"Just a dream, sir. That's all."

Taylor got up and put on his jacket.

"What time is it?" he said.

"Just after one," said Dixon.

"At night?"

"Afternoon, sir."

"Anything happened?"

"Home Secretary's asked to see you, sir. Three o'clock."

Outside, the weather had changed. It was overcast. The oppressive heat had gone. In the distance, beyond the hum of the traffic, a thunderstorm rumbled. Rain was forecast, the first for three weeks. More apparent to Taylor than the change in the weather was the change in the town's atmosphere. Troops and police stood in little groups at the major crossroads and in the traditional areas of public assembly, but the tension had gone. Normality of a kind was beginning to return, though behind it still hung a suspicion. Taylor wondered if the earlier normality, the normality they had all taken for granted, would ever quite return. It seemed that some previous confidence had been permanently shaken, some previous image permanently soiled.

Taylor rang Enid Markus. She sounded a long way away— remote, as if she knew it had all come to an end. It was almost as if she had to delve into her memory to remember exactly who he was. Yes, of course she'd meet him. The Home Secretary was at number 10, wasn't he? She'd be in Downing Street a little after three. Never mind if he couldn't be sure when the interview would be over; she'd wait.

Evans was still confined to his bed. He was smaller than Taylor had expected. His face was gray. A day's growth of stubble gave the impression of deeply sunken cheeks. Within the limits of his tiredness, Evans was enthusiastic. He said, "Bloody good effort, Chief Inspector. I wanted to thank you personally. I'm arranging for a citation."

"Thank you, sir," said Taylor. "It was—"

"I know what you're going to say, Chief Inspector. 'It was nothing' or 'All in the line of duty.' Bit melodramatic, don't you think? Others might have thought the same. The fact is they didn't. You've given me back my confidence in some essential human sanity—that's really what I want to thank you for."

"I see, sir," said Taylor. "Thank you, sir."

"You won't have heard about Monckton, Chief Inspector. It'll be in the papers. Hanged himself in Brixton about twenty minutes ago. Used the belt of his tunic—they'd left him that. Mad as a hatter, you know. Still, it's over now. Finished."

Enid was waiting for him outside, standing a few yards up the street. She took his arm, but she didn't say anything. They walked up Whitehall and into St. Martin's Lane. He led the way through to the back room of the Embassy and they sat down. A waitress brought them tea and a plate of small cakes. They were alone in one of the alcoves, separated from the rest of the room by a trellis with climbing ivy.

"Monckton's hanged himself," said Taylor. "I've just been told."

She looked at him for a moment, then put a hand over his. "What else was there for him?" she said. "It was his last chance."

"Well—it's over," said Taylor. "It's finished at last."

"Yes," she said, "It's over."

He looked at her and said, "I'm sorry."

"But couldn't you stay? If she's left you—isn't there a job for you down here? You'll be quite a figure when the story really comes out."

"Perhaps," said Taylor.

"What is it then?"

"This, perhaps," said Taylor, pointing to the room full of gossiping couples. "It's your life, your town. It's not mine. I'm not used to it. I belong to a small community. I might not like it, but it's where I belong."

"Shall I see you again?"

"I'll be in London again," said Taylor. "It drags us all back in time."

"But nothing more—an occasional visit in the line of duty? That all? I'd begun to think—"

Taylor looked at her for a moment, then he bent and kissed her cheek. "Come on," he said. "Let me get you a taxi."

"He's been no trouble," said Mrs. Jeffries. "I'd soon have told you if he had."

She was holding Jimmy by the hand and looking down at him. He was grinning up at Taylor. Taylor put a hand on the top of his head and ruffled his dark hair.

"You've been very kind, Mrs. Jeffries," said Taylor.

"Well, for God's sake!" she said, pushing her graying hair off her forehead with the back of a hand. "What did you expect me to do? Somebody had to give an eye to him. You've got to be neighborly, haven't you? You've got to do what you can for folks."

"Come on, lad," he said to Jimmy.

He walked down the street with Jimmy hanging onto his hand. He was wondering where he could get some advice on how to look after him. But damn it, the sun still shone. The town was back to normal. There was the rest of his life to find out about that.

71 72 73 10 9 8 7 6 5 4 3 2 1